BE THOU MY GOOD

BE THOU MY GOOD

The Devil's Foundry • Book 1

JOSEPH MARCIA
AKA ARGENTORUM

Podium

Podium

BE THOU
MY GOOD

CHAPTER 1

You Either Die a Villain, or…

I stumbled out of the smoke, hacking and coughing as my lungs tried to eject themselves by way of my throat.

"God…" I half doubled over, eyes stinging. "Damn it…" I waved a hand frantically through the air before giving it up as a bad job and collapsing to the sand—*sand?!*—beneath me.

"Well." My voice was raspy from the smoke. "This wasn't part of the plan…"

I scooped up a handful of sand, the white grains standing out starkly against the smooth black leather of my glove. Last I'd checked, I was *supposed* to land in Antarctica. Albeit that was before my escape portal had exploded in my face like a poorly planned gender reveal party.

Just an occupational hazard of being the most famous, and attractive, Supervillain in the continental United States.

Even still, as I pushed myself up, I couldn't keep the small moue of disappointment from crossing my face. I'd escaped, but I'd failed, and my DoomTron 5000 had exploded along with the portal.

Ah, those would be bits and pieces of my life's work sticking out of the sand. I blinked slowly at the sight of millions upon millions of dollars in rare alloys, precision circuitry, and *years* of my life smoldering on a beachfront in the middle of nowhere. All because of—

"Empress! Stop hiding already!"

I sighed.

Electra.

"I don't know what you did," the Hero called, "but it won't be enough to escape this time!"

I cast my eyes towards the sky. *God, if you ever did exist, strike me down right this instant.*

Unfortunately, I remained unsmote.

Checkmate, atheists.

Wait.

With another sigh, I pushed the stupid thought away and strode out of the smoke. A gust off the ocean cleared the air, revealing my nemesis. "Behind you."

Electra spun, sparks of blue-white lightning racing up through her spiked blond hair. *"Empress."*

My name dripped like a curse from her tongue.

I allowed myself a small smirk. "Try actually looking around next time."

The Hero clenched her fists. "You won't get away this time."

"You said that already." I cocked my head. "Did the lightning fry your brain too?"

She smirked, air ionizing around her in a series of short pops. "I'd be happy to fry yours."

Just as arrogant as every Hero.

"There's just one problem with that." I pointed down.

Electra glanced at the sand before. "Wha—shit!"

She leapt to the side, dodging a small wave as it lapped against the sand.

I laughed. "You really should keep a better lid on your weaknesses, Electra!"

The Hero danced back from the surf, lightning sparking at her fingertips. "How'd you even find out about that?"

I began to walk to the side, idly twirling a lock of black hair around my finger. "Well, I *may* have paid a visit to your organization's *super secret servers.*" I smirked at her. "I also made sure to update your fanpage, by the way."

"You *ass!*" She threw out her arm, releasing an explosive blast of electricity. I danced back, laughing again as it grounded on a jagged hunk of metal.

That would be the DoomTron 5000's codpiece if I remembered correctly. What a shame.

"Careful! You wouldn't want to hurt someone."

I continued to circle, even as I dodged the following blasts of electricity. With a few steps, I'd put Electra between me and the ocean.

"I'll show you *exactly* how much I want to hurt you." The Hero flexed her hands, sinking down into a sprinter's crouch.

"How much power do you have left, by the way?" I asked. She paused. "I know my robot exploded before you could eat his power core, you glutton."

Electra glared at me, hands sinking into the sand. Arcs of electricity dancing around her form, lighting up the blue fabric of her costume. She didn't expend the ones that grounded back into her body. Instead, she just preserved the charge like some kind of perpetual motion engine.

Gee, I wish *I* had an ability that broke physics over its knee. Do you know the things I could have *done* with a room-temperature superconductor?

Even one that came in such an *awkward* shape.

"Well?" I spread my arms. "Come on then! Weren't you going to show me what for?"

She frowned. "You're baiting me."

I smirked. "Is it working?"

Electra stood, moving to the right as I tracked my way down the beach. I felt my smile grow wider. "You want me to bet it all, don't you?" Her lips quirked into a smirk of her own. "You think you can get me to blow my load like a virgin at a sorority party."

"You'd know all about sororities, wouldn't you?"

"About as much as you know about virgins, yeah!" She snapped her fingers up into a gun.

My eyes widened. I threw myself to the side as a lance of lightning pierced the air. The *boom* beat against my ears. I sprawled across the sand, ducking behind another scrap of metal just in time to dodge the second shot.

"You're not the only one who can be smart!"

I grunted. A hit like that wouldn't *kill* me through my armor, but it would knock my lights out for sure. And here I wanted a nice civil battle where she wore herself out doing no appreciable damage.

"You're more of a smart *ass* in my book." I rolled to my feet. Electra's gun snapped to me.

I threw the piece of scrap metal I'd scooped up. The electricity arced to and grounded itself against the sand.

I charged.

Electra's eyes widened in surprise.

Us 'smart' villains were supposed to keep our distance, after all.

I grabbed a large metal rod as I sprinted, throwing it like a javelin. My form was *crap*, but sometimes the destination mattered more than the journey, no matter what your useless guidance counselor told you every day for four years.

Electra's next bolt of lightning was stronger, enough to send spots dancing through my eyes. It hit my impromptu javelin. I jumped.

The arcing bolt curved in the air.

But not to me.

Oh, it was *closer* this time—Electra wasn't dumb, just an idiot—but even she couldn't make an ionization channel so impervious that it could go *through* a conductor without grounding itself and also curve up towards me in *nonconductive armor*.

Instead, the bolt of literal lightning hit the sand with a *boom*, kicking up a spray of water and dirt that popped as it hit Electra's costume.

Unfortunately, this also meant I was airborne, suspended above the Hero whose arm was already tracking up towards me. Sparks raced to her fingers as she geared up for another shot.

I kicked.

It wasn't a very good kick, to be honest. I was always more of a stay-at-home-and-study type of girl.

But that just meant I folded people into pretzels with my mind instead of my fists.

And Electra, if you could pardon the phrase, fell *right into my trap*.

She stepped back into the surf.

In a heartbeat, a massive jolt of her charge drained out of her, grounding into the absolutely *magnificent* conductor of the ocean.

"Jesus!" Electra leaned forward, hopping out of the water.

And then I hit her like a shit-ton of bricks.

I might not have been the heaviest thing in the world, at five foot nothing sans heels, but my armor was a different story.

We crashed into the waves, and my hands clamped down on her wrists as Electra lit up like the Rockefeller Center Christmas Tree. The lightning surged into the water in a massive blast, forcing me to close my eyes against the steam.

Of course, in my insulated suit, the most I got was a slight tingling sensation as every hair on my body stood up.

And then it was over.

Electra glared up at me, water lightly lapping at her blond hair, messing up her press-conference-perfect updo. I patted her once on the cheek, just to drive it home. Then I stood. "Well…that's my cardio for the day." I waved at the Hero as I walked a few steps away, coming to sit on yet another piece of my DoomTron 5000.

Poor DoomTron. You will be missed.

After a second, Electra sat up as well.

Utterly drained of her charge, her electric blue costume no longer sparked in abstract circuit patterns. She was still taller than me, of course, but that didn't change the fact that she was at a pretty big disadvantage now against me in my suit. She'd *seen* the wrist-mounted laser already.

So instead of doing something *truly* idiotic, Electra stayed sitting. "That's it?"

I raised an eyebrow. "What's it?"

"You're just letting me go?"

I laughed "Go where?" I waved towards the ocean.

She pushed herself to her feet, blinking at me warily. Really, what did she expect me to do? Kill her?

How droll.

"I could call for reinforcements, you know." Electra still stared at me. "Or I could just take you out anyway. Did you forget that part?"

I rolled my eyes. "Well, if you want, we can go back to you lying faceup in the ocean, and I can do my best to drown you."

A complicated expression flickered over her face. "I'll pass. Thanks for offering."

"You sure?" I smirked. "I wouldn't mind paying you back for what you did to poor DoomTron."

"*That's* what you decided to call it?"

I frowned. "Better than *Electra*. Or was it just a *Freudian slip*?"

She blinked. "What's that got to do with my name?"

"You tell me, Mrs. Anti-Oedipus Complex."

She just stared at me for a second. "I'm…going to call for a pickup."

I placed my head in my hands. "I was defeated by an imbecile." Still, nothing for it. I stood, casting my gaze over the destroyed wreckage of my last robot. There wasn't much left that wasn't overloaded, shattered, or overloaded *and* shattered.

There should be enough for me to scrape together a death ray, at least, right?

I nudged a circuit board with my toe. It cracked in half.

I sighed. I needed to not be here when the Heroes showed—

"I'm not getting a signal!"

I glanced up at Electra. She had her communicator out. It was a circular device sized to fit comfortably in her palm, but the holo-interface showed only static. I blinked. Those things were supposed to connect automatically.

Electra rounded on me. "It's supposed to connect automatically!"

No, really?

I coughed. "Why are you looking at me?"

"What did you do to my comm?"

I blinked again, tilting my head. "What makes you think it was my fault? Last I checked there was only one person here who could fry electronics on command and her name started with *not fucking me*."

"My comm is hardened against my power!" she said, "It'll work anywhere on Earth. Your teleporter must have broken it."

I pointed. "But the interface is still working."

She paused, looking back towards her comm. I could almost *see* the steam coming out of her ears. "But…if it's not broken, and it's not getting a signal…"

The realization hit me a second after she spoke. "And we went through a collapsing wormhole…"

Electra swallowed, looking at me. "Where was it set to take us?"

"Not *here*." I waved a hand. "I had a nice hidden facility all set up." In Antarctica, not that I needed to tell her *that*. "And before you ask, no, there was nothing that would stop your stupid Hero Comms from working."

I'd been trying to get my hand on one of Dr. Impossible's devices for *years* to figure out how they worked. So far, this was the closest I'd ever been to one.

"So that means…"

I thought about it for a second, trying to come up with another solution that matched the data. Unfortunately, as a great detective once said, after you've exhausted every other possibility, whatever remained *must* be the truth.

"We're on another world."

Electra jumped slightly. "You mean like an Isekai?"

"What the fuck is an *e-sky?*"

She opened her mouth, but then a wave hit my knees, causing me to stumble. I blinked, eyes going to the water, which was *much* higher than I remembered a few moments ago.

"Crap! The tide's coming in!"

I all but threw myself to the ground, sweeping up whatever I could get my hands on that didn't look entirely busted. Electra, of course, just stood there like a *tree stump*, staring out towards the ocean.

"Stop thinking about Ise-whatever and help me!" I shouted. "We're gonna need this stuff if we're ever going to get back to our own world, you idiot!"

"Um." Electra raised a hand. "Not to burst your bubble, Empress, but…I think we have…bigger fish to fry…"

My eyes followed her finger, coming to rest on a…

A…

"Oh," I said.

Electra took a step back. "Yeah."

Peeking out of the waves about a dozen yards away was a grotesque, bloated, *misshapen,* tentacle. Well, you could call it a tentacle except for the part where all of the suckers were actually bloodshot eyes.

And all of those eyes were looking at us.

As Electra and I stared, a second tentacle rose out of the water, and then a third, and a fourth and a fifth and—

You know, some small dark corner of my mind added, *the human brain can't really conceptualize any number bigger than five.*

Because anything more than that was *way too fucking many.*

It was okay though; it was out there in the water, and we were here on the—

The thing heaved itself up onto its misshapen tentacles taking a step forward onto the...

...land.

CHAPTER 2

Something Fish-ed This Way Comes

"Run!"

Electra followed her own advice, booking it towards the beach and almost bowling me over.

"Gah—!" She knocked me off my feet, and I crashed into the surf. It drove the air from my lungs and scattered my armful of salvaged parts into the waves. My hands snapped out, but I caught nothing but air. The *thing* let out an ululating cry.

The sound hit me like a blow. I gasped, sound driving through my head like nine-inch nails. Someone started screaming. I didn't realize that someone was me until I'd already clapped my hands over my ears. Blinking rapidly, I saw the mass of tentacles advance on me in a roiling mass.

I realized with abstract clarity that I was about to die.

Then a hand came down on my shoulder. It cut through the fog surrounding me. I only had time to blink before Electra hauled me to my feet.

"Come on!" Her voice sent my head spinning again, but in a good way, back to the real world and away from whatever mess the monster had left me in. "We have to run!"

I nodded, turning with the Hero to dash towards the shore. As I ran, I snatched up what bits of metal and wire that I could, thoughts churning as frantically as the waves beneath my feet.

Unfortunately, I was also much shorter than Electra, and the water was *pouring* up the beach now as if someone had upended a pitcher the size of a stadium onto the coast. I scrambled, arms full of salvaged parts, but I barely managed to make any headway.

Beneath my feet the waves pulled back at the sand, making me feel like I was running on a treadmill as I struggled not to slip yet again.

Ahead of me, Electra pulled farther and farther away with each step. The water only came up to her calves, but for me, each step felt like I was running through molasses.

In addition to the twenty pounds of metal in my arms but I couldn't drop it.

Not if we were going to make it out alive.

Electra glanced back over her shoulder, and I felt my heart fall to the bottom of my feet as her expression paled. "Just run!" She waved her hand. "We don't need that stuff!"

I shook my head, breath heaving.

So much, I thought, *for no more cardio today.*

"You're gonna die!"

"Without"—I heaved a breath—"this, we"—I almost fell, my ankle screaming as it twisted—"die anyway!"

I could see the moment she realized that I wasn't going to make it. Electra's face flickered through a dozen emotions in the span of a heartbeat before settling on resignation. She was going to leave me because I was too slow.

I bowed my head, legs striving frantically against the waves. It didn't matter if Electra was just out to save her own skin! I didn't need her help! I'd save myself just like I always—

I had a moment to blink as a pair of hands grabbed me, looking up just in time to see Electra toss me over her shoulder.

"This is why!" She turned, legs pumping. "You never skip leg dayyyyyyyy!"

I gaped.

"That's what you're going with?!" I glanced back, stomach twisting in knots when I saw how close the tentacle thing was.

"You're the one"—the saltwater sprayed beneath her feet—"who can't run to save your life!"

I swallowed a retort. Even with me on her back, the Hero was going nearly twice as fast as I'd managed. I looked away from the monster as my head started to throb. "Just get us to the sand!"

"I'm trying!"

I growled, trying desperately to keep a hold of the metal and wires in my hand. I bit back a curse. Would I even be able to get it set up in time?

It seemed like I'd have to.

Somehow, I felt a grin spreading across my face.

"Brace yourself!"

My head snapped up at the words. Electra crouched. I felt her muscles tensing beneath me like a steel spring and then she *jumped* out of the water.

I went flying, mouth agape. As I tipped over backwards, I saw Electra a foot behind.

I closed my eyes and curled into a ball, hitting the raised berm of sand with all the grace and poise of a boulder. The impact drove the air from my lungs and my precious cargo from my grip for the second time.

"No!"

I forced myself upright, staggering as another mind-bending scream shattered the air. I dove across the sand, snatching up the wire and the metal coil, tossing them farther from the water.

Even now, the waves continued to crash against the shore like a storm. We'd gotten to higher ground, probably the normal high tide mark well above the ocean's reach.

Now, though, we had at most a minute until we were back in the drink.

Of course, the giant tentacle monster was the bigger concern. It was speeding up, too, like it was getting used to walking on land.

I pushed the thought from my head. Now it was my turn.

"Keep running!" Electra skidded to a stop beside me, grabbing at my shoulder.

"Where?" I was already working, frantically twisting a length of scrap metal into a U shape. "We don't have anywhere to run! The water's not stopping!"

"It'll stop!"

"And if not?" I shook my head, pulling out a length of wire. "Cut this for me, here!"

With a growl, she yanked a thin utility knife from its thigh holster, slicing through the metal with a flick. "We don't have much time, Empress!"

"You think I DON'T KNOW THAT?!"

Add the insulator to the metal. There, done. Here's hoping it wouldn't burn out.

I ripped my omni-tool from my belt, jamming the head into a crease in my suit's chest plate. With a twist, the panel popped open, revealing the suit's reactor. It was a hexagon of metal and glass-steel, generating enough energy to power this suit for the rest of my natural life.

Or, alternatively, something else for one massive load.

Of course, I couldn't just pop the stupid thing out. I grabbed the length of wire again, cursing my good sense. I'd installed a minor force-field generator, a precaution that was supposed to stop some enterprising Hero from ripping it out and rendering me powerless.

Now, of course, it was more likely to kill me than protect me, so it had to go.

I jammed the insulated piece of metal into the capacitor bank right next to the reactor. This wasn't *why* I made them open, but it would do the trick. The suit jerked as part of its power flow was cut off. Still, I didn't design my armor to have a single point of failure.

Only now I was realizing that the single point of failure was *me.*

"Any day now!"

I glared up at Electra. "Then maybe stop distracting me!"

"Just want to make sure you—!"

"Shut! Up!"

I pushed past the tremor in my hands, winding the length of wire around several key junctions bypassing fuses and resistors. With a grunt, I pushed the other end directly into the charging port, yanking my hand back as the material of my gloves nearly popped from the sudden surge of electricity.

With a whine, the servos in my armor went dead as countless precise circuits and fuses were overloaded all at once, welding them shut.

And like that, my armor died.

All I was left with was a hunk of metal, already bent out of the way, and a glowing power core.

My field disabled, and the much more mundane issue of electrical discharge taken care of, I grabbed the handle in the center of the hexagon, giving it a sharp twist. With a hiss, the entire reactor popped free, resting in my hands with a gentle red glow.

Not that it produced anything but white light; I'd just tinted the glass-steel red when I'd made the thing.

I couldn't stop myself from smiling faintly. This little, unassuming core was my life's work. My magnum opus. It was powered by exotic materials I'd painstakingly stolen, crafted at laboratories that had been destroyed, and marooned a literal world away.

I'd probably never be able to make one again.

"Empress! Not sure about you but—!"

A massive tentacle crashed into the sand about a meter away from us.

I sighed. It really was a shame.

"Hey, Electra." I rolled my wrist.

"What?"

"Catch!"

I lobbed my power core through the air, watching it tumble end over end towards the surprised Hero. My last thought before she grabbed it was, *It would really suck if she had a maximum capacity.*

Like, really, *really* suck.

I saw Electra open her mouth, only to freeze when her fingers made contact with the metal cathode of the core and approximately *all* of the electricity.

She exploded in an orb of white-blue lightning. Arcs of electricity struck the sand with so much energy that entire swaths of the beach were turned to glass.

For a second I even lost sight of her before a glowing figure appeared in the center of the maelstrom of electricity.

I pointed at the thrashing monster. "Any day now!"

The Hero blinked at my words, eyes going solid white as the power coursed through her. It took another second, even as she continued to absorb every last drop of power from my reactor, until the idiot finally realized what I'd done.

She turned towards the massive mound of flesh and *eyes* as a dozen tentacles reared out of the air above us, ready to slam down and do—

Well, whatever it was that tentacles did to defenseless young women, I assumed.

It was an immense splotch of red and black against the horizon, taking up nearly all my view with its beady black eyes and thrashing limbs. As it raised itself over us, it was as if the beast was the darkness itself.

But Electra? Electra was *light*.

"Sorry!" She raised an arm. "But you're in the wrong genre, freak!"

I rolled my eyes.

Well, I would have.

But the flash of blinding light, the physical *force* of the thunderclap, blew me onto my back.

The monster *screamed* again, but this time in pain.

Electra laughed, her body rising off the ground from the sheer power coursing through her. Each wild arc bent through the air, slamming into the creature as it writhed. The very water around it became charged, flash boiling as it fed the harnessed lightning back into the monster's bulk again and again.

And then, with one final surge, it was over.

I blinked the spots from my eyes. The image of Electra suspended in the air like some kind of Zeus wannabe was literally seared into my retinas. Slowly, I pushed myself to my feet, rubbing at my face.

My ears wouldn't stop ringing.

"Did we kill it?" I winced. I could barely hear my own voice.

"What?" Electra turned to look at me, eyes back to their normal dull blue. At some point, she'd fallen back to the ground. "I can't hear you!"

"I said"—this time I yelled for real—"did we kill it!?"

Then the *It* moved.

We both spun towards the monster.

If possible, it looked even more grotesque than it had before. All the eyes I could see were *popped* from the force of the current, great gouts of rancid yellow ichor pouring down its burned and boiled flesh. The thing twitched and spasmed, stretches of its skin sloughing off to reveal blackened muscles and bones beneath.

Its cells, in the billions, realized that they were dead.

I shivered at the sight.

I forced myself off the sand, staggering back. To my side, Electra's legs gave out, and she collapsed to the ground.

"I don't"—she doubled over, panting—"think I can run, anymore."

"SKRUUUERRRRSIAAAAAAAAA!!!"

I clutched at my ears, fingers coming back red. "I don't think it would let us even if we could." The beast's movements became even more frantic. My heart began to sink as I realized that we hadn't killed it.

Or rather, as tentacles and eyes and blood all cascaded down to the frothing waves, we hadn't killed *enough* of it.

The monstrosity raised itself up from the water, almost drunkenly, flesh and tentacles sloughing off to reveal a single, massive eye at its core. The cross-shaped pupil widened before looking at me, boring into the depths of my very soul. And I fell into the void of its gaze.

I would have screamed, but I could not find my mouth.

I was nothing.

The darkness was everything.

I struggled, breathlessly, against it, but I couldn't do anything but hold it back for a second longer.

Tendrils of darkness reached towards me.

Then—

I gasped, snapping backwards as the real world surged back to fill the void.

In front of me, the massive eye rolled back into the creature's morbid mass.

And it crashed down into the waves.

"Is it…" Electra staggered upright. "Dead?"

Ding!

I blinked as a blue box appeared in front of my face.

System Message

For defeating a creature from beyond and communing with forces beyond mortal comprehension, you have unlocked the Demogogue class!

What?

No, seriously, *what?!*

"Oh, hell to the yes!" Electra leapt to her feet. "I knew it was an Isekai!" She turned to me, grinning. "This is gonna be great!"

I stared at the woman, dumbstruck. Then, slowly, I reached up to pinch my nose. "We almost got killed by a tentacle monster from beyond *time and space*, and you think it's gonna be 'great'?"

"Well, yeah." She punched the air. "We got skills out of it! That means we have a system!"

"A *system?*"

She gave me a concerned look and for some reason that made me even more irritated. "No offense, Empress, but did you not like, have *books* growing up? TV?"

I glared. "I read *real* books, not whatever garbage you're insinuating is literature."

She gasped, placing a hand against her chest. "You take that back about my light novels!"

I shook my head, pushing away the creeping feeling of dread and giving into my irritation. "Light novel? So, they're not even real books then?"

"Yes, they are!" She stalked forward, grabbing onto my shoulders.

I glared—unfortunately—up at her. "It's in the damn title! *Light—*not real!"

"There are heavy light novels!"

"That's just a novel, you imbecile!"

"Who killed the giant tentacle monster! Was it you!?"

"Yes! It was my invention."

"But it was my power!"

"So, you're the light, and I'm the novel?"

"What?"

"Exactly my fucking point!"

CHAPTER 3

Prosperous New Relationships

Wow."

Electra grinned at me. "Right?"

She'd just finished explaining the concept of an Isekai to me. I shook my head. "I just don't know what to say."

"Amazing, right?"

"That's not the word I'd use." I ran a finger along the smooth material of my power armor.

Electra frowned. "C'mon, you can't call it stupid if we're *in* an Isekai."

"I mean, you're here."

Electra's frown narrowed into a glare. I would have cared more if she hadn't blown her entire charge killing the giant tentacle monster. "That's just rude. Did you forget who saved your ass?"

I raised an eyebrow. "Villain, remember? Or is 'we fought together so now I respect you' or some garbage a 'thing' in…*Isekai*?"

Electra coughed, glancing away.

I blinked. "What, really?"

"Well, it's more of an anime thing?" She poked her fingers together. "But that's where Isekai came from, so…"

"From those not-novels." I nodded. "Got it."

"*Light* novels." Electra crossed her arms.

"That's what I said."

"God, you're such a bitch."

"*Villain.*" I leaned forward. "VILLAIN. I'm not going to pretend to like your favorite book just to get in your pants like Wonder Man."

She blinked at me. "He wanted to get in my pants?"

"Electra, look in the damn mirror." I waved a hand at the statuesque woman, with her shimmering blond hair, baby blue eyes, and cheeks that could cut glass. "Every straight guy in the continental United States wants to get into your pants. Have you seen your fan website?"

She shifted, rubbing the back of her spiky blond hair. "I…tried not to look at it much, actually." She paused. "And hey! Whattaya mean *continental* United States?"

"Hawaii has Riptide."

She raised a finger before lowering it. "Riptide *is* pretty hot, I guess."

I raised an eyebrow. "You guess."

"Well, yeah?"

I shook my head. "What am I going to do with you?" While her head snapped to me, I reached up and fiddled with the control panel of my suit. My fingers found the small lever hidden into the frame of the control panel, and I pulled it.

With a soft hiss, the different pieces of my armor fell off, disconnecting from my undersuit.

She blinked. "If you could start by not stripping in front of me after making ambiguous statements, that'd be nice."

"Don't be a fucking prude." I stepped out of the armor panels. "I'm wearing an undersuit; it covers exactly as much as your own costume." I tilted my head. "Or did you not realize how big your butt looks in it?"

Electra's face shaded red. "*You're* a butt."

"Ah yes, I am rubber, and you are glue." I waved a hand.

She glared. "*You're* the one who said you didn't know what to do with me."

I paused, turning to look at the Hero.

We'd moved from the cove to a small cave we'd found in one of the surrounding cliffs. It was a bit darker in here, but not dark enough to cover up how she was already half on her feet, hands up in front of her.

I shook my head. "*You* need to calm down. I'm hardly going to attack you *after* taking off my power armor."

"Yeah, well, that sounds like something a villain would say."

"How strange." I rolled my eyes. "It is almost as if *I*, a villain, said it." I turned to face her. "Are you done yet? We have important things to discuss."

She cocked her head at me. "We?"

I pinched my brow. "What, are you going to try and arrest me instead?"

She stared at me for a moment more before huffing and lowering her arms. "No. But that doesn't mean I don't trust you as far as I can throw you."

I stared at her a moment before sighing. "So, we're doing this, then."

She shrugged. "I mean, you're the one who keeps reminding me you're a villain."

I raised a finger, then paused. "…Be that as it may." I glanced off to the side. "That doesn't mean we aren't connected. We both share a similar goal."

She blinked at me owlishly. "We do?"

Dear god, please smite me where I stand.

Unfortunately, god remained as dead as he had been since the beginning of time.

"Getting back to Earth."

"Oh, *sure*." She rolled her eyes. "'Cause, you'll just take us both back, with no strings attached."

I frowned at her. "You're right. I will."

She laughed. "Is this that 'honor among thieves' shtick people talk about?"

"There is no honor among thieves. Some thieves"—I placed a hand on my chest—"just happen to have honor all their own."

"That's what you're tryna sell?" Electra crossed her arms. "How do I know you won't just add a mind control beam to the teleporter or dump us both in your secret lair and take me prisoner?"

I glared. "Where else would I even take us back to? Never mind that even gaining access to a different dimension wouldn't be nearly that exact." I'd have to be careful not to dump us in an ocean, in all honesty.

"Headquarters, preferably."

"Oh, I see. It's a crime if I do it, but I'm supposed to just walk right into your base so you can slap handcuffs on me." I nodded. "Of course, why didn't I think of that? And why is it that *I* know all of your bases are shielded against teleportation, but the *Hero* who *works there* doesn't?"

At least she had the grace to look embarrassed. "Well, that's not the point. People have broken in plenty of times."

"What do they even *teach* you people about technology?"

"That tech villains can do anything, and you shouldn't give them time to get set up."

"NO!" I stopped. "Well, *yes*. Actually, that, that's rather flattering. My compliments to whoever wrote your handbook." I paused. "*But* that's not the point. It takes resources, time, and *energy* to make the impossible happen. And right now, I don't have any of those. It will take an incredible amount of time and effort even with your help to make a teleporter that even gets us back to the same dimension. Never mind slapping on…mind controllers, or shield piercing effects, or whatever other nonsense you've come up with!"

Electra blinked. "Uh."

I stared at her. "Or did you forget that *someone* blew up my giant robot? And then *someone* drained my power core, using enough energy to *kill* the sustaining reaction entirely. And then *someone* still assumed I could whip up some miracle teleporter, despite all that, that could take us right home for lunch?"

"Okay, okay, I get it!" She held up her hands. "No need to bite my head off, Empress."

I let out a deep breath. She was right, which of course only made me more irritated, but getting into another fight was the worst thing I could do right now.

"It's not important." I ran a hand through my hair. "Just…I wouldn't bother with that other nonsense. A teleporter itself will be hard enough."

She frowned at me. "Why me though? You don't need me, so why are you acting like you're gonna make sure I get back home as well?"

I scoffed. "You saved my life twice, idiot." Electra jumped at the words, eyes going back to me. "The very thought that I'd leave you marooned here without even making the barest attempt to pay you back? It's unacceptable. The equivalent of winning by default." I smiled at her. "And when I defeat you and your little band of Heroes, it's going to be because *I* was better, not because of a technicality."

Electra stared at me for a few seconds, working her jaw silently. "That…" She shook her head. "And here I thought you were gonna say something nice."

"Nice." I tilted my head. "To you?"

"You're really not making me want to work with you."

"Fine, then." I waved a hand. "Go do whatever you want. I'll be sure to collect you after *I* solve our problems. Why mess with what works?"

Electra grumbled. "Jeez, humble too."

I smirked. "So long as we're on the same page."

She met my eyes for a second before groaning and looking away. "We'll stick together until we find civilization or something. It'd be a shame if you bit it after all the work I put into saving you."

"How generous."

"Yeah, well." Electra crossed her arms. "It's the best you're going to get."

I huffed. Fine, it wasn't as if I needed her help. *Yes*, an electro-kinetic would be useful, but no more than actual copper wiring. If she was being stubborn, then I didn't have the time or energy to waste babysitting her.

"What's your class, anyway?" I asked.

Electra gave me a suspicious look, and I rolled my eyes again.

"If we're going to be trekking through the wilderness together, we should at least know what the other is capable of."

"Sure…" Electra rolled her neck. "I got a thunder mage thing. Hopefully, I'll be able to use it to recharge my power as well. What's yours?"

I quirked my lip. "Demogogue."

She blinked. "What's that even do?"

"You know, that's the first good question you've asked all day."

"Hey! I asked you to give up at the start of this mess, didn't I?"

I didn't even offer a response to that inane statement. Instead, I focused on the idea of a 'menu.' Electra mentioned it was a staple in Isekai settings. And while part of me wanted to call the idea that fiction would apply to reality idiotic and misguided at best—

Ding!

Name	Via Rodriguez
Class	Demogogue

The mighty Demogogue summons beings from the beyond to do their bidding, binding their servants in cages of words.

Skills	[1/5]
Summon Demon: Level 1	*Summon a creature from beyond. Be wary of your words.*

Status	
Physical	Strength 1
	Endurance 1
	Agility 1
	Dexterity 1
Ethereal	Charm 1
	Faith 1
	Attunement 1
	Soul 1
Unspent Status Points	5

Well, it wasn't stupid if it worked.

"It looks like I summon demons, for some reason." I shrugged. "Not sure what demagoguery has to do with that but—"

"Wait, wait!" Electra waved her hands. "Demogogue. Demon. *Demon-gogue.*"

I blinked. "No."

Electra grinned. "I'm pretty sure that's what it is. That would explain the weird spelling, at least."

"Why is *my* class a pun, but yours is something normal like 'Thunder mage'?"

She gave a little laugh. "Actually, the name of my class is Buzzkiller."

I froze in place. "That's…horrible."

Electra just laughed again. "I think it's pretty funny, actually."

"You would." I sighed. "Still, hopefully, that'll be enough to see us through for the time being."

"Oh, don't worry." Electra held out a hand. "If you get in trouble again, *I'll* save you, Empress."

I took her hand, removing my domino mask. "My name is Via." She blinked, and I rolled my eyes. "Please, secret identities hardly matter in a place like this. Calling me Empress will just confuse people."

If we managed to find any at all.

"Well…uh, sure, if that's what you want." She let go of my hand. "But *I'm* sure as heck not giving you *my* name."

I grinned. "Whatever you're comfortable with, Elenore."

This time it was her turn to freeze. "Where'd you hear that name?"

"Well, I *did* tell you I hacked into your organization's servers, didn't I…" I paused. "Elenore?"

She glared.

And I just laughed and *laughed*.

Revenge, dear reader, is always best served *immediately*. Whoever told you 'cold' is selling something.

CHAPTER 4

It's the Destination

After a bit of searching, Electra and I had found a path up and out of the cove. We marched up into the surrounding jungle through luscious palm trees with verdant green foliage growing thick on the ground.

And the jungle was *hot*.

"God there are so many *bugs*." Electra slapped the back of her neck.

"Really, Elenore?" I sent her a cheery smile. "I hadn't noticed."

"Don't call me that." She glowered at me. "Why aren't they bothering *you*?"

I shrugged. "Karma?" I stepped over a branch. "I don't get sunburns either." I'd always loved my tan, but never more than right now.

"Karma my lily-white ass…" She slouched after me, arms hanging limply by her sides.

I tapped my chin. "I mean, maybe I was just a saint in my past life." I shrugged. "But really, do you expect me to feel sorry for you?"

She slapped her arm. Again. "God, ow! These things are the size of *birds*." She hunched over. "Where are we even going anyway?"

"Somewhere not here."

"Why bother though? You saw those guys in armor coming into the cove, right? We coulda just asked them for directions." She glanced away. "Plus, there weren't any hecking mosquitoes on the *beach*."

I sighed. "Rule number one, never get caught at the scene of the crime."

She raised an eyebrow. "Even though it wasn't our fault?"

"*Especially* if it wasn't our fault." I shook my head. "The number of times I pinned my earlier jobs on some guy who just happened to be there… Almost too many to count honestly."

"What, really?"

I nodded.

"No way, I don't buy that for a second."

I raised an eyebrow at her. "Remember the Ascott Ruby?"

"What, the massive synthetic gem the Phantom Thief stole?"

"That was me." I laughed. "And she got put away for it too! God, she was so pissed after she escaped the prison. We had a little feud going for *months* over that."

Electra blinked. She opened her mouth to deny my claim before pausing. "We never did find the ruby…"

"Sure you did."

She stopped, looking at me with a complicated expression on her face.

"What do you think formed the matrix of my power core?" I gave a nonchalant little shrug. "Though, you slagged it pretty thoroughly. How's it feel to be the accessory to a crime?"

"Oh, you little…"

"Whoops!" I smirked at her. "I can see the headlines now, 'Rising Hero Destroys Evidence in Key Investigation!'"

She laughed. "Yeah, right beneath 'The Most Feared Villain in the US Captured.'"

"So you admit I'm the most feared, then?"

"Please." She rolled her eyes. "You're small potatoes after Cypher. There's just no one else *left*."

I stopped, glancing away into the dense jungle.

"Um, Empress?"

"Yes." I started walking again. "I suppose Heroes are rather good at what they do."

For a few minutes we walked in silence.

"So, why are we marching through the stupid jungle again?"

"I can't hunt for shit. You can't hunt for shit. The only source of water was the *ocean*." I gave her a look. "Gee, Elenore. You tell me why we left."

She blew out an annoyed huff. "Okay, now you're just doing it on purpose."

"Doing what?"

She huffed, waving a hand in the air. "Couldn't you have just whipped up some…water foodinator or something?"

"Yes, of course, why didn't I think of that?" I pressed a hand to my head. "With the three springs and one circuit board from my armor, I could make a device that synthesizes food from the ambient idiocy! It's so simple!"

"What, really?"

"No, idiot!" I hit her on the shoulder. Elenore just danced back, sticking her tongue out at me. "I don't have the parts, and even if I did, I don't have the tools to work them." The small tool kit on my belt, which I'd kept with me, of course, was for spot repairs only, not high-precision engineering.

She hummed as we continued to hike along, just above the coastline. "What about your new skills, then? I mean, you must've gotten something useful from your class."

I shrugged, pulling up my status screen and expanding the skills section with a mental flex.

Skills	[1/5]
Summon Demon: Level 1	*Summon a creature from beyond. Be wary of your words.*

"I have something called 'Summon Demon,' but the description is…less than comforting." I shrugged. "You?"

"Ah, uh." Her eyes did that flicking thing I was coming to associate with someone looking at their menu. God, I hope I didn't look that dumb when I did it.

"I have 'buzzer bolt.'" She lifted her hand. "Actually, that sounds kinda useful. I could probably give myself a jolt with my power, then shoot it at something like a bird, or some wild pig or something."

I blinked. "Are there even wild pigs on most islands?"

"I dunno." Elenore shrugged. "I think I read it in that one book, you know, the one with the conch and the big fire? They had piggies, right?"

I felt the urge to fall over and die. "There was a character named Piggy."

"What? That's horrible."

I nodded. "Which was, more or less, the point." I smiled. "It's fine, he died in the end."

"That's not fine."

No, it wasn't. But that was the point.

"Aren't you going to shock yourself?" I tilted my head at her. "I could use a good laugh."

She puffed up. "What, you think *I'm* gonna mess myself up with *lightning*? You've gotta be thinking of some *other* fiendishly attractive blond Hero who wrecked your base. Like Wonder Man."

"No," I said dryly. "That would be the one who tripped over a storage hatch and fell into the trash compactor, like something out of a bad movie."

"So you were watching!"

"I actually made that up." I turned to look at her. "What, did he really fall into an access hatch? My robot didn't even *have* a trash compactor."

She coughed into her fist. "Ah, anyway, I'm gonna start testing my power now..."

I laughed. "You do that, Elenore."

She shot a glare at me before turning back to the task at hand. "Usually, it's just pretty obvious right?" She nodded to herself, and I crossed my arms. "Buzzer Bolt!"

I waited for a second before raising my eyebrow. "Was that it?"

"N-no, I just, I don't know how to trigger the spell." Elenore flushed. "I mean, most of the time it's as simple as just saying it!"

"Really?" I tilted my head, "And that would be in those books of yours? The...*light* novels?"

"Don't you start on my novels again," Elenore said. "Or I'll blast you instead of me."

I hummed once, nodding along as she chanted the name of her ability like it was some kind of mantra. "Have you tried using, oh, I don't know, your *brain*?" I tilted my head. "Like you do with your power normally?"

She paused. "Uh."

"Elenore, please."

Her eyebrows furrowed as she tried to ignore me.

"Buzzer Bolt!"

A spark of what looked like electricity jumped across her arms.

I say *looked like* because normal electricity didn't knock Electra, the electric Hero, off her feet like someone kicked her in the stomach.

She hit the ground with a thud, steam coming off her suit as the heat flash evaporated any moisture she'd picked up during the trek.

"While that doesn't look like the most comfortable way to get clean," I said, "it certainly dried you off."

"Ugh…shut up."

"What, you mean you *didn't* mean to blow yourself off of your feet with your own electricity?"

"What the heck happened?" She pushed herself back to her feet. "That didn't feel like electricity at all!"

I hummed, tossing a few ideas around in my head. "Well, probably because it wasn't."

"Huh?"

"You just used 'magic.'" I waved a hand through the air. "Why *would* it work the same way real electricity works? If some random wizard invented thunder magic, what's more likely: He actually does the *research* necessary to understand the movement of electrons from areas of high potential to areas of low potential…or he just makes some spell that causes a line of glowing, superhot *something* to flash across the air from his fingertips?"

Electra's frown deepened. "Ugh, when you put it like that, it makes more sense that magic wouldn't be the same thing as electricity. God, that sucks though."

I nodded, placing a hand in front of my mouth. "Oh, my. Does the Hero need help from me again, so she can use her power?"

She huffed. "I can still use it in a thunderstorm."

"Oh, of course, a thunderstorm." I nodded. "You mean those ones with the clouds, and the *rain*."

She stared at me for a second, a betrayed expression on her face.

I patted her once on the shoulder. "Just trying to keep you grounded, El."

"I'll keep *you* grounded."

She reached out, grabbing me before I could get out of the way.

"H-hey, what are you doing?"

"Hmm? Just limit testing is all." She grinned sharply, fingers tightening. "My spell didn't really do that much damage, y'know? Gotta see if that's normal."

I squirmed, but without my armor, I was just a shorter, less athletic woman. "Can we talk about this?"

"Oh sure, sure!" Electra laughed. "It's easy. Stop calling me by my *name*."

I paused, glancing to the side.

She scowled. "Buzzer…"

"Okay! Okay! I promise I won't call you Elenore anymore!"

She frowned at me.

"Yep! No more Elenore from me, no sir!"

"Okay, you can stop saying that."

I grinned. "Saying what? That I won't use the name Elenore for this girl, Elenore, that I—"

"Buzzer Bolt!"

I let out a shriek as the surge of something that felt *remarkably* like lighting ran through me.

A second later, Electra let me go, and I staggered over to a tree.

"Ugh, fuck you."

She snorted. "That's right."

I staggered upright, glaring over at her. "I'll have my vengeance, Electra."

"Let me know how it goes, 'kay?"

"Oh, believe me." I was gonna figure out how fake magic electricity worked so I could build her a generator that made that instead. "You'll be the last to know."

She tilted her head. "Don't you mean the first?"

I smiled at her. "I know *exactly* what I said."

She leaned back. "Can you just not?"

"Hmm?" My smile grew wider.

"Uh, that's…" Her eyes flicked back and forth before locking onto something behind me. "Hey look, a city!"

I paused, glancing over my shoulder. "Huh, well look at that. Looks like we found one."

I could make out the towers and the top of a wall over the trees. After a few more minutes of walking, we caught sight of what looked like a small medieval city, complete with walls, dirt roads, and horse-drawn carts.

Electra glanced at me. "Think they'll have what you need?"

I sighed. "Probably not. But at least they'll have food, so we might as well go."

"Sure." She laughed. "What's the worst that could happen?"

CHAPTER 5

Murphy's Law

You just had to say something!"

"Halt!" Behind us, the guards were closing in fast.

"Shut up and run!" Electra yanked me down a side ally, our feet churning the muddy road.

"Stop there, criminal scum!"

Neither of us obeyed. Electra, of course, wasn't a criminal, so she had no reason to stop. And I had no reason to stop because I *was* a criminal.

Now, you're probably wondering how we got into this situation.

"Duck!"

I ducked, nearly tripping over my feet as we ducked beneath a wagon. The streets of Silverwall were packed with merchants and tradesmen. So, I think I could be forgiven for thinking we could slip into the city with the rest of the people coming in on the main road.

"Dammit, Empress, stop getting distracted!"

I sucked in a breath. "I'm…trying!"

It didn't go very well for us.

"This way, you hecking snail!" Electra jerked me half off my feet, a spear *thunking* into a wooden sign where my head used to be.

"Don't—haaa—call me that!" All I could do was follow Electra's commands. *She* was used to this type of rough-and-tumble mess. Not that either of us had expected the guards at the city gate to take one look at us and decide we needed to be apprehended with *lethal force!*

"If the shoe fits!" I blinked as Electra caught me by the collar, dragging me into yet another twisted alley between two perilously stooped buildings. I grunted as she tossed me to the ground in a deep puddle of mud and…leavings, crashing to the ground on top of me a moment later.

"I'll get you for this," I hissed.

"Quiet!"

The thunderous clatter of men in armor rounded the corner a second later, racing past our noxious pile of refuse without looking back.

God damn it. If it worked, I couldn't even be mad at her for it. Never had I wanted a plan that I hadn't directly sabotaged to fail so badly as I did right now.

The two of us waited in silence for a moment more, just enough time for a second pair of guards to stroll past on the main road—if indeed a slum like this could have 'main' anythings.

"Think they'll catch 'em?" one of the men asked.

The woman spat to the side. "Not if we lost 'em Northside. People here wouldn't know the law if it crawled up their ass."

The first nodded, placing a hand on the hilt of his short sword. "Almost make you wish we could stop caring so much about rare-classes and take care of this fucking pigsty."

"Keep it in your pants," the woman replied. "Don't get paid to make more trouble."

Electra got off of me as they rounded the corner, pulling me up with her.

"It's in my *hair.*" I didn't know how much of the gunk coating me was garbage and mud and how much was…*other*, but I didn't *want* to know. "Jesus Christ, did you have to dump us in it?"

"Can it!" Electra hissed at me, eyes furrowed. "If you think they're gonna give up after one sweep—"

"If you think I need help from you at evading the law, you've got another thing coming." I grabbed her wrist, pulling her back onto the main road.

"That's not what it looked like, *Via.*" Electra smirked. I held my breath. Working with this woman was insufferable.

As we made our way down the street, people in ragged clothes began to emerge from their houses and shops. They gave us leery glances; Even caked in mud, the two of us were obvious outsiders. I didn't linger long, this time heading back the direction we came from, back towards the city's main thoroughfare. It was the only street I'd seen with paving stones, though maybe that changed behind the city's second wall.

I frowned as I took in the rough-cut logs and thatched roofs surrounding us. There was a low-lying perimeter wall around the city, which showed medieval levels of stonemasonry. That was a rather clear sign of this society's level of technology.

In a word, disheartening.

I couldn't just wave my hand over a pile of scrap metal and yank the moon out of orbit.

Not...that I had experience with anything like that in particular. That was more Dr. Impossible's bailiwick. Thank god the man was a Hero.

But the point was that technology took precision, operating within incredibly small tolerances, and the devices to achieve that precision and measure those tolerances. Without that, in a world like this...

Well, to get us home, it wouldn't be a question of building the tools I needed to make a teleporter.

I'd be building the tools to build the tools to build the *tools*.

"Where are we going?"

I glanced over my shoulder at Electra. "Not here."

From what little we'd seen, it was clear that the city became more filthy and downtrodden the farther north you went from the main thoroughfare. Then there was the south side, which we hadn't seen, and that second set of walls with a castle peeking out from behind them, but I assumed that we wouldn't be getting into that place anytime soon.

I was leading us away from the area of the slums we'd been chased into. Breaking search patterns was the most important thing. The next would be finding an adequate disguise, preferably before our appearance drew unwanted—

"And who the fuck are you?"

—attention.

I didn't stop walking, keeping my head down, no matter how much it grated, as I tried to slip by the large man who'd stepped in front of us. Unfortunately, it was not to be.

Before I could even attempt to bull past him in all of my five-foot-zero glory, three other toughs slunk out of the nearby alleys. Which, in case you weren't paying attention, was pretty much every road in this part of the 'city.'

Electra pulled me back, pressing both of us into the wall of one of the stooped two-story buildings.

While there'd been people on the street a moment before, they made themselves scarce surprisingly quickly once we'd been singled out. Whether it was guards or thugs coming through, no one wanted to get caught up in someone else's problem.

"Well?" the big man asked.

He had a bald pate because, apparently, he decided to grow all of his stubble on his rolling double chin. Still, it wasn't all fat on that frame of his.

And more to the point, being *overweight* in a place like this was probably a sign that he could *eat* with anything approaching regularity. As opposed to Electra and me, who hadn't had anything for at least the last twelve hours.

I squinted my eyes. Descriptions popped into place above the man's head as I focused.

<Thief lvl 5>

That was the boss. There was a level 2 and level 3 thief as well. The youngest one in the back was marked a level 4 cobbler.

It seems that one had yet to blood himself.

"Just passing through." Electra took a step forward. "We don't want any trouble."

"Well, that's a funny way of saying 'we brought the damn silverbacks down on your heads.'" The big man stepped forward as well, and he had a *clear* foot in height on Electra.

"Oi, boss. These two got some rare classes on them."

The boss's eyes glinted at that. "Do they now?" He grinned, show-ing…surprisingly well-maintained teeth, actually.

I guess it would be irrational to assume he'd play into every stereotype.

"And on a pair of levels 1s too? Didn't your pap tell you to get some levels under your belt before you went flashing your new class around to everyone who can see?" He chuckled. "Makes a man get some… ideas."

"Not that I'd want to waste my time with these two!" another chimed in. "Smell worse than the pigs!"

Electra growled. I pushed myself off the wall, letting out an annoyed hiss.

Electra's one skill was weak, whether by design or on account of its low level, it didn't matter. That left me, and my skill that apparently summoned help.

Well, I could use some help right now, couldn't I?

I closed my eyes for a second. *Summon Demon*, I chanted in my head. I felt a drain, like someone put a hook in my navel and *pulled*. My mana ticked down as the thugs continued to posture in front of us.

They wanted to see what we could do first.

But this wasn't Electra's first fight either. She was holding back her skill, making threatening movements towards the men that sent them dancing back for another second.

My mana rolled over the halfway mark, and I felt a connection forming in the back of my mind.

What…do you require?

It was not my thought. It felt distinctly alien, crawling like a spider into my mind.

Something that can deal with these four, and nothing more.

There was an oily chuckle at my words. *Nothing more. Are you sure?*

Get to the point.

Another laugh. The men were closing in around us now.

What do you offer? What do you demand?

I swallowed. There was no manual for this stupid skill. But I thought the name of my class offered enough insight.

Their bodies, once slain, are my offer. I demand complete obedience to my words, and that whatever you are—or whatever I summon!—won't attack me or my companion.

Obedience? For a day, I offer.

"Get off me! Buzzer Bolt!" A skinny thief staggered back, but he kept his feet, and we were out of time.

Deal.

I was surrounded in darkness.

And then the voice said, *The bargain is struck.*

I snapped back to reality without a second having passed. Everyone was the same. The men were in the same spot, the boss grabbing Electra's face with one of his meaty hands.

But there was a small lump on the ground between us.

My eyes were drawn to it, taking in the too-long arms and its squat, almost squished, torso. From the back, I could only make out its pin-shaped bald head and massive nose.

Then the creature let out a gibbering shriek, mouth opening to reveal rows of serrated teeth. And it threw itself at the big man.

"Wha—ghrk!"

He had just enough time to be surprised before it took a juicy bite out of his throat. The man fell down to the ground, gurgling. My familiar paused for a moment, just enough for me to feel the connection between.

"Don't stop."

The thing seemed to smile before leaning down to take another massive bite.

Ding!

System Message

You have killed Thief lvl 5. For defeating an enemy more than twice your level, additional experience has been granted

Ding!

I pushed the *notifications* down. I didn't have time for that. "Kill the other thieves," I ordered. The thing looked at me mutely, even as the other men stumbled back in shock.

Capable of nothing else indeed.

With a growl I pointed towards the closest man, pushing my aggression across our bond. "Attack!"

With a gleeful squeal, it leapt forward.

And the rest, you might say, is history.

"I think I'm gonna be sick." Electra still had the last one, the cobbler boy, pinned to the ground.

The other three had been reduced to giblets, with my demon still crouched over its most recent victim, massive teeth munching happily on an arm.

Or was it a leg? The business end was already in its gullet.

"Are you going to deal with the last one?" I looked towards her. "Or shall I?"

Electra scrambled to her feet, stepping in front of the boy. "What? No way." She crossed her arms. "The fight's over. We're not killing him."

I raised an eyebrow, glancing towards the boy. If he jumped up and stabbed Electra, well, at least I'd have the chance to say 'I told you so' before she bled out. Instead, he just curled up into a ball, rocking back and forth.

I sighed. "Suit yourself." I turned, walking towards my little demon as it happily worked its way through a man's rib cage.

And yes, I could, in fact, feel its dull spark of joy simmering through the bond we'd made.

I glanced to the west, where the sun was sinking inexorably towards the horizon. "Be still."

It froze.

Now, I didn't know a thing about demons in this world, or the last.

But no one who ever trusted a demon lived to regret their decision.

Who knew what definition of 'obey me for a day' we were going with? The *last* thing I needed was to be carting this thing around until its sudden and inevitable betrayal.

So, I did what any successful villain would do in my situation. I picked up a discarded knife, grabbed my first familiar by the top of the head, and drew the knife across its spindly little neck.

It fell backwards, and I swore I saw something dark and mist-like rise out of the corpse before vanishing back from whence it came. The bond between us snapped, and I sucked in a breath.

In the back of my head, I heard the voice again.

This contract is thus complete.

I swallowed.

Then, in a completely normal voice, it added, *A pleasure doing business with you! Contact us again soon!*

I blinked. "What?"
Behind me, the cobbler threw up on Electra's feet.
"Oh, what the—"
I brushed myself off. "I did offer to kill him for you."

CHAPTER 6

Wash Your Back If You'll Wash Mine

I all but dragged Electra down the street.

Of course, my other hand was wrapped around the cobbler boy's neck, marching him in front of us towards the promise of a bathhouse.

If I had to spend another minute covered in this slowly drying blood and filth, I'd…

Well, I wouldn't be against killing a few more people if it got me a shower.

Priorities.

"Can't believe you killed all of them."

"Not *all* of them."

The boy shivered in my grip.

"His name is Rel."

I raised an eyebrow.

Electra snorted. "You're a bundle of joy."

"Oh, I get it, *I'm* the murderer, but you're the buzzkill."

I felt like I was herding *cats*.

Annoying, isn't she? the voice asked.

And the noisiest one of all was in my head.

You have no idea.

After 'completing' my first contract, the voice in my head had stuck around for a chat.

So, where were we? it—he? I was gonna go with 'he'—asked.

Why did you sound like that at first?

Like what?

I grit my teeth. *We hAVe sUCh sIGhTs tO sHoW yOU.*

Wow, that's pretty good! Have you considered applying for a job?

Just answer the damn question.

Oh, it's nothing much. I could practically hear the grin in his voice. *We do the voice with everyone the first time. Studies show it increases the likelihood of a new summoner offing themselves by three point two five percent.*

I blinked, parsing that bit of information.

That implied that telling me this increased the chance of *me* dying.

I waited a moment for a witty retort, but there was nothing. *Hopefully*, that meant this voice could only hear thoughts I *sent* as opposed to everything that went through my head…. Unless he wanted me to think that.

I worried at my lip. That way was a bottomless well of 'but what if he knows I know?'

I turned around a corner. We were nearing the central thoroughfare again, though this time as just another part of the crowd. The farther we got from the scene of the crime the less people paid attention to us.

Well, barring the fact that Electra and I were both covered in mud and shit, but that seemed to be a rather default state of affairs.

"How do we even know he's not leading us into a trap…" Electra grumbled.

"Jealous I solved all of our problems?" I would have tossed my hair, but I didn't want to get any more gunk on my face.

"Bite me."

I half lunged, snapping my teeth towards her pretty face.

"Fucking—!" Electra jerked back. I cackled, letting go of Rel as I walked towards the bathhouse.

There was a man there in front of the door. He stepped forward, cutting us off, "Where the hells do you three think you're going?"

Electra glared at him, but I waved her off. "We're here to use the bath."

"Right." He gave us a once-over.

I shrugged. "Shitty cart driver."

At that, he snorted. "Yeah, I can smell it."

I waved a hand. "I know it's all the same to you, but kind of want to get clean sometime *today*."

He paused for a second. "You'll need to pay for a private bath. One silver."

I rolled my eyes, tossing him the pouch of all the money we'd taken from the gang that attacked us. Well, the money that *I* took anyway. Electra was too busy trying to get Rel's puke off her shoes to really contribute. "I don't imagine you want to touch my hands."

I watched carefully as he counted out twenty-five copper coins before handing me back my purse. Twenty-five copper to a silver? At least it made more sense than *some* fantasy currencies I'd come across.

"Only open one is last on the right. *Don't* head to the left, or I'll toss you out into another cart full of shit."

I rolled my eyes. "How charming."

I turned to Rel. He was mostly clean, just some stains on his shirt. "You can use the normal bath."

"Ahaha, I'll jus' wait out here?"

I shared a glance with Electra. She shrugged.

I smiled at Rel. And he swallowed. "Won't move an inch, swear on me heart." He drew a cross on his chest.

"You do that." With that, I turned and marched into the bathhouse.

"He said there was only one free." Electra frowned at me. "I'm not sharing."

"Well, you can wait your turn, then." I certainly wasn't. I could *feel* the gunk drying in my *hair*. "Or you can find another bathhouse and pay for it with all the money you happen to have. Oh, wait."

She grumbled to herself, but when I slid the door open and asked, "Coming?" she got inside right away.

Fortunately, there was more than one stool.

The private bath was a tiled room with a cistern set into one wall. The water was cool, but not cold, and there were blessed blocks of soap resting in a small cubby in the wall. On the other side of the small sitting area, there was a slightly raised section of floor partitioning a tub full of steaming water. It moved slowly, as though the water was draining out and constantly being replaced.

Well, good to know this place had *some* kind of running water at least.

I plopped down on one of the stools, picking up a wooden bucket that had been left next to the cistern. Electra sat down next to me without a word.

We both let out a sigh as we dumped the cool water over our heads and started scrubbing away the worst of everything. I worked a thick lather of soap into my hair, sighing at the inevitable tangles I'd have once it dried. But that was a problem for future Via. All that was left was to scrub.

Well, and one other thing.

You still there? I asked mentally.

Oh, don't worry. We're always waiting with bated breath for mortals to contact us. There was a low chuckle, a decidedly odd feeling when it was in the back of my own head. *What do you desire?*

I wanted more information, of course, but coming out and saying that probably wouldn't get me anywhere good. *So how do I know what... demons I'm going to get? The skill descriptions are singularly unhelpful.*

Hmm, and why should I tell you that?

Because you want my immortal soul, I answered wryly.

The voice laughed again. *Well, it's simple. I don't spill the beans to just anyone, but it's been a solid millennium or two since we've gotten a real Demogogue in here.* I waited for him to continue. *We don't give the full orientation to just anyone, you know! Usually, we let you humans just muck around yourselves.*

I frowned, filing that nugget away for later. *So does that mean you are going to give me the full orientation?*

It's simple, really: give us orders, payment, and mana, and we will give you a demon.

I clicked my tongue before pausing and spitting out some soap. What a stupid idea, me. *So...I could theoretically summon a much more powerful demon? Say, by asking for a devourer of worlds, and offering something to the tune of...every soul in this city?*

Girl, I love the way you think, he replied. *But no, your mana is used to make the portal. The more mana you have, the more you can summon. Of course, we take our own share no matter what you ask for.*

It was a theoretically simple transaction on the surface but, for some reason, it left me more wary than if I'd had to carve circles on the ground and chant in bastardized Latin for my power.

Oh, and before you ask, all skills that reach out to the heavens or the hells work the same way. We keep a leash on the power we hand out. Even if we're much more hands-off than the angels. Another chuckle. *Consider that a free bit of advice, Outworlder.*

I blinked. *Outworlder?*

Silence.

I frowned down at the bucket in my hands. At least I'd managed to clean myself off, but somehow, I was left with even more questions than before. Outworlder, huh?

I guess Isekais were a thing after all.

With a sigh, I stood, tossing the bucket down to the ground beside my feet. I pressed a small stud near my collar, and there was a *fwip* noise as my undersuit split down the side and loosened, allowing me to step out of it.

"Whoa, whoa, whoa!" Electra held up her hands. "What do you think you're doing?"

I raised an eyebrow, making no move to hide myself. "Getting in the tub."

I wouldn't mind if she looked but making her uncomfortable was even more satisfying.

I kicked the fabric off my feet before slipping into the tub of water.

I couldn't hold back the groan that slipped from my lips at the heat. There was even a ledge just inside the pool for me to sit on. "Best silver I've ever spent."

"The only silver you've ever spent."

I waved a hand. "There'll be more."

Electra just sighed. A moment later, she also climbed into the tub, though her own suit stayed on. I didn't envy her for it. Watertight supermaterial or not, the fabric could never quite wick away all of the sweat.

We sat in silence.

After it became clear that she didn't have anything else to say, I decided to open my menu again.

A rush of notifications went through my head, letting me know that I had, in fact, killed three thieves.

More important was the list of level-ups.

System Messages

You have reached level 2. You have reached level 3. New skill unlocked. You have reached level 4. New skill unlocked. Summon Demon level increased by 1

I blinked. New skills? With a mental push, I flicked over to my skills.

Skills	[3/5]
Summon Demon: Level 3	*Summon a demon from beyond to do your bidding. Greater mana capacity allows for the summoning of greater demons. Always be sure to hold up your end of the bargain.*
Banish Demon: Level 1	*Never call up what you can't put down.*
Demon-itize: Level 1	Claim Them

There were changes to my status as well.

Status	Unspent Status Points: 9

I rubbed my temples. Of course, the horrid puns couldn't be confined to just the name of the class. At least there was some new information for my first skill.

Funny that the ability to send your demons back only came after you gained a few levels by summoning them in the first place. It struck me then that the voice hadn't told me *what* percentage of new demon summoners killed themselves on their first contract.

Best follow the advice of my second skill until I figured that out.

Next, I focused on Attribute points.

Increase one of your base attributes by one.

Interesting.

All of my attributes were set to one, which meant they were a baseline. The question then was if I could improve my baseline and if the stat bonuses were additive or multiplicative? For now, I put a few points into the 'defensive' states while holding the rest in reserve.

Even if I intended to use my new summons for everything, there was a lot of value in *not* getting hit.

Speaking from experience.

Status	Unspent Status Points: 3
Physical	Strength 1
	Endurance 2
	Agility 4
	Dexterity 3
Ethereal	Charm 1
	Faith 1
	Attunement 1
	Soul 1

The mystical stats would have to wait until I found out which one, if any, *I* needed. It would be a waste to put points into Soul, only to learn that demon summoners actually needed Attunement, or something stupid like that.

I had the seeds of a plan germinating in the back of my mind. If I could summon any demon based on my needs, I might be able to get one that could dredge the coast for some of my tech, or even do specific tasks like melting iron to make steel.

If they were all as dumb as the first one I summoned, things would still be difficult, but leveraging my abilities correctly might actually let me slingshot this world to the level of development I needed within *my* lifetime.

It would be nice to make it home before I was old and gray.

Across the tub from me, Electra stood up, water cascading from the form-fitting lines of her bodysuit.

I took a moment to admire her; it wouldn't do for a villain of my standing to have a mediocre nemesis, and really, Elenore was nothing if not *standout*.

"Well?" I asked.

She looked down at me. "I'll never agree with your methods," she said. I just raised an eyebrow. "But it's clear to me that this world has deeper problems than just one woman who doesn't know how to use nonlethal force."

I sighed. "Still hung up on that? Honey, what did you think those three were going to do? After they raped us, I mean."

She crossed her arms. "If you'd given me a chance, I could have taken them out of it."

"Forgive me for not trusting in your abilities any further than I have to."

"And forgive *me* for not wanting to play second fiddle to whatever scheme you're cooking up."

"Oh?"

Electra nodded, more to herself than to me. "This world needs a Hero."

I laughed. Well, it seemed like I wasn't the only one coming up with big plans. "Let me know how that goes for you."

Electra grinned down at me, eyes sharp. "You know, maybe I will."

I'd leave her to it.

I had an industrial revolution to plan.

CHAPTER 7

Roads Less Traveled

No one spoke until we exited the city.

I'd spent the last of our pilfered coin on some cloaks to cover up Electra's and my own more distinctive garments, and for some reason, Rel hadn't scampered off the moment I took my eyes off him.

Minion material indeed.

Still, it wasn't all bad; the boy had led us to a chink in the wall, called the Miner's Gate by the locals. The people who worked the lava tubes used it to avoid the tolls at the main gate. Apparently, they pooled enough to pay off a sympathetic captain too.

Just one more sign that this world was no better than the last one, no matter how enamored Electra seemed with it. I'd be lying if I said the thought of magic didn't spark some childish joy in my heart. But I was well past the age where I could find happiness in—

Okay, no, I couldn't even think that with a straight face. Demons or no demons, I was going to enjoy breaking this world's magic system over my *knee*.

"What are you smirking about, Empress?"

I turned my gaze to Electra. We were a short distance away from the city now. "Nothing you need to worry your pretty little head about."

Her eyes narrowed. "In case you missed it, that was my job description."

"Is it?" I tilted my head. "Well then, by all means, feel free to be my minder. I'm sure I can find some use for you."

I turned, walking towards the eastern coast of the island as the sun continued to sink behind me.

I heard a snort as Rel scampered in my wake. "Don't get yourself killed, Empress," Electra called.

"Nor you." I tossed one last parting smirk over my shoulder. "It would be a shame if my nemesis proved so…fragile." My smile grew. "I haven't gotten around to breaking you yet."

I caught the hint of a shiver running through her at my words. It's true, back on Earth I'd cultivated a bit of a…reputation, regarding such matters. For all I joked, Wonder Man had actually lasted much *longer* against me than most.

But it was, as I'd said, nothing to worry her pretty little head about.

We parted ways there, Rel and I heading east towards the coast, while Electra turned west towards the road. At my side, Rel pattered on silently, eyes downcast. Now that just wouldn't do.

I waited until we were out of sight of the wall and any prying Heroes before I turned to face the boy, catching his chin in my hand.

I wish I could say I looked down on him, but even this street urchin was much taller than me. Still, my past gave me plenty of experience looking down at people *regardless* of height.

"Ah, uh…?" He tried, voice squeaking into a higher register in his anxiety.

"Tell me," I tightened my grip slightly, "why did you stay? You very well could have run, and I wouldn't have had the time or the inclination to track you down." I smirked. "At least, not before you managed to flee the city." He shivered at the implication that I would have found him eventually if he hadn't stayed.

But that was just good business sense. If you were a tailor, it didn't pay to leave loose ends. The same only went double for a villain.

"I, uh…didn't have anywhere tah go?" He shrugged his shoulders. "Been running with the boys for near on a month now. Da…" He shook his head. "Just didn't have anywhere else to turn."

I hummed. "Acceptable."

He blinked, eyes looking up at me.

"Still, I won't stand for you holding yourself like you're some kind of common riffraff." I let go of his chin. "You're a cut above all of those lowlifes you used to cower behind, do you understand?"

He nodded but it was clear from his eyes that he didn't.

I sighed. "Rel. Rule number one. Never lie to me, understood?"

He jolted. "Uh, y-yes ma'am!"

"So." I narrowed my eyes. "Do you understand?"

"…no?"

I sighed. This is what I had to work with.

Still, like Mama always said, it's a poor craftswoman who blames her tools. If I remembered correctly, Father used to blame his tools quite often. See where that got him. Where that got all of us.

"You work for me now," I said slowly. Wouldn't do to overload his brain. "Which means the way you act reflects on me. And I'll *not* have you carrying yourself like a piece of trash, am I clear?"

At that, Rel frowned at me. "You wan' me to act more…"

"I want you to act more like you deserve to be here. Can you do that for me?"

Rel just scratched his head. I sighed. "For now, just look *up*. Keeping your eyes on the ground just marks you as something worth stepping on. From now on, you'll look people in the eye." I met his gaze and held it. "Even my own."

I took a…different approach to minions. So far it hadn't led me astray.

Or at least, not so astray that a few security protocols and a death ray couldn't fix it.

"What if someone does decide to…" He gulped. "Step on me?"

"Then I'll break their legs." I nodded sharply. "If you work for me, then you are under my protection. I believe that's the premise of gangs, isn't it?" I smirked. "Though, unlike the group you were with before, I make it a point to actually keep my promises."

A nervous, frenetic laugh won free of his throat. "I-I understand, ma'am."

"Good." With that, I turned. There was still much work to do, especially if I was to grow my magical power to the point where it was actually useful, instead of just summoning random, useless hobgoblins too stupid to follow my orders.

"Now, let's get to work. First, I want you to tell me if you unlock any new classes. I'll let you know which one to pick."

He jumped again. "That's uh—" He looked down again, cutting himself off.

I sighed. This was just going to be one of those days.

"Speak."

"People don't…pick classes for other people."

I filed that away. Good to remember for the future, if only so I didn't step on any toes. That aside, there was a little misconception I needed to fix. "Oh? You mean those boys you ran with weren't going to make you become a thief?"

He hunched his shoulders.

"I don't have to hide my intentions," I said, looking over my shoulder at Rel. "Don't think I plan on sticking you with something *useless*. I will make sure our classes can work together."

"W-why?"

I paused, raising an eyebrow. "Why what?"

"Why me?" He shook his head. "You had that other girl, and she already had a rare class. I'm just a c-cobbler. Nobody special…just some g-guy you found in the dirt o' north side."

I hummed. "Because you showed me something far more important than any rare class," I said. He looked up at me in askance. "You showed some modicum of loyalty." I smiled sharply. "Even if it was motivated by fear, that much can be hard to come by." Judging by the expression on his face, he knew it was true as well. The more things change, as they say.

"When people are true with me, I am true with them as well," I said. "And so, I decided to keep you. And no one of mine will be a 'worthless bit of trash' by the time that I'm done with them."

True, some of them had been *atomized* bits of trash. But that had been *their* career choice.

Rel looked at me, eyes blinking slowly before a different expression came over his face. One that I found quite a bit more pleasing than his usual groveling expression. "I-I understand!" He gave a small smile. "I'll try tah be better."

"Good." I nodded. "You can start by telling me a bit more about how jobs work. First of all, how do they level up?" I crossed my arms. "I just got my rare class, so I need to reassess."

Rel rubbed the back of his head sheepishly as we continued walking, but at least he didn't look at the ground anymore. "I dunno that much, ma'am…"

"Just tell me what you know."

He gave a short little nod. "Uh, Da always said you can upgrade your class by getting all of your skills to level 10. Uh, he didn't say if you had to be level 10 as well for that, but I never heard of anyone getting their skills that high without leveling up themselves."

"And skills, are we really limited to five?"

"You can switch 'em, I think. But then you lose all a' the status points from the old skill. I heard some of the guards bragging about how they had more skill slots after they ranked up, but I think most of 'em were making it up." He wrinkled his nose. It made him look almost cute, and I had to hold back a giggle. "I think maybe the captains have got their second class, if it's even a thing."

I hummed. "I see."

So there *were* people much stronger than the ones I'd fought so far. That could prove troublesome, at least until I was able to build up enough to face them head-on. Still, at least he made it sound like it took a long time to reach level 10 and unlock this second class.

But that was as a destitute child living in the slums. Who knew what was available to the people with time on their hands to actively hone their skills and increase their levels?

I'd have to make contingencies.

I came to a stop, placing my hands on my hips as I surveyed the coastline. Some distance to the south, closer to Silverwall, there were ruined bits of ships and what looked like stone docks. As I summoned a few aquatic demons and sent them off with orders, I nudged Rel. "What's up with the docks?"

"Oh, uh…" He shifted back and forth on his feet, knees knocking together. "I heard an outworlder showed up here…Da told me that where outworlders go, calamity follows."

"Calamity?" I smiled.

Rel's gaze snapped to me.

Well, that giant squid thing could certainly count as one before we'd cooked it like *calamari*. But as for what I intended for this world, well…

"Calamity is certainly a *fitting* description."

CHAPTER 8

What Lurks in the Shadows

We waited by the coastline as the sun continued to set.

By my side, Rel shifted nervously every few seconds.

A crisp, clean wind blew off the ocean, something that I'd never really gotten to experience in my last life. I think the cleanest air I'd ever breathed was at my secret base in Antarctica, and even then, you could smell a trace of oil from the drilling platform a few miles away.

The air here was pure, and I breathed deeply before sighing. "What's got you so jumpy?"

Rel jumped again, shrinking backwards some. "O-oh, nothing, ma'am."

I rolled my eyes. This was why I didn't do minions. "Tell me." I didn't move my gaze from the water. Case studies had shown that the gaze of a Supervillain was rarely a positive in the mind of the minion.

Questionable scientific ethics aside, there was no reason to make the boy even *more* on edge.

From the corner of my eye, I saw him glance back and forth from me to the horizon several times. "The m-monsters'll come out at night. Da always said we had to be back inside the walls before sundown, or they'd come 'n gnaw our bones."

Normally, I'd dismiss such talk as nothing more than a children's fairy tale, but in a world like this, with magic and status screens…well, who was to say there weren't also monsters lurking in the night, waiting for some intrepid Hero to come and slay them for loot?

I, of course, had a much more proactive way of gathering the materials I needed.

I hummed as my jellyfish demon resurfaced from the water. I'd netted the thing by offering an hour of freedom on this world after it completed my tasks. A single slimy limb rose from the water, tossing another scrap of metal towards the shore.

I'd had it gathering bits of metal and electronics for the past hour. After a moment, I sighed, giving it the mental nudge that its duty was done. With a burble of water that sounded like sobs, it sank back beneath the waves.

Demons were weird.

"We'll see what we have here, and then head back."

Rel cast a glance towards the waves. "Can we just…let it go?"

I raised an eyebrow. "I already did, didn't I? I'll dismiss it in an hour."

"R-right!"

Rel scampered in my wake as I made my way over to the pile of trash on the beach.

Most of it was just corroded iron or steel from ships, or perhaps armor from a noble or a knight who'd gone overboard half a century ago. But here and there I saw scraps of my own neo-titanium alloy. I quickly separated it from the rest of the trash. "Here." I shoved the lot of it into Rel's hands. "We'll be needing these for later."

I didn't have the tools to work the metal yet, but then, I didn't have the tools to make any more either.

Sometimes you had to run before you could crawl.

Beyond that, there were a few smaller components and a circuit board or two that didn't look like a complete loss. I added those to the stack.

I rose to turn from the rest of the debris when I caught sight of the last thing the demon had tossed upon the shore.

"…Now that's interesting."

I reached down, pulling the sword from the sand. It was a simple straight sword, long since rusted into its sheath. But what drew my eye was the ruby set in its handle. I turned it over in my hands, noticing how the setting hadn't corroded through. Even the handle itself was in much better condition than the sheath.

If nothing else, I could use the precious stone.

I slipped it into my belt with a smile.

"It's not much, but it's a start." I turned towards Rel. "With this, I might even be able to make something worthwhile."

Then Rel tilted under the weight and fell to the ground.

I blinked once as metal and electronics scattered everywhere, crashing against the sand and the rocks. I sighed. "So that's how it's gonna be, huh?"

"I-I'm sorry!" He snapped to his feet, scrambling for the parts, but I caught him by the scruff of his neck. Rel trembled in my grip.

"You, carry this." I shoved the sword into his hands, not like I had a use for it or anything. "I'll handle the…important bits."

"Th-that's, I can—"

"Drop it all over the ground again?" I asked. "Step on something fragile a few times, maybe?" He hunched over and I sighed. "Just carry the sword. I should have known I'd have to feed you before I made you do any heavy lifting."

Rel swallowed. "Y-yes, ma'am."

"And stop calling me fucking *ma'am*," I muttered. "It makes me feel old."

"What should I…uh, call you?"

How about you just don't. I bit back my instinctive response. I'd heard that line too many times in *way* too many bars. Oh, and my sign was *fuck off,* if you're curious.

He wasn't hitting on me though, and I had a bit of pity for the poor boy. He was so far out of his depth that he could see sharks.

I'd been in the same situation myself, a year or two ago, hadn't I? After Cypher's identity…

I shook my head, gathering up the scraps of metal and electronics that I'd deemed salvageable. I sighed at one cathode induction array that had shattered against a rock. Easy come, easy go.

"You can call me Via, or Lady Via if you have to." I rolled my eyes. "I'm not a fan of titles," I smirked to myself at the joke, settling the junk parts in my grip. I'd picked the name Empress for myself *because* I'd ruled nothing. A thumbing of my nose at the established hierarchy.

Of course, my enemies had just claimed it was a sign of megalomania.

"Let's go." I turned back towards Silverwall. "And…try not to drop the sword, at least."

"Y-yes!"

I sighed. He was painfully earnest. It made me feel almost bad about exploiting him.

"And if you fall, *don't* land on me!"

"Yes!"

It had been a short walk out to the coast. However, the sun cast long shadows as it dipped beneath the horizon, making the march back slower and more treacherous. Not to mention that I was carrying a stack of metal and could barely see where I was putting my feet in the *first place*.

For the second time since coming to this new world, I made a promise to myself.

I was tired of being *dainty*.

And sure, maybe I'd never be able to go toe-to-toe with someone like Wonder Man—I'd settle for having a perfect record against him in tic-tac-toe thank you very much—but at the very least, I shouldn't be struggling to carry twenty pounds a mile or two.

Okay, maybe I should. I wasn't exactly a titan.

But I didn't *want* to!

Ugh, it was just, there was always so much to *do*! New designs to prototype, to test, to innovate. Schemes to plan, to refine, and then to execute.

Heroes to defeat.

Banks to rob.

People to see.

It had been a busy life.

There was a crack from the jungle. I stopped, head snapping to the side. "What was that?"

Rel trembled. "Uh…maybe nothing?"

There was a rustling of leaves, and I felt a chill creep down my neck. "Keep moving. We're almost back to Silverwall."

By now, the sun had almost fully set, leaving just the last few rays of sunlight that were quickly fading beneath the horizon. I quickened my pace, even as I started breathing more heavily.

"Never," I muttered, "skip…leg day."

"W-what's leg day?"

"A giant fucking…" I took a breath. "Meme."

From the corner of my eye, I saw Rel blinking at me, confusion writ plain on his face.

Not, I noted, that it was anything new.

"If you have time to talk, you can move faster."

"I'm…" He shot another fearful glance towards the jungle. "Going as fast as you?"

I glared.

"Eep!" Rel picked up his pace, and I did my best to follow.

Madre de Dios, why was everyone taller than me, even in fantasy land? Weren't medieval people supposed to be short from inadequate nutrition or something? I swear I saw something like that on TV once, after the guy with the crazy hair.

I panted for breath as the chink in the walls came into sight.

It wasn't fair! Why did Mama have to be so short? Why couldn't I have inherited any of my father's tall genes?

There was a roar from the jungle. In front of me, Rel stumbled, casting a glance over his shoulder.

I just leaned forward. "Run!"

He didn't need to be told twice. This time, anyway.

My feet pounded against the ground, even though it felt like I was barely moving faster than a walk. But we were almost there.

I heard thumps behind me, the sound of leaves and branches snapping aside.

Never look back. That was my motto.

I just…never thought I'd be applying it so literally.

"Go! Go! Go!"

My heart was pounding out of my chest when we made it to the Miner's Gate. We ran through the chink in the wall just as I heard shouts coming from the top. Something *big* crashed into the stone behind us. I collapsed to the ground to the sweet symphony of crossbows being unloaded into the thing outside.

There was another annoyed screech, then the creature turned and ran away from the walls. I forced myself to my hands and knees just in time to see a shadow slipping back into the jungle, something massive, a long-muscled tail, knocking over one last tree as it went.

I turned to look at Rel, who was staring back at me with wide eyes.

Slowly, I pushed myself to my feet. "Next time…we'll go in the morning."

Rel nodded fervently. I hauled him upright. "We'll need some place to store all of this."

He thought for a second. Well, if nothing else, today had shown that the boy wasn't *slow*. Naïve, utterly lacking in confidence, and with little ability to plan, perhaps, but that's what *I* was here for.

"There're…a buncha abandoned buildings near the old docks. Warehouses 'n the like."

Despite my near brush with death, I found myself smiling. "Warehouses, you say?"

CHAPTER 9

Friendly Neighborhood; Spiders, Men

Come on…dammit!"

So, the warehouse thing wasn't quite as good as I'd hoped.

"Just a bit more…"

I twisted my fingers, leaning forward I tried to force the stupid gem out of its setting. The scabbard was jammed between the wall and a chunk of stone. So much for defunct equipment I could cannibalize for parts.

With a huff, I put a bit more weight onto the hilt. I would have just pried the damn thing out with, like, a file or something, but the entire blade and scabbard were rusted straight through. If I put too much weight onto it, the whole thing could snap right off.

Which, of course, meant that the one piece I needed was the only bit *not* corroded to hell and back.

"Fucking piece of…hah…shit—!" With a grunt, I popped the gem free. It bounced across the dirt floor of the warehouse before rolling to a stop next to a pile of unused bricks.

Well, calling them "bricks" was a bit charitable. In reality, they were crude adobe that had long since cracked. Anything of value had already been stripped from this place. The walls likely remained simply because no one wanted to collapse the ceiling.

With a sigh, I discarded the blade and made my way over to the real prize. I held it up to a beam of light coming in through a broken window. The gem was a bit smaller than I'd expected, but that worked in my favor. It would fit perfectly into the core.

"What d'ya want to do with the sword, L-lady Via?"

I glanced over at Rel, who was busy moving things out of the way. We were staying in a half-collapsed building, but that didn't mean it had to be a *dirty* one. "The sword? Do whatever you want with it." I shrugged.

There'd been only one gem set in the pommel: the ruby I now popped into the small power core I'd managed to salvage. I pressed it gently into the prismatic facilitator array before closing the access hatch on the orb. With a twist, it started to hum, growing warm in my grasp. Good, it hadn't been damaged after all.

"And they said it couldn't be done."

I moved over to the 'worktable,' which was a slab of raised stone that no one had cared enough to drag away. I'd assembled a crude metal shell from some of the smaller sheets of my alloyed titanium. The tools in my belt pouch weren't made for big construction, but I could man-age this much, at least.

The hard part was the limbs. I'd managed to salvage enough for four, but only by stripping out the servos and 'ligaments' in the hand sections. In the end, I was left with a lumpy oval and its four little spider legs. Its eyes were a mishmash of whatever sensors I still had, in the hopes that at least one of them would work. That only made it look even more like a spider. I hummed to myself.

"I wonder if Electra has arachnophobia?"

Was the little robot useful? Maybe not, but after recovering the parts, the urge to build had made my fingers itch until I'd finally given in. I'm sure I'd find *something* for the little guy to do eventually.

Of course, I thought, as I slipped the core into the housing, none of this would matter if the motherboard I'd salvaged was more damaged than I thought. There was nothing I could do about that. *Yet.*

I nodded to myself as the little robot started to hum.

Soon, I'd be able to build all the things I could back in my home dimension. This was just the first step. A…proof of concept, if you will.

Behind me, Rel cursed, voice squeaking, as he almost dropped a wooden beam on his foot. I sighed. And also, hopefully, a slightly less bumbling helper, if the fabricator assembly I'd hooked up to its 'front' still worked.

There was a short series of chirps and whirrs as the machine spooled up. I waited, palms flat against the stone table. A spark, a plume of smoke spitting from the crevasse in its housing. I bit my lip.

Then its eyes lit up, more sensors than I'd expected flickering back to life. It stood.

I cackled. "It's alive!"

"Meep!" Rel staggered into something, but I couldn't bring myself to be upset with him as my little robot stood up on four wobbly legs.

"I always wanted to say that." I grinned. "Computer, display readiness and functional status."

The little robot made a clicking noise, head bobbing up and down on its little legs. Then it let out a series of beeps and mechanical whirrs.

I sighed. "Language centers damaged. That figures." I shook my head. "Still, at least it seems to be able to run." I wasn't a coder first and foremost, but my father had taught me a thing or two. I'd always had a knack for writing programs that could function even after catastrophic damage like this, call it an adaptation to my own shitty life. "How's your fabricator, little guy?"

Another beeping whirr. It opened its mouth, revealing the feed port. Deconstructors sparked once before flickering out. I shrugged. Call it two for three. "We'll get to that; for now, see if you can't fix your speech centers while you help Rel out," I said.

I straightened up as my creation whirred again. It walked forward, and for a second, I thought it was almost going to jump off the table. Then it reached the edge, foot missing its next step, and my robot let out a single surprised beep as it started to tilt forward.

And fall.

"No!" I lunged, catching it an inch from the ground.

I breathed out a sigh of relief as I set the little guy down. It tilted back, sensors looking up at me. I rubbed my forehead. "Computer, amend instructions. Run full diagnostics and modify movement algorithms first."

The pseudo AI I'd put together for my doombots was adaptive, but I guess expecting it to realize that it was in a body less than a quarter of its normal size was a bit much.

I let out a laugh. "God, imagine if it just fell over and broke. A day of work, just down the drain." With the way my luck was going, the whole thing would have probably exploded.

I patted the little robot once as it let out a soft hum before folding its legs up and going into standby mode. With the processor damaged and a nonstandard power core, that would take a while. As long as it wasn't a complete wash, I'd have to be satisfied.

That was one thing done, now on to the next. "Rel."

"Yes, Lady Via!"

I closed my eyes, debating whether I should just make him call me Via or not.

It probably wouldn't help. "Come with me." I moved to exit the warehouse. "We have things to do."

The old port district was, if anything, even more dilapidated than it had looked last night. I could see where there used to be roads and buildings, maybe even a port authority office. But all of that had been left to rot, or else completely swept away, as was the section closest to the wall.

I could see a dip in the ground where a massive blow had carved divots into the ground. There was a gate set a little farther south, Rel had said, which led to the new fishing docks next to the Merchant Quarter.

But whatever interest this Silverwall had in its shipping industry had died along with this section of the city.

"Where are we going?" Rel popped up next to me. Then his stomach growled.

I felt the same way. I hadn't eaten in a day, preferring to get a base of operations set up first. Even in standby mode, the little robot I'd created would defend the warehouse in case of intruders. Now that my spoils were secured, it was time to look towards new conquests. Like food.

Honestly, you'd be surprised how many villains put off consolidating their own gains, and then next thing you know, you're out to get a taco and you come back to find—

Well, I'm sure we've all been there.

"Food will be the second order of business," I said. "First, we'll need some money."

Rel glanced to the side. "Um, if we're gonna steal, why not just take the food?"

I rolled my eyes. "Why steal from a street vendor when you can cut a rich man's purse?" That was me, a regular Robin Hood.

"With that in mind, let's—"

I stopped.

In the middle of the road in front of us stood three men. They were loitering idly against the wall of another abandoned warehouse, rusty knives and thick-looking clubs displayed prominently. At my side, Rel pulled back.

I sighed. "Ah, the welcoming committee."

The leader, a man with spiky blue hair—and what was it with fantasy settings and off-color hair anyway?—pushed himself off the wall when he heard me.

"You got that right." He grinned, showing a missing tooth or two. Just another reminder to never take a job without dental. "Heard from my boys that you went in and squatted on our turf last night." Behind him, *his boys* leaned forward menacingly.

"Do you call them that in the bedroom?"

He blinked. "Wha?"

"Do you call them your 'boys' in the bedroom?" I tilted my head. "Seems a bit weak, thought pretty boys like you preferred…" I made a rude gesture. "Men."

It took him a second before he snarled at me. "Bitch." He spat to the side.

I smirked, raising my hands. "No! No! I'm not *shaming* you for your preferences." I cast a glance at Tweedle Dee and Tweedle Dum. "It's just pretty clear who wears the pants in your relationship."

"Hey," Tweedle Dee said. "What's she talking 'bout?"

"It doesn't matter." Blue Hair crossed his arms.

Tweedle Dum scratched his head. "I think she's sayin' we fuck boss in the ass?"

"I said it *doesn't matter!*"

But we were already off to the races. "Ooh, yeah, now that you mention it, boss is real nice looking from the back." He gave a small grin. "I always liked short hair."

Dum shook his head. "No, long hair's where it's at, gotta get something to hold on to like—"

"I swear to god if the two of you don't shut up, I'll make sure you never stick your tiny little things inside *anyone* ever again."

Dee and Dum shared a glance. Dum raised a…rather large hand. And you know what they say about those. "Actually, boss."

"I. Do not. Care."

I hid a chuckle behind my hand as Dum lowered his hand again. Blue Hair continued to glower at me for a second, hand clenching around the hilt of his rapier.

"You know…" The man ran a hand through his spiky hair. I was tempted to make some comment about product, but he wouldn't understand. "I was gonna take it easy on you, show you the ropes." He leered at me, and I raised an eyebrow. "Maybe even teach you a thing or two."

"I don't think your thing has much to teach." I checked my nails. "Whatever it is you're selling, I'm not interested."

Behind me, Rel let out a keening whine.

"No, no, no…" He shook his head, sneer coming back as he mimicked my earlier words. "It's not us who's selling anything, but you." He waved a hand. "See, that warehouse you were using, it belongs to the Red Scars. And *you're* squatting without permission."

There was a moment of silence before Blue elbowed Dum in the side.

"Oh, right!" Dum steeped forward, doing his best to loom menacingly. "We don't take kindly to that 'round here."

"So…*you'll* be—"

"No." He blinked as I interrupted him. I sighed, placing a hand on my hip. Maybe if he'd approached me with a *deal,* I might have humored him for a bit longer, but no. "No, I won't be doing whatever idiot thing that was about to leave your lips." Because I was *Empress*, not some little girl lost and alone in the dark.

And Empress does not kneel.

CHAPTER 10

Good Help Is Hard to Find

Blue Hair snorted. "Well, looks like we get to do this the fun way then."

"Lady Via…" I could practically hear Rel trembling behind me. "W-what—"

"Why don't you go back to the warehouse." I shook out my hands as the men drew their weapons. "It appears negotiations have broken down."

Blue jerked his head. "Kill her."

My hand snapped up, focusing on that feeling of mana as I channeled my new skill. "Demon-itize!"

A crackling bolt of *black* leapt from my hands as I felt my MP take a precipitous dip. Blue Hair's eyes widened as he threw himself to the ground. My skill raced over his head, splashing harmlessly against a building on the far side of the road.

I bit back a curse as Blue sprang back to his feet.

"Don't just stand there, you imbeciles! Get her!"

Dee and Dum shared another glance before turning back towards me.

I growled. "Demon-itize!" Another black bolt leapt from my fingers. Blue swore explosively as he ducked again.

This time, it left a discolored streak through his hair—mind the spikes, gents. He howled as he saw a strip of it fall out to the ground. "I'll get you for that! Bitch!"

"Why don't you come and make me?"

Dee and Dum charged.

I turned, sprinting after Rel into the collapsed building. My MP was over two-thirds depleted now. Whatever my new skill actually did, it was clear I couldn't just go throwing bolts around like party favors. I bit back a hiss as I saw my MP bar tick up slowly in the corner of my vision.

Wasn't this what…Int or Wis was supposed to help with? Why did this stupid system have to use stupid nonstandard stats as well?

I sprinted through the broken doorway of the warehouse, ducking as a piece of metal cut through the air above my head. "Not me! Hit them!"

"Ah!" Rel jumped, voice going high-pitched in surprise. "Sorry."

I snatched the rusted sword from his hands. "And if you're going to use it, hit them with the other side!" I shoved it back into his hands by the rusted sheath. And he blinked up at the pommel for a moment before the sound of footsteps jerked him out of his stupor.

I need to summon another one of those demons!

There was a moment's pause as I cast out with my skill.

Then. *Hmmm?* The voice sounded bored. *What was that?*

I raced deeper into the warehouse. "Computer, activate self-defense protocols! Assign all new encounters Designation: Adversary!"

My spider bot beeped once as it came online again, interrupting whatever diagnostic process it was undergoing. It skittered into the shadows.

Another one of those demons from two days ago, same deal!

Dum ran through the doorway, only to get clocked in the head by the hilt of Rel's 'sword.' The man staggered backwards, clutching at his face.

Unfortunately, while it drew blood, Rel didn't exactly have the best upper body strength. The big man didn't go down and managed to block the second swing with his own club.

Well. The voice clicked its tongue. I paused; did it even *have* a tongue? *Normally, I'd say that based on your previous actions I can't find anyone willing to take your contract…*

I glared, raising my hand as Dee and Dum forced their way through the door, Rel stumbling back in shock.

Buuuuut hobblefiends are too dumb to think about any of that stuff.

Great. My eyes narrowed. *Then get me the* same *kind of demon I summoned yesterday, for the same deal.*

I felt more than heard the smirk in his voice. *Coming right up! Oh, and again, they're called hobblefiends.*

I pushed the rest of my mana into the summoning circle forming in front of me. It expanded, growing big enough for another one of those red imps to fall out of the air with a chittering screech.

As one, every occupant of the warehouse froze.

"Demon!" Dee (or was that one Dum?) shouted.

"Get the big ones!"

The hobblefiend gibbered gleefully at my command, dashing forward on its lumpy arms and legs. It leapt over Dum's first swing and sank his claws deep into his leather jerkin.

I grinned as the man screamed in alarm, flailing around in a panic until he tripped and hit the ground with a massive thud.

Right on top of my demon.

The creature gave a piteous cry as it was smushed beneath his immense bulk. A single visible arm flailed, three-fingered hand clawing at the air before it stiffened and vanished.

I blinked. Come to think of it…I *had* killed it with a single stab the other day.

"D-did it die?" Dum pushed himself to his hands and knees.

Dee tilted his head. "I think you got—"

Rel slammed his sword into the back of Dee's head. The man collapsed with a dull moan.

Rel blinked. "I…did it?"

Dee roared, turning and swinging at my minion. Rel meeped, holding up the sword in front of him, for all the good it did. Dee still practically tossed him across the room into a pile of bricks. Then the man turned towards me.

He slapped his crude club against a meaty palm. "Gonna have fun with you."

I laughed. "Try it and I'll rip your balls off."

I raised a hand, and he flinched back. "So why do you take your friend and get out of here before I have to get serious."

For a second, it almost looked like he'd go for it, then Blue shoved his way into the warehouse. "She's obviously out of mana! Get her already!"

I clicked my tongue. Everything was so much easier when my enemies were idiots who overestimated me. It was the main reason I did so well against Heroes.

I leapt back as Dee charged, running behind a collapsed pillar.

I didn't have any weapons; they were all integrated into my armor, which, for those of you who weren't paying attention, I'd stashed back in the cove on the other side of the damn island.

"Get back here!"

"No, you!"

I ducked beneath some crumbling masonry, a club crashing through it a moment later. One of the walls half collapsed behind me, taking a chunk of the roof with it. I staggered out, coughing. My instincts screamed at me.

I ducked.

Dee's club ripped through the air right above my head. I could feel the wind from the strike. Given that the oaf outmassed me by a factor of two, if his hit had connected it probably would have taken my head off.

But there *were* advantages to being so small.

I decked him in the junk.

Dee howled, staggering backwards.

I rolled to the side as his club hit the ground, nabbing it as I jumped to my feet. Choking up on the haft of the club, I reared back and put my best golf swing right up between his legs. He let out an agonized wheeze, the ultimate expression of agony, and toppled like a ten-foot oak.

I grinned. And here Mama always said schmoozing with execs at Aegis Corp was a waste of time.

I mean, she was right, but I *had* learned my way around a club.

"Blade Flurry!"

I jerked back, holding my club up in front of me like a shield, just in time for Blue Hair's rapier to cut it to pieces. I staggered backwards as a line of fire cut into my cheek.

Blue grinned at me, showing off his nasty teeth again. "Got you." He flicked his rapier, sending a line of my blood across the floor of the warehouse. The blade glinted in the dusky light of the warehouse. And here I was without weapons.

Blue took a step to the right, circling me. I moved back, eyes casting around the warehouse frantically, looking for something I could use to turn the fight back in my favor.

My stupid little spider bot hadn't made an appearance either. Its combat protocols were probably half corrupted with saltwater. I was of half a mind to just turn and run, but…my eyes glanced over towards Rel. That would mean leaving him here, at the mercy of this little gang.

And *that* tasted even worse than defeat.

I came to a stop, flipping the remains of the club over in my hand.

Blue grinned. "Finally decided to stop running away?"

I swallowed. Had to get him talking for just a moment longer. "Maybe I've decided I want to just beat your face in and get it over with."

He chuckled, twirling his sword. Pansy ass. "Oh, you'll have a hard time with that. Get her."

I blinked, eyes widening. There was a roar behind me, and I spun—

Only for Dum to catch my arm in his massive hand. I swore, pulling away, but the man pulled me into a bear hug and lifted me off my feet.

"What's your skull fucking made of?" I kicked at the air. "Titanium?"

Blue laughed again, walking closer. "Oh, you'll have a long time to learn about skull fucking when I'm done with you."

"Really?" I glared at him. "That's your best material? Fucking hell, and here I was starting to think you were half-competent."

Blue glared. "Beat the shit outta you well enough."

"Oh, look at the big strong criminal!" I simpered. "It took him two whole thugs and himself to take out a woman and a little boy! I'm so *scared*!"

"I'll show you scared, you little cunt—"

Then my spider dropped from the ceiling onto Dum's titanium skull.

He screamed, grip loosening. "Get it off! Get it off!"

I jerked my arm free, grabbing on to Blue's jerkin.

"Demon-itize!"

This time the oily black bolt sank right into his chest. He gasped, staggering backwards, hands flying to his…undamaged shirt.

Blue let out a laugh. "Well, that wasn't so—"

His left arm exploded. He screamed.

I blinked.

Well…it hadn't *really* exploded, now that I took a second glance. Instead, his pink human skin had more sort of…popped like a balloon to make room for a new scaled arm with massive talons.

He caught the scaled arm with his other hand, arm straining to hold back the new demonic appendage.

"Wh-what did you do to me?!"

I tilted my head. "You know, now that I think about it, the name Demon-itize is actually pretty obvious once you get past the pun."

He blinked stupidly at me.

Then the rest of him popped too.

Dum dropped me in shock and I landed just in time to step away from the blood splatter.

Left in Blue Hair's place was a hunched-over lizard thing, with dark green scales and a scrunched-up face. There were two extra arms coming out from the middle of its chest—kind of like a T-rex—and a short mane of blue hair in…homage, perhaps, to the man who'd spawned it.

I felt a connection spring into place between myself and the demon the moment we made eye contact. But, unlike the hobblefiend or the little jellyfish demons I'd summoned before, this creature felt more like an extension of myself than a living, thinking creature. I narrowed my eyes, willing it to move to my side.

It bounded forward, claws carving divots into the dirt floor.

I jerked back, shrieking.

Then it landed next to me, sat down and stared at me. Almost like a cat asking why the human was being so stupid—it did what I wanted it to, didn't it?

Maybe I was just projecting…

With a shake of my head, I turned to face the other two thugs. Dum was cowering in the corner as my spider bot menaced it with its forelimbs, and Dee was still lying on the ground, moaning softly as he cradled his jewels.

No, he was sobbing.

I sighed, walking over to Rel. He looked at me with his large eyes, blinking slowly as I pulled him to his feet. I gave him a nod. "Good job."

He blushed slightly, glancing to the side with a shrug.

Then I turned to face my newest…acquisitions. "Now then." I crossed my arms. "I trust there will be no further problems?"

Both men nodded violently.

It was a start.

CHAPTER 11

Basic Operations

"Put it down over there."

Dee and Dum did as I said, dumping the last few armfuls of thatching in the corner of the warehouse. I didn't know where they'd gotten it from, but that was secondary to getting our base of operations up and running.

"You two, finish repairing the eaves." I held out a roll of parchment I'd found on Blue. "I drew the design for you. *Don't* damage the parchment."

I never thought I'd be working with a sharpened stick of charcoal, but the needs must when the devil drives.

Or demons, as it were.

With a sigh, I moved over the chair I'd gotten myself. It wasn't even upholstered, but after the day I'd had, I'd take anything to rest my feet. I plopped down, the wooden frame creaking slightly. I smirked to myself as I ran a hand over my mechanical spider's metal carapace.

It beeped once, tilting slightly and sensors flashing, before settling back down on its perch. "Good work, General Tock." I'd decided to name him after his stellar performance at the warehouse. His diagnostics seemed to be going pretty well.

Beneath Tock, my newest demon rumbled, craning its neck. With a huff, I gave him a few scratches as well. "Haven't forgotten about you either, Blue."

My lizard let out a low trill, resting its head on the ground as Dee and Dum got to work.

I turned to my final follower. "Run over that report again."

Rel nodded. "Y-yes, my lady." I held back a sigh at the 'my lady;' next thing he'd be wearing a fedora or something. "The uh, Red Scars were a pretty small street gang. They had—uh—another two or three guys." He shrugged. "Prolly long gone by now."

I nodded. "So, no one *else* is likely to come after us?" Truth be told, I had been expecting to be noticed eventually. I just thought I'd have a bit more time to prepare before people came calling. It wouldn't be due to be caught unaware twice in a row.

"Uh, not for a few days?" He shrugged. "No one really cares about the ol' docks."

"Hence why these louts were here in the first place." I rubbed my face. "What territory did they control?"

"A bit o' the docks? Not much, mostly they just shook down anyone caught out after the evenin' bell."

I nodded. "Well, *that* will have to change." For the first part, mugging nobodies was a terrible business model. Even if you robbed a million people, a million times zero was still zero.

Sometimes, you needed to add something first.

"But, uh, the Red Scars paid some tribute to one a' the other gangs on the north side."

I nodded again. "You told me, the Tarnished. How long until their next payment comes due and they send people sniffing around?"

"The boys uh, don't know?" Rel wrung his hands. "They said their boss took care of that stuff."

"I'm sure he did." All the better to hide how much of the take he was pocketing. He'd had a full enough purse, covered in blood as it was. I wanted to track down the rest of his stashes, but that was a fool's errand. I had more important matters to attend to.

I rubbed my brow. "We'll need to start talking to the locals, then. I assume people still live around here?"

Rel shrugged. "A few? I dunno. My Da said it was only fishermen and people who couldn't put a roof over their heads."

At that, I smiled. "Perfect."

Rel blinked.

I patted him on the shoulder. "Never underestimate the ability of desperate people." I smiled a bit wider, thumbing the bulging coin purse tied to my belt. "There's a lot we can do with a bit of money, and hopefully, we won't even have to resort to extortion."

There were other matters to be worried about as well, of course. The guard, tax collectors, the other bigger gangs. But for now, it looked like I had time to get situated, start laying the foundations I'd need for my own little industrial revolution.

Hopefully without children working in coal mines this time around. There was enough *gilt leafing* this world already. Besides—I raised a hand, pooling a bit of mana into my palm—I had plenty of disposable labor to work with. I wondered if there were *forge* demons, and what they'd take for barter.

"Good work." I turned back to Rel. "If there wasn't anything else…?"

I wasn't just sitting back and making Dee and Dum put up a new roof. I had plenty of my own work to do as well. Summoning was… frowned upon in this kingdom, apparently—not that anyone in my little band of misfits had ever been beyond the city of Silverwall. But I planned on abusing it for all it was worth.

"Um…"

I raised an eyebrow at Rel. "Hmm?"

"There was somethin' else too."

"Well?" I waved a hand. "Don't keep me waiting."

"You said to tell you when I got a new class."

I nodded. "I did. So? Was it a rare class?"

"Uh, yes, Lady Via." He frowned. "Least, I think it is, I don't really understand it."

"What's it called," I asked.

"Filet Minion."

I groaned into my palm.

Rel shuffled, voice squeaking. "Uh, Lady Via."

"Just…read the unlock description."

"Fer, ah…defending your mistress with blades."

I nodded, face still resting in my hand. "It would be something like that, wouldn't it?" If I ever met the gods of this world, I'd kill them. "I'm just surprised they counted that rusted old sword of yours as a blade." It seemed that you unlocked classes based on some esoteric sense of 'achievement.' Apparently, it happened rather easily as well.

Though hopefully there weren't any more Filet Minions running around. I'd hate to have to…*cut down* the competition.

"What should I do?"

I let out a deep breath. "I don't suppose cobblers have much in the way of interesting skills?"

"No, ma'am." Rel tugged down on his cap. "I can repair shoes… Nothin' like what you have. Least thugs like the boys get blunt weapon mastery."

Yes, another interesting distinction I'd discovered in this world. The rarer the class, the more active abilities it had, while common classes had more simple passives. Given time, rare skills like mine were supposed to unlock passive abilities of their own. Of course, all of this information was based on hearsay.

Forget a portal, I'd kill for access to a Wiki about this world.

"Take the class," I said. "We don't have much need for new shoes here, at the moment." My own suit had inbuilt boots I'd trust over anything this world could provide. And the boys, all three of them, looked like they'd recently stolen a pair or three.

"Yes ma'am."

I saw him go slightly cross-eyed as he manipulated his menu. I really needed to work on that tell, for myself if no one else.

"Done…Lady Via."

I tilted my head. His posture had straightened slightly, hands going back down to his sides. "Well, what does that class of yours do?"

"I…assist my mistress in a-achieving her ends wherever possible?" His eyes glanced to me. "And…predicting her desires."

I hummed at that. "Well, I suppose you've been better than the usual minion I've had to work with in the past. And your skill?"

He quirked his lip as if holding back a laugh. "Cutting Words."

I sighed. "And there we go again." I waved him off. "Get some practice with that. Outside."

Rel looked at me sheepishly, closing his mouth. "Yes, Lady Via."

"Good." Reaching into my coin purse, I pulled out a handful of coins. "After you're reasonably sure you can control whatever your skill does, go to the market district. We're going to need some additional supplies." I glanced over towards Dee and Dum, who by now seemed to have gotten the hang of things and no longer needed my diagram. "I'll make you a list."

I opened my mouth to add some more instructions, such as what to prioritize, and what to do when he ran out of money, but then I paused. His class was supposed to make him a better minion.

Might as well see what that meant.

With a small smirk, I wrote up a list, containing both the essentials, food, basic building materials, and the like, along with a short wish list of things, capping it off with a lodestone.

If I could get my hands on that and some copper wire, the possibilities would be truly limitless.

I handed it to Rel, who swallowed, before tucking it up his sleeve. "I…I won't let you down, Lady Via!"

I raised an eyebrow at that. The boy was really coming into his own, wasn't he? Still, it wouldn't do to make him overconfident, so I just gave him a wan smile.

"You haven't yet."

CHAPTER 12

Relly Good Deals

The man glared. "Ten copper, final offer."

Rel nodded, handing over the coins with a smile. The shopkeep grumbled as he handed over a bolt of linen. It was rough material, but still worth much more than the ten copper Rel had paid for it.

Bartering came easier after unlocking Cutting Words, but Rel still didn't know what to think of the whole Minion class, especially the part about knives and all of that.

But it was better than being a cobbler.

Into the bag the linen went, along with the rest of Lady Via's purchases. Rel tucked the rest of the coins away, stepping out into the street. A man bumped into the minion, sending Rel staggering for half a step, cap almost flying off.

With a muttered swear, Rel caught the hat, jamming it back on and scampering out of the way of the two burly men walking down the street.

With a furtive glance towards the street, Rel ducked into a nearby alleyway, before reaching into her tunic and pulling a small case out from beneath her bindings. Rel held up the small, barely palm-sized mirror, hissing when she saw a long strand of dark brown hair had fallen loose from her cap.

She quickly tidied it up, tugging her cap low and cursing her bright blue eyes for what was not the first time and probably wouldn't be the last. When Rel had been growing up, she never thought she'd have to work so hard to look like an underfed street urchin.

Well, underfed Filet Minion now, whatever that was supposed to be.

With a nod, Rel tucked the mirror away again, letting out a sigh of relief when the metal was pressed against her skin once more.

It was one of the last things she had from her mother.

Pausing once more to make sure her cap was *firmly* affixed and to check that she hadn't lost her coin purse, Rel stepped back out onto the street. She let out a low sigh, before screwing up her courage and continuing through the market district.

Lady Via had given her a list of items to find. Thus far, she'd managed only the basics, some things were either too expensive or else entirely impossible to locate. Why would anyone turn copper into wire? At least she'd talked to a smith who said he could probably do it; she'd have to confirm with Lady Via before committing to a deal.

Rel stepped to the side of a large cart, heading back towards the old docks. The sun was high overhead, and the canvas bag she'd picked up to carry everything was digging into her shoulders, but Rel still had one more stop left to make.

Her feet pounded down familiar dirt roads as she moved away from the old thoroughfare. Stone buildings gave way to wood, and she ducked her head at the sight of familiar faces.

Not that she thought anyone would recognize her; it had been years since she'd left home.

But old lady Mara was still cooking stew in a pot right outside her door. Rel remembered her parents sending her over there for lunch, and the old woman would tell them tales of famous adventurers and daring knights. She taught them how to read too, even though Rel had hated it at the time.

It turned out that knowing her letters was the biggest reason she'd managed to survive after…leaving home. Most craftsmen wouldn't take on a dirty urchin, but one who knew their letters and could count higher than ten? That was a different matter.

Rel patted the parchment scroll tucked up her sleeve. Lady Via was the most recent in a long line of jobs, but she was the first woman Rel had worked for.

Rel didn't know how to feel about that. Her…Da and Lady Via wouldn't get along, to say the least.

She came to a stop in front of her old house.

If possible, it looked even worse than she remembered it. The wooden steps leading up to the door were half-sunk into the mud, and what little paint she remembered had long since been stripped off. She remembered painting that door with her Mom's crew, before.

Rel shook her head; there was a reason she'd saved this stop for last. At this time of day, all of the miners were working. She walked up to the door, lifting it by the splintery handle until the battered wooden hinge slipped clear of the latch and let her push the door open. Just like when she was a kid.

She closed it behind her, sucking in a deep breath at the dusty and grimy interior of her childhood home.

Even the warehouse looked cleaner.

She took a step forward, old boards creaking beneath her feet.

"Huah?" Rel froze at the voice. "Who's there?!"

She swallowed as a tall, gaunt man came around the corner. Her eyes caught on the near-empty green bottle in the man's bony fingers.

"Who the feck are you!"

Rel shivered, but…she wasn't the same girl who'd run away from here nearly five years ago. She was…she was better now, she had a *rare* class, and Lady Via had trusted her to find the things they needed, while Dee and Dum, career toughs, were busy putting up a new roof.

So, she raced her head. "Hello, Da."

The man blinked, eyes squinting at Rel before his chapped lips cracked into a grin. "Relly!" He spread his arms, teetering slightly. "I kn-knew you'd be back."

Rel didn't step forward. When her Da was on the bottle… She shook her head. "I'm just here to grab my stuff."

His smile collapsed into a sharp glare. "Eh? What stuff?" He straightened up slightly, towering nearly a foot and a half over Rel. She'd always had her mother's height. "Sold everything you didn't already steal."

Her heart clenched in her chest. "Thought you said you knew I'd come back." Her voice was rough; she hated it, clutching tighter at the bag at her side. "I dun care, just let me through, I want to look at my old room."

Da spat. "Thought I raised you better than that, Relia, didn't raise me no back-talking little shit, did I?"

She glared at him. "You didn't raise me at all!" She spread her feet. "Ma did, and the day she died you—you—ugh!"

Her Da chuckled, leaning forward. "You always did look just like her, Relia." He took a staggering step forward, hand reaching towards her. "Look, I know we didn't always see eye to eye, but yah came back. "We can"—he licked his lips—"talk about it."

Then his hand came down on her shoulder and Relia lost her shit.

"Don't *fucking* touch me!"

The words cut the air, not just in their volume, but with physical force. Her Da staggered back, clutching at his chest as her skill drew a thin line right below his clavicle. His hand came away bloody.

His eyes lost focus for a second, and she saw the exact moment he realized she had a new class.

Rel drew herself up to her full height. She was tall for a woman, taller than Lady Via certainly, but she knew she didn't look very intimidating.

Luckily, she had a class for that.

"Just let me go through my room, and I won't have to hurt you."

The man looked at her for a second. "Relia, who'd you get mixed up with? If it's one of them gangs I can help out, I've got connections and—"

"I dun—I *don't* need your connections." She took a trembling breath. "Go back to your chair, and I'll be gone before you finish that bottle."

She met her Da's eyes, and he looked away.

"'S not your room anymore."

"I don't care."

She walked forward, forcing the man to give way, shoving past him into the main room of the house.

It was a small building, but still bigger than most places she'd lived since running away. There was a rickety staircase leading up to a small loft where her Da's bed was, and a tiny little nook in the back that was her old room.

She opened the door and froze.

On her bed was a girl, barely older than Rel herself. She was asleep, but Rel could see the telltale graying skin around her eyes and fingernails. She shot a glance towards her father, stewing on his chair in the corner.

What she'd taken for just wrinkles were actually signs of Miner's Root. She bit her tongue, shoving into the room. She'd thought…

It didn't matter what she'd thought, obviously she'd been wrong.

The door banged against the far wall of her little room, and the girl on the bed stirred. "Aker?" Her eyes fluttered, pupils dilated. She looked around sleepily. "Again?"

Rel felt her gorge rising as the girl spread her legs slightly, letting the thin sheet fall off them.

She looked away, kneeling on the floor at the foot of the bed as the girl fell asleep again. Miner's Root did that, she knew people who took it just to sleep away the day. She just…never thought her father would be one of them.

Never thought he'd have a girl with hair the exact same shade as—

Relia bit her lip so hard it bled. The sharp tang of iron on her tongue drew her back to why she was here. Her Da said he'd sold everything, and she believed the—the bastard. But there was one thing he didn't know about.

She found the plank easily, even after all these years. Her fingers were bigger now, but she wormed them right into the crease in the warped board. She hissed as a splinter dug into her thumb, working the board upwards with short jerks.

It popped free. Rel's hand darted into the hole, yanking out an oilskin pouch. The fabric was dry and cracked, but it was unbroken. She undid the tie, peeking inside.

With a sharp nod, Rel pulled it shut again and stood.

She needed to get out of this place before she threw up.

Rel didn't spare a glance towards her father as she left the house, ignoring his plaintive whining. She stormed down the dirt roads of her old neighborhood, practically daring someone to get in her way.

For once in her life, no one did.

Before she even realized it, she was back in front of their warehouse. It was only a little deeper in the old docks than her house had been.

She remembered these streets; she'd been all over this part of Silverwall before her Ma had—

Rel swallowed, walking into the warehouse.

Dee and Dum were finished with the roof and were adding some more support beams to the walls. Rel picked out Lady Via on the far side of the room, deep in thought.

Shaking off the last of her shivers, she started forward again.

Part of Rel, a *large* part, still wondered why she kept coming back. She'd had ample chances to leave; hells below, a pouch of silver was even enough to buy an apprenticeship with a real merchant, one that wouldn't try to get his 'money's worth' after he realized she was a woman.

But for some reason, she returned all the same.

Lady Via looked up, lips pulling into that sly smile. "Good, you're back."

Rel gave a nod at that, setting her bag on the ground in front of the Lady.

Maybe it would go the same as every other time. Rel would get a new class, gain a level or two, and then leave. That was fine. Rel got a rare class this time, and in Silverwall, that was worth its weight in *gold*.

Via opened the bag, going over the contents. "Better than I expected, honestly." She shrugged. "I suppose it was a miracle to expect copper wire."

But…Lady Via trusted her. Lady Via had plans. Lady Via was an *outworlder*.

It was clear Lady Via wasn't a good person, but *good* people hadn't ever done right by Rel either. And there was always the chance it *wouldn't* turn out the same as it always did. That Rel wouldn't be turned out on the street yet again with nowhere left to go.

She'd had nowhere to go since the day her mother died.

Relia swallowed. "I found a smith who said he can make copper wire, but it's not cheap."

"No, it wouldn't be." Lady Via smiled. "But that doesn't mean it's not worth it."

Relia wanted to know how this woman always seemed to know where she was going, always seemed to have everything all figured out.

"I also have…this." She held out the oilskin pouch.

Lady Via raised an eyebrow, taking the pouch and weighing it in a single small hand. Then she opened it. Her expression lit up as she pulled the small compass from the bag. Even after all these years, the brass case was just as bright as the day Rel's mother had given it to her.

"*Be good,*" Ma had said. *"Be good and I'll bring you with me on my next voyage."*

But then she'd sailed away and never came back. And Rel had *tried* to be good. She'd tried and tried and tried, but all being good had gotten her was an empty stomach and another set of bruises.

"Oh." Lady Via's eyes widened. "Rel, you've outdone yourself." She grinned, and Rel felt a spark of pride growing in her chest. "Lodestone." The woman laughed. "We'll turn this world upside down!"

And Rel nodded, because being good had never gotten her anywhere.

So maybe it was time to be a bit wicked.

CHAPTER 13

Who Needs a Map?

Electra nearly collapsed in relief when the village appeared on the horizon.

"Finally!" She jogged down the last hill, a grin growing wider on her face. "Where were you a *day* ago?" With a huff, she tossed the worn piece of parchment over her shoulder. The map spiraled in the air, wrinkled parchment caught by the breeze before flying off to the ocean.

"Gonna need to convince Empress to 'invent' some GPS later," the woman muttered. She ran a hand through her sweat-slicked hair. The island was *hot*, and the road was so dusty it sometimes made her eyes water.

Still, the hard-packed road was better than the thick jungle that dominated the rest of the island. Electra breathed a sigh of relief at the sight of farmland. She was *not* cut out for jungle living.

She shook her head. All that mattered was that she made it. And also, that she made it before she ran out of water, but that was a secondary concern! She was a Hero, and Heroes didn't balk at things like rationing and stuff like that, not if it meant helping people.

"Hello there!" She waved a hand at the first farmer she saw. The man was stocky and built like a linebacker. He glanced up from his field, squinting at Electra as she jogged down the road.

"Yes?" He eyed her warily, but Electra ignored it.

Woman in armor comes running up to you? She'd be more surprised if he wasn't a bit suspicious. "Is this Ineir?"

"…It is."

"Great!" She placed her hands on her hips. "Heard you had a monster problem."

The man blinked before a grin broke out on his face. "You're here for them? Praise the Rain." He leaned on his…whatever he was using. Electra didn't really know about farm tools. "'Bout time the Guild sent someone!"

Electra chuckled. Well, she wasn't really *with* the Adventurer's Guild—though she would be soon, if all went well. "Where can I get more information about the job?"

"Hmm?" The man scratched the back of his neck. "Old man Hilv said he sent it all to the Guild with the request. Probably wasn't such a good idea…there were a lot of the damn hounds."

"Well, I'm not exactly with the Guild."

He blinked again. "You're not?"

Electra shook her head. The man looked like he was about to tell her off, but she clapped him once on the shoulder. "Last I heard the Adventurer's Guild marked this quest as too dangerous for any tier one Adventurers." She *had* done some research, of course.

Though, that research also included the current Guild entry fee, which she was hoping to save up for. She'd always wanted to join an Adventurer's Guild, so the fee was a bit of a bummer. But it was a temporary setback at best.

The man slumped. "Ah. Well…if the Guild won't take it, I don't think you should either, miss."

Electra laughed. "Relax. I can handle a few Strong Maws." She jerked a thumb towards herself. "I'm a Rare Classer."

"Well, sure, you could probably deal with the hounds, but…"

Electra tilted her head. "Did you have another problem?"

"No, no!" The man waved his hands. "Just, Hilv sent payment already, you'll…uh, have to talk to him about all of that."

Electra clicked her tongue. "Well, no one said adventuring was gonna be easy."

"That's why most of us don't do it." The man shrugged, looking away from her. "Best not to get in over your head."

She held back a huff of annoyance with the ease of long practice. "I can handle myself. Where can I talk to Hilv?"

The man grunted, shading his eyes for a moment. "At this time of day…probably at his house. It's the biggest one, right in the center."

"Thanks!" She smiled. "And don't worry, I promise I'll have this handled in a flash."

The man quirked a thin smile as Electra started past him. He shot a single glance over his shoulder before shaking his head and returning to his field. He had a lot of rocks to clear today. "It's not the monsters you need to worry about, miss."

Electra, for her part, just continued down the hill none the wiser.

She found the biggest house easily enough. It was the only one with more than a single story, including the 'inn.' The village…honestly, it looked a bit quaint, but they *were* farmers. Everything couldn't be all nice and shiny like in a book, after all.

She knocked on Hilv's door. After a moment with no reply, she knocked again, louder. There was shuffling from the inside, and a moment later the door swung open.

The man on the other side was certainly *old*.

He was bald, with a long straight beard going gray. The man rubbed his eyes with a single wrinkled hand. "Yes, miss?"

Electra put on her press-force smile. "I'm here to handle your Strong Maw problem." She paused, glancing off to the side. "I'm not with the Guild though, in case you were wondering."

"The Guild, pah." The man opened his door wider, beckoning her inside. "Shoulda known they wouldn't bother sending anyone." He gave her a toothless grin. "Still, it does an old man some good to see the young'uns taking a stand for us small folks."

"…Right." She followed him inside. The house was dirt-floored, and what she'd taken for a second story was actually just a loft area with what looked like a bed.

"Take a seat, take a seat." Hilv gestured to a small wooden table in the corner of the room. He pulled down a teakettle from a nail over a shuttered window.

Electra did as she asked, accepting the cup of tea a few minutes later. Hilv sat down across from her, bowing his head over the small plume of steam. "Now, you wanted to know about the hounds."

"Yes." Electra took a sip of her drink. "And also, about payment. I understand if you can't offer the same amount as the Guild. One of the farmers told me you already sent some money to them?"

"Hmm, should be able to cancel it. Still, it'll be a while 'fore we see any of that coin back." He nodded to himself. "If you kill those monster hounds, I'll be able to offer you…half a silver a head. Don't have much more to spare than that."

She held back a wince. The Guild notice had offered twice that much in payment, but Electra had just walked through the village, and they were not in good shape. She'd caught sight of more than a few buildings that were half-collapsed, and there were several overgrown fields as well.

After a moment she sighed. "That'll be more than enough." These people clearly needed the help, and the reward would cover the Guild's entry fee. Hopefully, she'd be able to get some food for her trip back to Silverwall too. "What can you tell me about the hounds?"

The man smiled, letting out a sigh of relief. "Rain bless your heart, miss." He cleared his throat, taking a sip of his tea. "Right, well, we don't know exactly where they are, but I can draw you a map of the general area. I know my letters well enough."

Electra felt her smile turn a bit brittle as she looked at his shaking hands. "Could I get a guide instead? Just someone to show me most of the way."

The man chuckled. "We need the men for the harvest, and none of the boys know the land as well as I do. You'll have to head a ways into the jungle, but they're not subtle creatures, them Strong Maws. Once you're headed in the right direction, you should be able to see their marks easily enough."

"Haha, of course…" But then, that was also what the merchant who sold the map had said. "How close to the village did you say it was, again?"

"Oh, less than a day's walk." He stroked his beard. "Maybe a full day, if you get a bit tangled up in the undergrowth."

"Great…" Electra nodded as Hilv stood up to fetch a stick of charcoal and some cloth. The moment he disappeared into the back room, she slumped. "Fucking maps." She shook her head, straightening a second later. "Focus, Electra. You've dealt with worse."

She managed to get a smile back on by the time he came back, shakily drawn map in hand.

At least she wouldn't have to go as far this time.

With one last nod, Electra took it and went outside, shaking her hand as she looked at the slowly sinking sun overhead. She sighed again. There was no way she'd be able to find them before nightfall. That meant she'd be sleeping rough.

Again.

"Well." Electra rolled her shoulders. "I'm probably doing better than Empress, right?"

Rel watched as sparks leapt from the coils of copper wire. Her eyes were so wide they felt like they were about to pop out of their skull.

Empress continued to laugh, features cast into stark relief by the *lightbulb* that glowed without a single drop of mana.

"Unlimited POWERRRR!"

CHAPTER 14

Dress to Empress

The sound of metal ringing against metal was music to my ears.

The warehouse had transformed over the last week and change. Whereas before it had been an empty expanse of dirt floors with crumbling stone walls, now it was an empty expanse of dirt floors with *completed* stone walls and a roof. Really, if you wanted my honest opinion, that was much more impressive than the little hand crank generator I'd put together.

I had power, but I still needed things that could use that electricity before my 'generator' started paying any dividends.

Of more immediate utility, one of the warehouse walls had been converted into an ad hoc foundry. I didn't know the first thing about smelting metal; luckily, there was a class of demons who agreed to work with metal so long as they were allowed to sleep in the forge itself. They were called Foundry Imps and currently I had two.

They were stumpy little wrinkly baby things with soot-gray skin and hands like miniature hammers. Really, they were about the most adorable thing I'd seen since coming to this new world. Unfortunately, as I peered into the forge, they were nowhere to be seen.

I sighed. Working with demons was hell.

"Hey!" I banged on the warm brickwork over the mouth of the forge with my palm. "Where'd you two scurry off to?"

A sooty gray head popped out of the burning coals. Large, dark eyes blinked up at me as the first of my imps sat submerged in the immolating coals the same way I might relax in a nice Sunday bath.

"Hrrga? Krrupbl Mrrrbaba!"

I could understand her—I'd decided this one was a 'her'—in the same way I could understand all my demons: an odd mixture of intention and emotion.

I frowned. "Yes, I know you finished the daggers on time," I replied. "Where's Mr. Burns?"

"Mrrrgl va Frrrra." This one, who I'd named Coaline, waved her arms. They were surprisingly large for such tiny creatures, with sharp claws not to be used as weapons but to engrave the metal of their forge with detailed filigree, they could ball them up into fists like little wrecking balls too. Coaline and Mr. Burns were excellent smiths.

They were *less* excellent roommates. "What do you mean you don't know?"

"Va Frrrrra!"

I bit my cheek in irritation. "That's not an answer."

Coaline gave a little shimmy of her ashy shoulders, horned head tilting side to side. "Crrramsha da Varrrmia mul."

I sighed. "Coaline, you both live in the forge. He couldn't have gotten lost."

"Mrrrvka."

"What did you do to him?"

"Mrrrgle va Frrrrra!"

And we were back to this shit. I rested my head against the mouth of the forge, the heat of the coals bathing my face. I was about to just order Coaline to tell me, our agreement allowed me that much, when another clawed hand sprouted from a mound of charcoal towards the back of the forge.

Fortunately, I had an expert poker face.

"Oh, so you have absolutely no idea?"

Coaline nodded eagerly.

I leaned back, smiling as Mr. Burns, a slightly smaller forge imp but with a bigger head (which was why I decided he was a *he*) hauled himself from the ashes. "Then I refuse to be held responsible for anything he does when he…shows up again."

Coaline tilted her head. "Vrrakama?"

"Graaaaaeeeeeeee!" Mr. Burns tackled Coaline into the forge with a war cry. I sighed as they tumbled across the interior of the forge, gray forms a dark blot against the otherwise glowing foundry.

They got along like a house on fire.

I tapped the mouth of the foundry once more. "Make sure you get started on the next batch of daggers when Tweedle Dee and Tweedle Dum show up with the metal."

I got what looked like a thumbs-up from Mr. Burns before he returned to noogie-ing the other forge imp so hard steam rose off her scalp.

With a sigh, I turned away. And people wondered why I didn't want minions getting around underfoot all the time. I had just enough time to take a seat in the stone chair I'd set up when the side door of the warehouse opened again.

"Lady Via."

I looked up as Rel slipped back into the room. "The boys are back, my lady."

I sighed, standing. "No rest for the wicked, huh?" I brushed off the leggings of my bodysuit, throwing my cloak over my shoulders. "Let's see what they found."

Dee and Dum shuffled into the room, eyeing the blue-maned lizard lounging next to the forge. Blue was a good boy, but he *did* take a lot of mana to maintain. Thankfully, he was lazy.

"Boss," Dum grunted, taking a step forward. "Did whacha wanted, cart full of metal is outside."

"Excellent work, Dum." I grinned.

He rubbed the back of his head. "Was nothing."

When I'd first...*convinced* the two lunks to work for me, I'd expected to learn their names, only to be told they didn't really have any. Their mother had called them 'boy,' when she bothered to call them at all, and from *that* lovely relationship, they'd graduated to a series of gang bosses or lieutenants who proceeded to call them much the same thing.

They seemed to like being Dee and Dum, especially after I explained how the names were connected. What a world, am I right?

In any case, they'd been happy enough carting metal in for the foundry imps. My budding industrial revolution was a hungry beast already, but the oceans were full of salvage that I could send demons to drag back to shore. It was effective and cheap; exactly what I needed right now.

Not that I would waste time with it myself when there was so much else to be done.

I turned to my first minion. "Rel, how did the first batch of daggers go?"

The boy ducked his head in the approximation of a bow. "It was hard to sell them in the market, too many guards. Plenty of gangs in the southern district were happy to pick up cheap weapons though."

I nodded. "As expected." The foundry imps worked fast, and even if we were still fine-tuning the right way to make steel (I remembered it had something to do with charcoal and the imps were eager to fill in the rest), cheap iron weapons by the cartload were sure to sell.

"How much did we make?"

"Less than a gold for the lot."

I shrugged. A good sword apparently went for a few gold pieces each, depending on the maker, and most good weapons fell in the same range. "The smiths can keep their specialty pieces," I said. "We're trading in bulk."

"Yes, Lady Via."

"Now." I turned back to Dee and Dum. With a crook of my finger, two little lizards, like smaller Blues, scampered down off of their shoulders. My little watchers, barely intelligent enough to follow my commands at all.

But more than enough to ensure there hadn't been any betrayal, at least, in the short term.

"The two of you have paid off your debt to me." I looked both of the stocky men in the eye, noting the way they straightened. "And maybe I'm an idiot, but I've taken a liking to your ugly mugs." They chuckled. I guess their boss hadn't been too kind with them either. "We're at the beginning of something here, something that will shake this entire city at its foundations. If you want to go on with your lives, you're more than free to go, but if you're interested in seeing more…"

I trailed off, waiting a moment as Dee and Dum exchanged a glance. Then I stepped forward, holding out my hand. "If you want to stay, then we can make a deal."

Dee paused a moment before stepping forward. "You treated us right, Lady Via." He grasped my hand, and I felt my new skill activate. "We'll work for you, as long as you do."

I shook Dum's hand a moment later. "I always do." I smiled at the three of them. We weren't anything impressive, but we would be. "First though! We have some important business to take care of." I waved my hand.

At my gesture, General Tock, my little spider robot, scuttled out from the corner of the shop, with three bundles of fabric on his back.

"Lady Via?" Rel asked. "What's this?"

"All good organizations have a uniform." I smiled. "This will be ours. I brought the design to the same seamstress that sold me this cloak." I plucked at the fabric. "It's hardly bespoke, but I wanted something special to commemorate the occasion." I had to hold back a giggle. "It's… been a while since I worked with anyone."

Longer still since I'd partnered up with anyone *competent*. Rel was turning out to be an excellent investment.

"I'll step outside so the three of you can get changed." Rel blanched. I raised an eyebrow at him. "Something wrong?"

"N-no! It's not that, Lady Via; it's just…" He shuffled, knees rubbing against each other as the boys shared a confused glance.

I sighed. "Rel, what did I tell you?"

"Right." He took a step forward, putting a hand up next to his mouth. "I-I'm a girl."

I blinked. "Wait."

He—she—nodded, blush rising on her cheeks. I gave Rel a quick once over, going over the details I'd picked up on before without putting them together. The slimness of her shoulders, how she always kept her hair tucked under her cap, the way she stood even.

"Well." I grabbed her by the shoulder. "I supposed it's good your uniform came with a hat." I yanked her into the small alcove I'd set up in the corner of the warehouse that doubled as my room, kicking the door shut behind me. "You can get changed in here."

Rel blinked owlishly at me before nodding slowly. I stepped back, leaning against the wall of my room to give her space to change.

Not that there was much space to be had. I'd set aside an area big enough for a small straw cot. Dee and Dum had their own places to sleep, and Rel had hung a rope hammock from the rafters. Guess now I knew why.

She pulled off her shirt, revealing that she wrapped her chest with strips of cloth, I held back a sympathetic wince at the lack of support. Still, I'd gotten her measurements right, and as she pulled on the clothes, I found myself nodding; they suited her just fine.

Rel struggled with the buttons though.

With a small laugh, I stepped forward. "Here. Like this."

She blushed again, glancing away as I did up the buttons on her shirt and vest. I ignored it, straightening out the fabric. It wouldn't do for my *Filet Minion* to look anything less than her best. I stepped back to take in the full effect.

"W-well?"

"Try not to stutter so much." I smiled. "It really doesn't suit you anymore."

Rel glanced down at her clothes before looking up at me in surprise.

I'd gone for a classic look, one that Cypher's henchmen had used before his fall: a black vest and white collared shirt to go along with black slacks. The *shoes* didn't match, but then, if I could find dress shoes on this planet, everything would be so much easier.

To top it off, I sauntered forward and placed a newsboy cap, black, of course, on her head. "You look sharp," I smirked. "Well, you would if you stopped tripping over your own two feet so much."

"L-lady Via!" She blushed. I just laughed, straightening out the little bits and pieces of her new clothing.

Fitted outfits were far more available here than they *should* have been in this time period. I'm sure Electra would have had some explanation for me, but I just put it down to bad writing.

Wouldn't stop me from taking advantage of it though.

With a smile still on my face, I pulled Rel back out into the main room of my little foundry. Dee and Dum were changed into their own outfits: black slacks, white shirts, and black coats. Simple, but classy.

I felt my smile grow wider. "It's a start."

Rel and the boys exchanged glances.

I clapped my hands. "Now! I have some new toys for all of you." General Tock scurried over once again, this time with a small sack. I picked it up. "Call it a...thank-you for your service." Of course, I planned to start paying them as well, but I'd need to figure out our profits from the daggers first.

For now, this would have to suffice.

I opened the bundle, revealing two metal rods and a small pouch.

"For the boys, I have these." The cylinders were a bit big for my hand, but they fit into Dee and Dum's meaty mitts perfectly.

Well, you know what they say about big hands.

Big beat sticks.

"Simply flick your wrist." I demonstrated, and the rest of the night-stick telescoped out, complete with the iconic weighted orb on the tip. "It's nothing special, but you'll find it much more durable than those sticks you were carrying around before." I pressed it shut again before tossing both to the boys. "They're made from some of my own alloy, so feel free to let loose. They won't bend an inch."

Dee fumbled his for a second before flicking it out and giving it a few swishes through the air. "Heh, sturdy." He gave a little dip of his head. "M' thanks, Lady Via."

I held back a sigh. "I keep telling you to call me Via."

"Sure thing, boss!" I gave Dum a deadpan stare before tossing him a weapon as well.

Lastly, I picked up the pouch, holding it out to a blinking Rel. "And this is for you."

Rel took it, letting the cloth wrapping fall from the very compass she'd given me a week ago.

Or at least it's outer casing.

Rel looked at me in askance. "Lady Via?"

I mimed opening it with my hands. "Take a look inside."

Rel blinked again, blue eyes going back to the latch. She pressed it, and the spring I'd painstakingly inserted popped the case open.

Her breath caught.

I smiled.

Rel's mouth opened slightly into an 'o' as she raised her other hand to cup the compass. Or rather, the ornate casing that had once been a compass.

I'd polished it with my tools, taking off the little bits of tarnish and bringing the elaborate filigree back to the fore. The inside was where I'd spent most of my attention. I'd taken out the rest of the bits and pieces of the compass, save for the etched rose itself. Behind that façade, I'd built a pocket watch, with twelve o'clock being north. The finishing touch was a small chain that could clip onto a button.

Rel's eyes followed the second hand as it ticked around the compass face. It…really hadn't taken me much more than a bit of time and having Mr. Burns make me some gears.

But I'd seen the expression on Rel's face when she gave that compass to me.

I didn't know where she got it, or who it belonged to, before it found its way to my possession. I knew that I was being given something precious, and as a villain, well...

I liked to think I saw the value in things and paid accordingly.

CHAPTER 15

Rolling Stones

"Knives are selling good, boss."

I let out a small sigh, patting Dum on the shoulder. "Selling *well*."

The man gave me a toothy smile. "Whatever you say, boss."

This was why I never hired minions. You do *one* nice thing for them, and suddenly they feel like it's okay to snark at you. "As long as we keep expanding our market."

Dee, who'd just pulled the cart back inside the warehouse nodded. "Been a lotta interest, people starting to grumble too. Muscling in on their business."

I nodded. "Please, as if I'd stop my plans just because a few smiths complain."

"Lots of guilds have a deal with the Adventurer's Guild." Dum shrugged. "Old Boss never wanted to mess with them much."

I cast an eye to Blue, my lizard demon. Currently, he was napping next to the warm bricks of the forge. "See where that got him." The boys both laughed.

There was an awful racket coming from inside the foundry itself. Part of me wondered if Coaline and Mr. Burns were actually working in there, or if they were trying their best to kill each other again.

I couldn't see them at the moment. But even if I could, I doubted I'd be able to tell with those two.

"Anything else to report?"

Dum shook his head. "Been looking for the rest of the things you need, no luck."

I sighed. "My kingdom for a table saw." At his slightly downcast expression, I patted him on the shoulder again. "It's nothing to worry about. I expected that I'd have to build most of the tools I needed."

There was a screech as Rel came in through the side door of the warehouse, cap tucked low. I glanced over as she pulled the rusty door once, cursing at the hinges before finally managing to pull it shut.

I'd trade my kingdom for some WD-40 as well.

She flicked out her pocket watch, glancing at the time before striding over to me. "Lady Via."

Rel had taken to her new outfit and her new role in my organization.

I caught her cheek with my hand. "So *quick* to hurry back."

You know, if she didn't blush so much *more* now.

"O-of course, my lady."

I smiled at her, moving back towards the forge. "So?"

"Oh, yes!" She clapped her cheeks once, returning to the competent minion I'd begun relying on more and more. "Some of the other gangs of the North Side are moving into the docks.

I tilted my head. "…So?"

Rel glanced over at the boys. Dee just scratched his head and shrugged.

"They're muscling in on your territory," Rel said.

I gave a little laugh. "Rel, we don't have any territory."

Dum leaned forward. "We don't?"

I huffed, crossing my arms. "How much money did your old boss pay you?"

Dee and Dum looked at each other. "Handful of coppers a week. Maybe a silver if we had a big score."

"And you're making more now, aren't you?" They nodded at my words. "*Because* we're not wasting our time with petty protection rackets and breaking into people's houses. Take from those with nothing and you'll *get* nothing." I smiled. "We're after much more lucrative marks."

A look of understanding went across the big men's faces. "That's pretty smart, boss."

I nodded. "And that's why I'm the boss."

"Yep."

"Lady Via…"

I glanced over at Rel. She was tugging at her sleeve, glancing off to the side. I sighed. Reaching out, I cupped her cheek again. Rel started. Honestly, I wouldn't do it so much if she wasn't so easy to surprise! "Didn't I tell you to always be honest with me?"

Rel nodded, eyes lighting up. "Yes."

I waved my hand. "Well?"

Rel rubbed her cheek where my palm had just been. I raised an eyebrow, and she blushed again, glancing to the side. "They're…hurting people."

I blinked. "The other gangs?"

Rel nodded. "The Red Scars kept a pretty light hand on things here. But the people coming in aren't going to be so kind."

I looked over to the boys for confirmation. Dee stepped forward. "We didn't have many people, just Boss and the five of us."

The other three of which had long since vanished. I wished them the best of it.

"Boss thought it'd be best not to 'over-extenduate' us," Dum said. "Gotta make sure we didn't bite off more than we could chew. But new gangs coming into open territory? 'S always bloody business."

"And where there's blood, the newcomers will want to make sure they get their share of coin." Rel crossed her arms. "Unless we do something."

I ran a hand through my hair, catching a lock around my finger. "Why didn't they do this before?"

Dee shrugged. "Wasn't worth it. Blue was all friendly with the Tarnished, see. Thems the big boys on the block."

I sighed. "And then Blue just up and vanished one day." At the answering nods, I tilted my head back, looking towards the ceiling of the warehouse. We'd just finished rethatching it this week. And there was still a lot of work to be done.

I looked back at my minions. Rel looked at me hopefully, while the boys…well, they certainly looked excited to bust a few heads. I guess they didn't sign up with me to be pack mules, no matter how good the money was.

I flicked my hair. "I suppose it would be a shame to have to relocate so soon."

Rel's eyes sparked. "Lady Via!"

"Yes, yes." I waved a hand. "Go grab a few daggers from the rack in my room. Boys, are you happy with the new clubs?"

Dee grinned, flicking out his nightstick. "Been loving 'em, boss."

I hummed. I swept up my cloak from the workbench, casting it over my shoulders. "How do I look?"

Dee and Dum glanced at each other in confusion. "Like…the boss?"

I tapped my cheek, glancing down at my outfit. It was still just my undersuit and the black cloak overtop. Sooner or later I *would* have to get some actual clothes. But for now… "It's missing something."

I cast an eye over my workshop, looking at the various bits and bobs I'd collected over the last two weeks and change. My ad hoc generator was still sitting in the corner for where I was working out some…connection issues. Then there were various bits of scrap metal yet to be fed to the foundry imps, and some other trinkets that my jellyfish demons had tossed up onto the shore.

Then my gaze landed on a familiar shape and I smiled. "Dee, grab me that leather belt from yesterday, would you?"

"'Course, boss." He lumbered over to a small chest in the other corner of the warehouse, going through the fabric there. I'd gotten some simple leather belts made for both of them along with the outfits, along with making the pants bigger than necessary so Dee and Dum could cinch them shut.

So, as expected, the pants fit perfectly, and the belts were too small.

Dee came back, handing me a length of leather that I wound twice around my own trim—*thank you very much*—waist twice before clasping it shut. Then I slipped the rusty sword and scabbard into the belt.

Rel had polished it up nicely after beating Dum over the back of the head with it. Unfortunately, she told me that no matter what she did, she still couldn't get the sword itself out of the sheath.

It looked nice though.

"There we go." I did a little spin, cloak flaring villainously. "Much better, don't you think?"

"Yeah." Dum grinned. "Looks dangerous."

"That's rather the point, yes." I crossed my arms, putting on my evil smirk #4. And yes, before you ask, I *did* practice them.

Every night in front of a mirror.

Rel came out of my room a moment later, several daggers sheathed at her waist. I could see a few more hidden under the folds of her vest.

"Hope you practiced drawing those," I said.

Rel smiled and nodded. "Only cut myself the first dozen times or so."

I blinked, opening my mouth to say something. But then she pulled off a glove, revealing a bandaged hand.

Instead, I just sighed. "What am I going to do with you people?"

Rel giggled, putting a hand over her mouth. She'd been less guarded around me since yesterday. "As long as you don't throw us away, you can do whatever you wish, my lady."

I huffed, trying to ignore my face heating up. Thank god for my tan. "Just tell me what we're dealing with already."

Rel continued to smile. "Of course." She crouched forward, drawing a crude map of the old docks in the dirt with her dagger. "The Red Scars didn't have much territory, pretty much just this slice near the wall." She outlined it. "No one else really wanted to fight on it. We're about here, by the by." She added a dot representing the warehouse.

"And who's coming to take this little bit of nowhere?"

"We got, sorry, we *have* two gangs." Rel scratched two crude arrows in the dirt, one coming from the south, the other moving in from the west. The southern arrow was much closer to our location. "From the west, we have the Black Tongues. They're pretty small time, same as the Scars."

"Bit bigger," Dum added. "But they never pushed in on us before."

"Right." Rel nodded, twirling the dagger across her fingers. "From the south is the bigger problem. The Tarnished." The boys let out a hiss. "Guess they figure they own all this territory because Blue used to be their buddy."

I smirked. "Here's the part where you tell me why I should be worried."

Rel rubbed the back of her neck sheepishly. "Well, they're a pretty big gang, probably figured they'd just run over the Black Tongues and anyone else who tried to move in. They've a couple of rare classes too, and the boss of the Tarnished is level 10." She leaned forward. "Rumor has it he's working towards his second class."

A gang boss only at level 10? Was this the tutorial or something? "So." I let my smile grow. "What you're saying is that if we beat the rust out of these Tarnished, the Tongues will leave well enough alone?"

Yes, yes, silver didn't rust.

Rel blinked. "Ah…pr-probably?" She rubbed the back of her head. "They probably won't take too kindly to that, since we did *used* to be the Red Scars gang that worked for them and all of that."

"Excellent. I love it when my actions can't be misconstrued." I whistled. Blue perked up from his place by the fire before bounding to my side. On all fours, the demon came up to my sternum and outweighed me by at least fifteen kilos, each and every gram packed full of chorded muscle just about to rip your face off.

Then I scratched him under his jaw, just how he liked it. Blue let out a happy little trill, hind leg thumping against the ground. "Who's a good boy? Yes you are, yes you are!" Blue butted his head against my stomach. "Want to go for a walk, boy? Want to go tear up my enemies for me?" He perked up, slitted pupils flaring in excitement. I grinned. "That's what I thought."

Dee and Dum threw open the doors to the warehouse and the five of us made our way out onto the street. I cast one last glance over my shoulder as Dee started to push the double doors shut. "Hold down the fort, General Tock."

My spider automaton skittered out of the shadows at the last second, giving me a jaunty salute right before the door slammed shut.

"Well." I turned back towards the dilapidated docks of Silverwall. "Let's go meet the neighbors, shall we?"

CHAPTER 16

Hello, Neighbor!

We marched through the streets in silence.

There weren't many people in this part of the city. No jobs in the old docks, no real houses either. All that was left for people was a place to stay if they had nowhere else to go. Of course, they took one look at the murder lizard padding menacingly at my side and found *somewhere* they had to be quick enough.

I took in the crumbling walls of old warehouses and other buildings. No wonder a 'gang' of six people could hold this section of the city; there wasn't anything to hold, much less *take*. Really, why would anyone want to be the 'ruler' of this little patch of dirt?

And people wondered why I preferred the company of robots.

"How much farther?"

Rel leaned forward at my question. "The people I talked to said people were busting down doors a little farther south. Where the houses start."

I nodded. "In other words, the only place with something actually worth stealing."

"Exactly."

It didn't take much longer for us to find the Tarnished. I spotted the small group of men the moment we rounded the corner.

They were dressed better than the Scars had been, with distinctive metal armbands that marked their allegiance.

I was hoping for silver but was unsurprised to see mostly unadorned iron. How typical.

Two men, barely more than boys really, stood in front of one of the bigger houses. One had a pickax clutched in his white-knuckle grip.

The other was struggling in a headlock.

"I suppose negotiations didn't go all that well."

"'Bout as well as they went with us, boss," Dee said.

"Well." I ran a hand through my hair. "We'll see about that."

The small group of Tarnished looked up as we came closer. The man holding the boy glanced towards his boss for a second before shoving his hostage onto the ground and pulling out a mean-looking dagger.

I took a moment to look over their levels.

<Cut Throat lvl 6>

<Thug lvl 8>

Those two were the two highest levels of the bunch, with another handful of the same thrown in. And, of course, at their head.

<Bale Blade lvl 8>

The Bale Blade, a young man with a long ponytail, saw us first and moved to head us off.

"Gentlemen!" I placed my hands on my hips. "What exactly are you doing here? On *my* turf?"

The man crossed his arms. "Heard this place belonged to the Scars." He grinned sharply, resting a hand on the sword at his side. "Or it used to before I moved in."

I sighed. "Like you moved back in with your mother?"

He snorted. "Think you're funny, huh?"

"Please, I *know* I'm hilarious."

The man flicked his sword from its sheath. "And who the fuck are you, anyway?"

"Why, I'm the new proprietor and this is my territory!" I waved my hands. "So, I suggest you go fuck in the *off* direction before I take care of you myself."

The man glanced over his shoulder, jerking his head towards his squad. One or two of them eyed the demon at my side, warily, but they moved forward all the same.

I sighed. "Maybe one day people will start actually listening when I warn them." Internally, I was already forming my first *Summon Demon*. By now, I had a feel for the spell, enough that I could skip the annoying middleman, so long as I knew what I wanted.

The other man just laughed, rolling his wrist. "Got a name?" He started walking forward. "You know, before I cut that tongue out of your pretty little face."

"Hmmm. You can call me Empress." I smiled at him. "Or you will when you're groveling at my feet."

"Get her!"

The thugs charged. I waved my hand, summoning half a dozen of my old standby, the hobblefiends.

Turns out Soul increased mana capacity, who'd a thunk it! Thank god I put some points into that before this whole mess. My gibbering army of demons launched themselves forward, with Blue only a second behind. I let out a satisfied grin as my little demons took down the first two criminals with ease.

Then I turned to look at the rest of my entourage with a raised eyebrow. "Are you going to make me do all the work?"

With a pair of bellowing laughs, Dee and Dum surged forward, flicking out their nightsticks. Rel ducked her head. "I helped last time." Then she was running forward as well.

Well, she wasn't really *lying*.

Ding!

System Messages

You have slain a Thug lvl 8
For defeating an enemy twice your level, bonus experience has been awarded

Oh, there went the first one.

I was just about to call it an easy victory when the Bale Blade leapt forward with a roar, spinning through the air until his saber looked like a solid disk of metal.

He twirled like a top, cleaving through my hobblefiends as Blue trilled and danced back in fear.

I blinked. I felt like I was missing something obvious.

A second later he spun to a stop, and I smacked my fist into my palm. "Of course!" The remaining fighters paused, glancing over at me with various expressions of surprise and shock. "You're named after that children's toy, aren't you?"

The man blinked before glaring. "I'll show you a—"

"Demon-itize!"

He threw himself into a roll as my bolt tore through the air. It smacked into one of the thieves, and the man shivered for a moment before popping as a slightly larger, uglier hobblefiend clawed its way out of his corpse.

Ding!

<You have slain a *Thief lvl 5.*>

<You have leveled up to level 5!>

"You'd think I'd get more used to it." I stepped to the side as a stray bit of blood sailed through the air next to me. "But really, it's just excessive, isn't it?"

"Get back!" I flinched; a wave of wind cut through the air right in front of my face. My eyes flicked over to Rel in surprise, but she wasn't looking at me.

I spun just in time to see her Cutting Words slam into the Bale Blade's sword, throwing off his stab. It scraped along the inside of my cloak, cutting a rent in the fabric.

I jumped back, hands coming up as a bolt of darkness formed around my fingers.

The man froze. A bead of sweat ran down the side of his head.

I held my hand steady. If I missed, he'd cut me down in a second.

But if I didn't miss…

Well. I could always use another demon or two.

Out of the corner of my eye, I saw the rest of the Tarnished pressed into a tight knot, fending off my demons and my followers. Rel was tied up dueling with the highest-level thug, her low level coming back to bite her despite her rare skills.

A real stalemate, then.

I gathered a second spell in my other hand, mana once again dripping down to near zero. Damn, *I* wasn't used to being the one with the stamina problem. The Bale Blade dug his feet into the ground, no doubt lining up for another spin.

Then I whipped my hand to the side and fired.

Pressed together as they were, the Tarnished couldn't even attempt to dodge my spell.

One of them screamed as he—

Well.

I've said it plenty of times already, haven't I?

Instead, I kept my focus on the last man in front of me. He cursed, eyes flicking back and forth between the fight and me.

Then he threw his sword.

"Fucking—"

I ducked to the side, bolt of inky blackness firing from my hand, but he was already running. My spell splashed across the wooden wall of a house and the Bale Blade vanished into an alley a second later. I shook out my hand, hissing softly.

Holding on to that skill really started to *sting* after a second.

I stayed watching for a moment longer, only turning when the first of the system messages began to push against my subconscious.

No second level up, but Demon-itize did go to level 2, netting me five more stat points.

With a sigh, I lowered my hand, turning back to the scrum in the middle of the street. The rest of the Tarnished were in a pile on the ground, Dee and Dum standing vigil over them. Whatever demon that had been birthed from that mess had apparently been trampled in the fight itself.

It was over quickly, but then, most fights were.

I looked to my boys. "Is there anything I should be aware of, regarding the injured?"

Dee shrugged. "Not unless you want to ransom them back, boss."

I quirked my lip. Then I turned towards the house that had started this whole encounter. An older woman had come out of the house; she ran her hands through one of the boy's hair, fretting over him. Maybe I was being hypocritical, but...

"Finish them off." I was never one for loose ends.

A quick glance over my shoulder found Rel. She stood over the body of the man she'd been fighting, a bloodied dagger clenched between trembling fingers. There was a gash on the inside of her arm.

That made me sigh. It was easy enough to tear a strip of fabric off of my already ripped cloak. Rel's eyes snapped up when I wound it around the gash in her arm.

Her mouth worked soundlessly.

"You did well." I tucked a strand of hair behind her ear. "Can you hold it together, for just a little longer?"

If not, I'd send her back with one of the boys. But it would be better if we showed no weakness.

I could tell she understood. A moment later she nodded.

"Just stand behind me, and…try not to faint." I favored her with a small smile. "I did, my first time."

Rel gave me another shaky nod, falling into step behind me as I moved to the family. I saw people peeking out of windows and doors as I came to a stop in front of them. The eldest one pushed his younger brother behind him, looking up—well, *down* but we don't talk about that—at me with hooded eyes.

"We ain't got nothing for you."

I rolled my eyes. "If I was looking for something, it wouldn't be *here*." I placed my hands on my hips. "Now listen up, all of you!" I turned my head, looking up and down the street. "This area, the whole territory the Red Scars used to hold, is under my protection. If you have any problems with outsiders, come find the foundry in the center of the old docks."

The boys shared a confused look. "There's…no foundry over there?"

I smiled. "There is now." With a satisfied nod, I turned and started walking. And with a snap of my fingers, the rest of my…*gang* fell in step behind me.

I ran my fingers through Blue's mane almost without thinking, my smile growing wider.

Empress had always been a solo act, back on Earth. I'd never bothered with organizations, or *territory*. At first, I'd been too raw to think about the future. Then I'd made the conscious decision to cut myself off from everyone. For their safety *and* mine.

But despite all of that, in this new world, well…

It felt *good* to be queen.

CHAPTER 17

Quest Complete!

Electra buried the hatchet into the Strong Maw's skull one last time.

Its body twitched once, limbs spasming as the doglike creature finally realized it was dead. "Shiii—sugar." Electra wiped her brow. She was breathing heavily, sweat matting her blond hair. "That was much harder than I thought it was gonna be."

She took a deep breath, straightening up, as she looked over the clearing. There were about six Strong Maws bleeding out on the jungle floor.

"Least I'm done here."

The jungle was thinner on this part of the island, so she hadn't had *too* much trouble finding the monsters. Strong Maws, now that she'd had *ample* up close and personal time with them, looked like a thickly furred dog, with a stubby nose and lots and *lots* of teeth. Electra could see why a village would have trouble with them, especially when farmers didn't really have a lot of combat-related skills.

Fortunately, they were weak to electricity.

Ding!

System Messages

You have defeated Strongmaw level 4!
You have leveled up to level 4!
Buzzer Bolt has increased to level 3!

"Heh." Electra grinned. "Not bad for a day's work." She'd only been level 2 when she left Silverwall, because Empress hogged all the kills from the first fight (not that they *should* have killed all of them, but she couldn't change the past). It was nice to finally make level 4. "Probably stronger than her now." Knowing her nemesis, Empress would probably be holed up in a building somewhere, making a magical super robot instead of grinding her levels.

With a sigh, Electra yanked the ax from the last monster's skull. She didn't have time to waste thinking about Empress. Next, she needed to cut off some ears or something for 'proof' of her kills and get back to the village. It was getting pretty late.

Not to mention that she was starving.

Electra turned just in time for a shadow to launch itself at her back.

She flinched, arms coming up defensively as one last Strongmaw lashed out at her. Its claws met her arm, only for it to be blown back in a blast of lightning.

"Frick and *frack*!" Electra jumped forward, chopping off the head of the whimpering mutt before it could regain its senses. She glanced into the trees wearily, looking for another attacker. Only after a few minutes passes with nothing else slinking out of the woodwork did she relax.

"Thank god for Lightning Reflex..." Electra muttered.

Skills	[2/5]
Lightning Reflex: Level 1	*Create a reflexive burst of lightning the first time an attack would hit you every fifteen seconds. Costs mana.*

She'd earned it from taking out a few of the stragglers late yesterday before finding her way to the main pack. Not how Electra expected to test it out, but hey, at least it worked! With one last nod, Electra slipped her axe back into her belt and started back towards the village.

Then she stopped, looked up at the sky, and turned around to march the other direction.

Her hand reached out, finding the mark she'd cut in a tree trunk less than twenty minutes ago. "Fricken stupid fantasy world without fantasy GPS." Luckily, after taking a day longer than she should have to find the Village of Ineir from Silverwall, she'd decided to track her location a little better. This time, it only took *two* hours longer than expected to get back to the village.

And at least forty-five minutes of that was because she forgot and had to go back for the ears.

It was evening when she knocked on the door of the village elder's house. "Hey! I'm back!"

After a moment and a rustle, the door opened to reveal the familiar face of Hilv. He'd hosted her while she scouted the surrounding village for the Strong Maws.

The old man's eyes lit up when he saw the clutch of ears in her grip. "You did it, then?" At Electra's nod, he moved to the side. "Quickly, quickly, come inside."

She raised an eyebrow, glancing over her shoulder towards the empty main road, but she let herself be pulled inside all the same. "Something up?"

The man sighed, rubbing a hand down his face. "I was hoping we could have avoided the Guild showing up in person."

Electra blinked. "What, the Adventurer's Guild? Didn't you cancel the quest with them?"

He sighed again. "I did. My hope was that such a small mission would be beneath their notice, but they sent several Adventurers to *assure* us we needed to hire them."

Electra frowned. "That sounds like extortion."

Hilv gave her a small smile. "And who'd listen to an old man talking 'bout that, eh?" He shook his head, puttering around the room. "We're simple farmers here, Miss Electra. Don't have the strength to muscle out the Guild."

She opened her mouth before catching herself. "They won't be happy with me for finishing that quest, will they?"

He chuckled. "Like as not, no." He patted her on the shoulder, but his wrinkled hands were steady and sure. "Don't worry, you'll get what we owe, I'll handle the Adventurers. Just…stay here."

Electra's frown deepened even more. "What will they do to you?"

"Make an example." He waved a hand at her outraged expression. "Don't worry, don't worry. They won't kill anyone. And the village will get its gold back at the end of the day. We'll just be paying in…other ways."

He moved to walk past her, but Electra caught his arm. "I'll talk to them."

Hilv looked up at her in surprise.

"It's my fault, after all," Electra said. "I didn't have the money to pay for the entry fee." The words tasted bitter on her tongue, but if being a Hero was easy, everyone would do it. "I thought I could make it solo. Didn't think things were like this."

The man shook his head. "Miss Electra, that's…" He waved his hand helplessly. "They're higher level than you, rare class or not! Even if you manage to defeat this group, there are *hundreds* of Adventurers in Silverwall!"

She cracked a grin. "Don't worry," she parroted. "I'm not going to fight them. Where are they, anyway?"

The old man sighed. "In the tavern."

"Least they're paying for food."

The man gave a small nod. "It will help pay for the damage."

Electra held back a wince. Damage?

Any intention she still had of fighting it out went up in smoke. She wasn't here to make these people's lives harder. She just…

Electra shook her head, putting on her best press conference smile. "Don't worry about it! I'll make sure it's all taken care of."

The man gave her a doubtful look but didn't stop Electra as she exited his house, marching across the simple dirt road in the direction of the tavern.

The group of Adventurers met her right in front of the entrance. The first was a man in leather slipping out the door. He held it open, letting two women step out. One was wearing armor, and the other a cloak.

Electra gave them a quick once-over.

<Warrior lvl 8>

<Rogue lvl 6>

<Archer lvl 6>

The man was the rogue. As made clear by his dark leathers. He had enough daggers to outfit a small gang to go along with it. The two women were the archer and the warrior, respectively. The warrior was the smallest of the bunch, but Electra guessed that classes and stats made size less important.

The warrior had muddy blond hair, and a big old 'frick you' ax hanging off of her back. The archer had a bow, and she was fingering the quiver of arrows peeking out from beneath her cloak.

Electra could tell in a heartbeat; these people were looking for a fight.

"Hello there!" The warrior raised a hand, giving a cheery grin. "Heard there was another Adventurer around here. Any chance we can see your Guild card?"

Electra sighed. "Sorry, I'm not a part of the Guild."

"Not a part of the Guild?" The girl put on a surprised expression. "Not a part of the *Guild*! This entire area is our turf, you know. You can't just go muscling in on our quests; it depreciates the value of our members."

Electra said nothing, holding her tongue by force of will, and many, *many* public relations courses.

After a moment, the warrior girl shrugged. "Well, I suppose we can make an exception for you just this once. As long as you say you're sorry." She leaned forward, fingers playing along the haft of her great ax. "You are sorry, aren't you, rook?"

"Yes." Electra ducked her head, swallowing the taste of acid on her lips. "I'm truly sorry, I didn't understand."

"Mmm, that's better." The warrior stepped forward, reaching under her own brown cloak to pull out a pouch. "Well anyway, here's what you'd get, minus the fee for canceling a quest." She gave a smile. "Of course, we'll have to make up our payment in other ways, but as a prospective Guild member, you don't have to worry about that, do you?"

Electra eyed the simple cloth pouch. Maybe it wasn't a lot of coin for a team of Adventurers, but a one-woman job like her? It was a lot of money.

She could also, of course, read in between the lines.

'Damage' and 'recouping costs'? Please, they were going to *make an example* of the whole village. They were being nice to *her* to tell her which side *she* was supposed to be on.

Electra…really fricking hated gangs.

But hating them wouldn't fix anything. Making a scene wouldn't fix a single *damn* thing.

So she just smiled and took the pouch. "I get it. But hey, it was my fault, you know? Let me cover your costs for these people." She leaned forward. "Not like they have anything worth taking anyway, right?"

She reached into the pouch, pulling out a handful of coin—less than half—before tossing the rest back to the warrior.

The woman blinked before breaking out into a more natural grin. "You're not so bad, rook!" She slapped Electra on the shoulder. The Hero held back a wince as she lost a few points of HP. "Knew you'd figure it out."

"Well, yeah." Electra smiled, rubbing the back of her head. God, this was almost as bad as that one time Wonder Man asked her out in front of an entire press corps. "Thanks for spelling it out though; I'm kinda slow."

"Everyone is, at the start." The woman laughed. "Hey, we're pretty much done here then, wanna come back to Silverwall with us? We can get you all squared away with the Guild." She gave Electra an appreciative once-over. "Rare class like yours, we'd love to have you on our squad."

Scratch that, it was worse.

Electra's smile grew a little strained, *especially* at the venomous glare the archer fixed her with over the warrior's shoulder.

"You know, normally I'd love to, but I've been hiking through the woods all day. You all go on ahead, I want to have a chance to clean off before walking for another day."

"Sure, sure!" The warrior patted Electra again. "Look us up when you get back to the city, name's Vire."

"…Will do!"

With that, the three of them turned to leave; apparently heading back to Silverwall at night wasn't a big deal for more seasoned Adventurers.

The rogue, a man with jet black hair, glanced over his shoulder. *I'm sorry*, he mouthed.

Electra blinked. She shrugged; nothing he could do about that. All too soon, they vanished back into the surrounding woodland.

Electra was left standing in the middle of the road, half a pouch of loose coin still clutched in her raised hand.

And no idea what she was going to do next.

CHAPTER 18

An Offer You Can't Refuse

Status	Unspent Status Points: 10
Physical	Strength 1
	Endurance 2
	Agility 4
	Dexterity 3
Ethereal	Charm 1
	Faith 1
	Attunement 1
	Soul 4

I looked at my stat sheet. The fight with the Tarnished had bumped two of my skills up a level, which left me with more stat points to spend.

I still didn't really get these stat points. Did they have second-order effects? The physical ones certainly seemed to. But would I become more *faithful* if I put points in Faith? Or were they just numbers plugged into my skills? On one hand, I wanted to run some tests on these, but every point was precious. The last three points that I'd invested in Soul had paid dividends in that fight.

I certainly wasn't feeling more *soulful*.

But what if they had larger effects later on?

After a moment, I huffed. Being all indecisive like this? It was a bad look. And here I'd made fun of Electra, while I was agonizing over where to put all of my points.

I heard a cough from the side. "Lady Via."

I rubbed my eyes. "More of them, already?"

Rel nodded. I could see a smirk playing around the corners of her lips. "It would seem so." She'd gotten pretty cheeky recently. Not that I hated it.

With a sigh, I distributed my stat points and confirmed.

Status	Unspent Status Points: 0
Physical	Strength 2
	Endurance 3
	Agility 5
	Dexterity 4
Ethereal	Charm 4
	Faith 1
	Attunement 3
	Soul 5

I'd stick with a balanced build for now, see if I could pick out any other effects that matched up later on.

Except for Faith.

Fuck religion. Not to mention that an actual, factual demon told me that there *were* in fact gods in this world and I did *not* want to attract their attention.

I turned to the front of the warehouse before my nose suddenly started to itch. I sneezed into my wrist. "Ugh. Dust." I ran a hand through my hair, flicking it back over my shoulder with a negligent twist. "Let's go."

Rel stared at me, eyes blinking.

I tilted my head at her leaning in. "Rel?" I peered up into her eyes. "Is something wrong?"

Her eyes widened and she stumbled back a step. "N-nothing."

I frowned at her, but my minion was already heading towards the front of the warehouse. After a moment, I shrugged. She'd tell me if it was important. I followed a step after her, smiling as Rel opened the door for me without asking.

I'd never say, but the cutest bit was how she still stuttered sometimes, especially as she tried to act more composed.

Outside my warehouse were four men and a woman, all older than me, just going by the wrinkles in the faces. Their classes were beggar and thief and not much else between them, just like every other group of people that came to the warehouse after I'd beaten back the Tarnished.

I held back a sigh. This is what I got for offering a decent wage to people who worked for me, huh? Hiring the first group had seemed like *such* a good idea at the time.

Well, the only reward for good work was more work, as they say. "I take it you're all here for a job, huh?"

There were some glances before they nodded silently. I placed a hand on my hip, looking down at each of them. They looked hungry and down on their luck, but that was nothing new. "There's a bunkhouse across the street. Go there, get some food in your bellies." I narrowed my eyes as the new recruits shifted. "Consider that part of the payment for the work you *will* be doing. Coin will come later, but I *don't* tolerate broken agreements, on either side." I waved a hand. "If you still want to work for me, go see Dee and Dum and they'll get you situated."

The food was just a simple stew, but making people work on an empty stomach? Please.

I had standards.

I looked down at them for a moment more before one of the older men sketched a little bow. "Thank you kindly, Empress."

I waved a hand, going back inside my workshop with Rel half a step behind. I made my way over to my workbench, where General Tock was organizing the tools I'd managed to put together. "At this rate, it'll start getting difficult to feed them all."

Rel stopped a bit behind me. She shrugged. "It's useful to have more hands. And your demons can start fishing as well."

I nodded silently. The old building across the street had been torn down and rebuilt into a bunkhouse in the fraction of the time it took me to put my little foundry together. There wasn't anything of *value* left in the docks, but piles of stone that used to be buildings? There were more than enough of those to go around.

"We're not exactly flush with coin all the same." I should know, I was the only one with a good enough grasp of math to do the accounting.

Considering all I needed was some multiplication and division, that said more about this place than it did about me.

"I can always tell the enforcers to turn them away, Lady Via."

I felt my lips quirk into a frown. "And leave them to starve?"

Rel shrugged again. "They've made it this far."

"Yes. They have." I leaned over my workbench. I'd known plenty of people who'd made it 'this far' in my life. For some reason, I wasn't too interested in making more of them. "We'll have to expand."

At that, Rel smiled. I scoffed at her happy expression. "Please, you didn't *really* think I was going to hang them out to dry." I gave her a gentle shove.

Rel took a step back before laughing. "I just…want to be helpful."

"You are. More than I can say." I rolled my eyes. "And I *don't* need you playing devil's advocate." I tapped my head. "Got enough of them up here already."

"Ah…r-right." Rel nodded. "What should we do then?"

I hummed, turning back to my workbench. On it I'd put a single iron ingot. Steel was harder to make, but we had plenty of charcoal now, our only 'expense' outside of labor. "There's always a need for more steel…"

I was drawn from my thoughts by a banging on the doors to the warehouse. "Boss! Got a boy from the Tarnished here for you!"

I shared a glance with Rel before pushing myself upright and marching back to the door. Outside was a man, but unlike the ones who'd been trickling in to work for me, he didn't look worn down by the world.

"Hello, *Empress*." He gave a friendly smile, running a hand through his dark red hair. I was immediately on my guard.

<Rogue lvl 10>

He wasn't a pushover, even then. Why would a gang we'd just sent running for the hills send someone to talk with me *alone*?

"And you are?"

"Devarin, at your service!" He gave me an elaborate bow. "My boss sent me because he thinks we've had a bit of a miscommunication and is willing to let bygones be bygones if we can…come to an agreement."

I crossed my arms. "Oh, and if I think that you are the ones who… miscommunicated?"

"All the more reason to work things out, face-to-face." Devarin smiled.

"A parley, then?" I sighed. Politics.

"Of course."

"Well." I folded my arms. "Tell him we can meet on the edge of my territory, there're plenty of buildings for him to choose from if he wants to sit down."

"Oh, I'm sorry, I should have been clearer." Devarin tilted his head, and I felt the hairs on the back of my neck go up. "You'll be meeting with him now, at the Poisoned Apple."

That was the name of a tavern close to the center of their territory. According to Dee and Dum, the Tarnished used it as a de facto headquarters.

I nodded, tapping my chin. "And why, pray tell, would I ever agree to do something as stupid as that?"

"Well, because you don't have a choice, really." Devarin clapped his hands.

I stepped back, hand coming up with my spell already formed. Devarin made no move to dodge.

Then I heard Rel hiss behind me.

Devarin smiled as I froze. "Go on, I promise I won't attack…first."

Slowly, I glanced over my shoulder. There was a person wearing a dark hood. They had their arms around Rel, pressing a knife to her neck.

<Assassin lvl 9>

There was a commotion across the small dirt road as the door to the bunkhouse flew open. More men with knives came out, pushing my people in front of them.

Last out were Dee and Dum, sporting more bruises and cuts than they'd had a few minutes ago.

Every single one of the Tarnished was a rogue or an assassin. Higher level than us, and they outnumbered us as well.

Slowly, I lowered my hand, releasing the spell. In my chest, the surprise faded, replaced by a growing volcanic rage. I thought the Tarnished would either stick to easier pickings, or else come at me head-on. Instead, they'd knifed me in the back before I even thought to look.

"Now then." Devarin held out his arm. "Shall we go?" He cast a faux careless glance over his shoulder. "I'm sure you don't want to be…late."

I did not growl at him. I didn't let a single speck of anger show on my face.

Control your anger. Never let it control you.

I pushed it down, building walls around my anger, like coals in a forge. They glowed bright hot, but on the surface, I remained as cool as ice.

"Of course." I slipped my hand into his elbow, putting on a smile. "I would love to."

I fell in step behind Devarin as his men moved to tie up the rest of my people. I cast a single look back at Rel. She met my eyes, question plain in her gaze, but I shook my head.

She wouldn't gain anything by dying pointlessly here.

"Something on your mind?" Devarin asked.

"No." And after this little display… "Nothing at all."

My revenge would be much more *personal*.

CHAPTER 19

One Day I Will Call Upon You

The worst part of the mess wasn't being held at knifepoint myself.

It wasn't even that I was being escorted into enemy territory to meet with people stronger and more influential than me. Really I'd been in this kind of situation more than a few times. And don't even get me started on the hot mess that was the Papaya Gambit.

No, the worst part was that my escort kept trying to make conversation.

"So, what brought you to Silverwall, anyway?"

Your mom. The puerile insult was on the tip of my tongue. You'd be surprised how many 'unflappable' enemies could be thrown off balance by stuff like that. However, I needed to be seen as…reasonable, for the moment. I needed to be *useful.* I knew how these types of people worked.

I was one myself after all.

"I decided that I needed a change of scenery." I looked over my shoulder, taking in the two level eight rogues shadowing us. "Though I was hoping the locals would be nicer for a change."

The man laughed. "Rare classes are in demand wherever you go." He raised an eyebrow. "Or didn't you get told when you tried to come into the city in the first place?"

I raised an eyebrow. So that's why the guards were chasing after me. "If I was the type of person who listened to the guards, we wouldn't be having this conversation."

"True." He smiled. He thought he was pretty charming, didn't he? A real scarlet pimpernel who was going to win me over by the end of the night. What a joke. "Usually, if you have a rare class, you have to serve the Baroness or the Guild."

"I've worked for the government." I rolled one shoulder. "It didn't agree with me."

"No." He leaned in closer. "You strike me as a free spirit, the type of woman who likes to make her own decisions."

I raised an eyebrow at him. "Like where and when I was going to meet your boss?"

He gave another laugh, this one a bit more strained. "Well, that's…"

"We're already here, aren't we?" I pointed to the somewhat larger building, clearly a tavern, that was set against the north wall. Just like Rel said, the Tarnished were pretty close to my territory.

"Yes, that's it." He slowed slightly. "But we don't need to…"

I pulled my hand from his arm, striding ahead of my escort. I could play the game if I wanted to; sometimes it was even fun.

But I only played on my terms.

Behind me, the rogues scrambled for a second before catching up to me. The man, whose name I'd already forgotten, had an annoyed expression on his face. "You can't just go on ahead whenever you want."

"Oh?" I smirked. "I was under the impression your boss wanted a meeting with me." I stepped onto the small porch at the front of the building. "Run along, junior. The adults have business to take care of." I pushed through the double doors without another second's delay.

The inside of the tavern was dimly lit, with a merry fire going in the fireplace. The chimney and firepit were set behind a small counter, probably where the owner of the inn cooked. Around the room were several wooden tables, well made and lacquered, even.

A handful of lanterns were mounted on the walls as well, though where I expected to see candles, instead most of them glowed softly with a blue orb of light.

They looked expensive, with worked brass casings and, if I squinted, I could see what looked like intricate patterns carved into the interior. Enchanted lights, then? They looked too expensive for this dive.

The lone man at the table glanced up as he heard me enter. There was a woman standing at his shoulder. They shared another look as I moved into the room, the three rogues trailing at my heels.

I came to a stop in front of the table. "I heard you wanted to talk." I waved a hand. "So, let's talk."

The woman, a <Warrior lvl 11>, frowned. I kept a wary eye on her. If she was level 11, did that mean she had a second class? I couldn't see anything.

The man laughed, slapping the table.

"And here you thought she'd be a meek little dove."

The woman's frown deepened. "I said that I expect you to keep her *in hand*." She narrowed her steely gray eyes at me, and I felt the back of my neck itch.

Now that I had a chance to look at them, it was clear the woman was no gangster. She had clean steel armor on, with a golden tassel hanging from her left shoulder. For a second, I thought she was a captain of the guard or something.

But then the man rubbed his chin. "Oh, of course." He waved at me. "Well take a seat, best get the particulars out of the way before the Guild gets any more anxious."

"We are not *anxious*." The woman folded her arms. "If anything, you should be worried about breaking your end of the deal."

I slid into the chair across from them. "He got me here, didn't he?"

The woman let out a breath of air, looking away.

"Don't mind her." I looked back to the man. He had laugh lines around his eyes and a short cut salt and pepper beard that made his smile look all the more welcoming. With a bit of focus, I could see that his class was <Card Shark lvl 10>. I suppressed the urge to frown.

At this rate, he probably turned into a shark made out of playing cards or something equally asinine.

"No promises."

He grinned, holding out a single hand. His fingers were worn and scarred. "Arlo."

I gripped it. "Via."

"Pleasure." He gave my arm a solid pump before letting go. I held back a sigh. One day, I'd meet a person whose hands didn't just engulf mine. I know that I'm tiny, world, you don't need to rub it in all the time…

"So." I leaned forward, placing my elbows on the table. "You came into my territory, I kicked you to the curb, so you decided that threatening my people, and dragging me here was the way to go." I gave the two of them my best smile. "Why don't you tell me what you want so badly."

"We want *you* to stop making waves and—"

Arlo held up a hand. "Thought we agreed you'd let me handle this, Delia."

The woman glared down at him. "If you'd handled it to begin with, I wouldn't even be here." The man just shrugged, and after a moment the woman sighed again. "Whatever, we'll do it your way, this time."

Trouble in paradise? How wonderful.

Arlo turned back to me, still grinning that lazy grin of his. "Let's set aside our little spat, to start with."

I raised an eyebrow. "Oh?"

"You can imagine my position, no?" He waved a hand. "A long-time friend of mine up and vanishes, and no one steps up to take care of his house. You can forgive me for thinking it was vacant." His smile turned sharp. "And maybe I can forgive you for killing my men when they walked into your house."

I glanced over my shoulder. "Your boys gonna be okay with that, old-timer?" I didn't bother mentioning how much I doubted he saw Blue as a *friend*.

Arlo laughed. "Oh, everyone's happy when a new position opens up." He grinned. "And don't worry about our little Bale Blade friend, he shoulda known better than to make decisions on his own."

"Well." I tossed my hair. "I do know a thing or two about boys making bad decisions. So, let's say I accept your gracious offer. What next?"

He shrugged. "Heard you been selling a lot of cheap daggers from that foundry of yours."

I tilted my head. "A girl has to make a living."

Arlo let out a deep chuckle. I got the feeling that not many things bothered this Arlo. Men like him were useful allies, but just as terrible enemies. "Yeah well, looks like you got someone's britches in a twist." He jerked his head towards the woman behind him. "The Adventurer's Guild doesn't like it when people mess with the other guilds, you know."

"Like the Blacksmith's Guild?" I raised an eyebrow. "I wasn't aware that they were such good friends of yours."

This time Arlo leaned forward, hand coming up as if he was sharing a secret. "That's the thing about Silverwall, *everyone's* a friend here. Until you aren't."

I hummed. It seemed that I'd stepped right into the middle of a protected market. "If they can't compete, that's their problem." I smiled at them both. "That said, I'm sure I could be talked into a more equitable arrangement, for my…friends' sake."

Delia's armor creaked but otherwise she didn't say anything.

"Don't we all?" Arlo leaned back. "Normally, no one would care, but you've been a busy little bee this past few weeks."

"I try."

Arlo nodded. "Now, between you and me." He leaned in. "I'd just wait for them to come down on you like a shit ton of bricks. But Delia here showed up, wanted to make sure I was keeping control of things in this part of town." He waved a hand. "So here we are."

I nodded. "You must be really good friends with them."

"Well." His grin grew sharper. "I try." He tapped the table. "So, to business. First off, I'm afraid you'll have to stop selling in the southern districts. Us gangs, we stay up here, and the Guild doesn't come and kill everyone, see?"

Delia stepped forward. "You'll also be providing some weapons to the Guild."

I raised an eyebrow. "Will I now?"

"Yes. Or I'll have Arlo here kill all of your men."

I felt the tiny ember of rage in my chest ignite once again, but I didn't let a bit of it show on my face. "So?"

She glared at me. "Don't try to play this game with me."

I tilted my head. "Last I checked, the only one playing a game here was you, Delia." Her glare deepened, but I continued before she could speak. "Let's see. You want me to stop selling my wares to appease your friends in the Smithing Guild." I checked it off on my fingers. "But then you want those cheap weapons for yourself, for free." I smiled at her. "Not happy that those pesky smiths came whining to you either, now?"

She huffed and pulled her spear off of her back, leveling it at me. "If you don't care about your people, I can always just kill you instead."

I smiled wider. "But who would make you those cheap steel weapons then?"

"You only make iron."

"I only *made* iron." I buffed my fingernails on my cloak. "Of course, steel isn't cheap to make, especially here where, well…" I leaned around the spear. "There's a reason they don't call it *Ironwall*."

After a moment, Delia pulled back her spear. I nodded, sitting back in my chair. I'd suspected that this island didn't have a surplus of iron when I saw the prices *other* metalworkers were charging, but Delia's reaction cinched it. There was a reason all of my iron was scrap I dredged up from the bottom of the sea.

"I'll provide you weapons at three times the old rate."

"Three times?" She shifted her spear again. "Maybe I should just kill you and save us all the trouble."

I raised an eyebrow. "If you think steel should be as cheap as cast iron then no wonder you're having trouble with the Smithing Guild."

She snorted. "We'll pay on delivery." She walked past the table, making sure to kick my chair as she passed. "Arlo will see to the details."

Arlo laughed, but I could see the annoyance on his face. "Of course, of course! Don't worry your pretty little head about it."

"Believe me." Delia opened the door. "I won't be the one worrying about my head."

The door slammed shut a moment later.

I tapped my chin. "She's a real joy to work with, isn't she?"

Arlo let out a darker laugh. "You don't do business in Silverwall without going to the Guild."

I turned back towards him. "Would you like to?"

Arlo blinked slowly, leaning forward. "I don't think you know what you're suggesting, girl."

"Well." I knitted my fingers together, resting my chin on the back of my knuckles. "If you'd rather stay Delia's errand boy…"

He put one muscled arm on the table, fixing me with a sharp look. But one doesn't become a gang leader if they lack *ambition*.

"…What do you have in mind?"

This time I was the one who extended a hand. "Why, a partnership, of course." I smiled. "Nothing untoward."

What's a bit of conspiracy between *friends*?

CHAPTER 20

Conspiracy Cute

I slammed the door of my warehouse shut behind me the moment I'd issued orders.

"My lady…"

"Shush, you." Dee and Dum were unbinding the rest of my men outside, who were then to be given food and rest after the last of Arlo's gang had left. Rel, on the other hand, I'd dragged inside to handle personally. I slipped a knife from her jacket, slicing the thick rope binding her hands and legs together.

"I'm sorry I couldn't escape."

"I thought I said 'shush.'" I ran my hands up and down her arms, looking over the minor bruises. I grit my teeth.

"But I—"

I pulled the stupid girl into a hug.

She was taller than me, annoying as it was. But at the very least she could stop talking about nonsense like 'breaking out' and killing half a gang by herself while everyone else was being held hostage.

"Enough of that." I took a step back, meeting Rel's eyes. "You would have just gotten yourself killed. And you're no good to me dead, Rel." I shook my head. "No, this is my fault. You should never have been put in that situation in the first place."

She said nothing for a second, mouth working soundlessly.

I sighed. "I just thought we'd have more time. I didn't think selling a few shitty iron daggers would be such a big deal." I crossed my arms. "And so they got the drop on me because I got cocky." The death of many a villain, even those bigger and better than me.

Especially those bigger and better than me.

"Listen." I cut Rel off again. "You're safe, and that's what matters. Now we can start focusing on the important things."

Rel nodded slowly, still giving me odd looks out of the corner of her eye. "Like...what?"

I felt my features slip into a deep glower. "Making sure they pay for every scrape and bruise they left on my people, of course." I folded my arms. "First, though, we have to play...nice."

Rel nodded again. "I'm here." She straightened out her uniform, brushing the dust off the fabric of her vest. "What do you need me to do?"

I sighed. "What I need is for you to be very upset with me."

Rel blinked. "Lady Via?"

"We made more waves than I anticipated," I said, casting my eyes around the warehouse. "And the Tarnished were a bit smarter than I gave them credit for." I huffed. It was much more fun when *I* was the person doing the outsmarting. "But we've had a lot of people joining up over the last few days, which is not the way things normally go, now is it?"

"Not exactly?" Rel tilted her head. "But we've actually been protecting people, we haven't even demanded any money for it. And then word started getting 'round that you were going to be hiring people for the smithy..."

"Foundry," I corrected absently. I had started pacing now, winding up and down the dirt floor of the warehouse. "And that would explain some people, especially in an area like this." I sent her a look. "But would it explain all of them?"

Rel frowned. "...Maybe not?"

I nodded. "And that's why I need you to be mad at me." I laughed. "It makes sense, doesn't it? This whole mess is my fault, but a normal gang boss? They'd be looking for someone to vent their frustrations on. And that someone is you."

Rel swallowed. "If that's what you need, Lady Via."

I blinked once as she bowed her head, twisting her cap in her hands. Then it hit me. "What? No!" I smacked her arm. "Don't be an idiot. I'm not upset with you, I just need everyone else to think I am. So put that hat back on and be ready to act all sullen when we go back outside." I paused. "I mean, if you think you can pull it off."

Rel paused for a second, glancing up at me through her fringe.

I sighed. "Oh, for god's—I'm not mad at you, so put your hat back on and tell me if you're up to the job."

"I think…I can act pretty sullen, Lady Via," she said, toying with a strand of hair. "But why, again?"

"Because I need to know if the Tarnished were the ones who brought in the Guild." In which case, my deal with Arlo was gone with the wind. "Or if someone *here* tattled instead. So, I'm going to offer them up a juicy new source of information. As long as we're on the outs, maybe someone will think they can flip you."

Rel's eyes widened in understanding. "And then I bring it to you…"

"Exactly." I nodded. "So be upset with me, and put on your best show. If we're lucky, they'll even offer you some money for going behind my back."

"Ah, uh." Rel paused, looking back and forth nervously. "What should I do if someone pays me to…you know…"

"Betray me?" I raised an eyebrow. "Take the money, of course; we can split it. Then…" I reached up, patting Rel on the cheek. "You come and tell me, and we show them exactly how I feel about traitors."

Rel nodded.

"Good." I spun away, mind moving a mile a minute. "That's a start on the potential mole problem. Next, I have to worry about the rest of this mess."

Arlo had agreed to work with me, provisionally. He'd even been kind enough to let me have a bit more 'turf' to 'recruit from' in order to meet my delivery deadlines.

The one thing he wasn't on board with were any plans to take on the Guild itself. They were too big, had too many friends, and he wasn't about to start a war he could only lose. Survival instincts were something I could work with though. All I had to do was show Arlo that we could do more than kneel beneath their boots.

Or else, force the issue.

The last problem was the forge. I needed to make steel. So far, the imps and I still hadn't managed to completely work out the process so, of course, I'd lied my ass off to that Guild lady in order to get a better deal. Fortunately, it had worked, and so I had a lucrative contract with the Guild that would earn me goodwill as a nice little menial who knew her place.

Unfortunately, it also meant I was on the hook to provide steel weapons to the Adventurer's Guild.

"We're going to need to scale up production." I opened my status screen, looking at my new stat points and the skill I'd earned after making a deal with Arlo.

"You said Soul is regeneration, and Attunement is mana pool?"

Rel nodded. "That's what I managed to learn."

"Good." I cracked my knuckles. "Now, we have some work to do." I felt a tingle go down my spine as I started to fill up my increased mana pool. "We're going to have to organize more people to go down to the ocean. I'll need more demons for this." I banged on the top of the forge. "As for you two, any progress?"

A sooty black head popped out of the coals.

"Zhruka m'darrrrrn!" Mr. Burns grinned up at me.

I blinked. "It worked?"

"Zhruka! Zhruka!" He scampered back into the forge. There was a brief moment of hissing and yowling before he and Coaline hauled a lump of iron out of the back of the forge. I paused. No, that wasn't iron glowing cherry red in the mouth of my foundry, was it?

I plucked a hammer that I'd acquired from the side of the foundry. "Hold it there." The imps nodded happily. I hefted the hammer and swung.

The metal rang beautifully as I hit it. But more than that, there was a noticeable dent from the hammer. Now, I wasn't a smith, but I'd worked with more than a bit of our melted wrought iron the past few days, and this, this was steel.

"Perfect." I grinned. "We'll have to tear out the wall to give you more room to melt the bars and add the carbon. The new charcoal, it worked?"

"Phrrkramer dvvvot." Coaline swayed her head back and forth. "Frmardrrrr gwrrkkwala zzzravak!"

I nodded. "I'll get you more, just keep track." I let out a breath. "At this rate, we might actually make that delivery deadline."

Two things taken care of, then. All that remained was my plan to stick a knife in the Guild's back. I sighed. That was also the hardest one of the lot. I was never the type of villain to say, 'damn the artillery,' which was the reason I was still alive and kicking. Idiots like Black Noon and even Cypher were so confident in their own abilities that they would take on impossible odds just because they knew they'd managed to win.

Past tense intended.

After a moment, I shook my head. For now, I'd have to work with what I was given. In a few weeks, I could turn my ragtag little gang into a force to be feared. In the meantime, I'd need much more firepower if I was going to hit the Adventurer's Guild.

I turned to Rel. "Ready to put on a show?"

Rel gave a sly smile. "Yes, Lady Via."

"Good. Let's go…rally the troops." I strode towards the double doors of the warehouse, Rel following half a step behind. From the corner of my eye, I could see how she'd hunched in on herself not daring to look at me.

Perfect.

I threw open the doors to the warehouse, stepping out into the evening light. Then I paused.

Standing in the middle of the dirt road was a blond-haired woman. "Hey there, Empress!" Electra raised a hand, sheepishly. At her feet, Dee was spasming on the ground. "Sorry, but he attacked me first?"

I spared a glance at Dee. He'd…probably be fine. "Get him into a bed, someone make sure he doesn't throw up or something awful." Then I turned back to Electra. "And why, exactly, are you here again?"

"Well, I came back from my first quest, you see." She rubbed the back of her head. "And I kind of ran into the Guild, not really a big fan of them right now, not gonna lie, and…Empress, why are you smiling?"

I felt my grin stretch wider. Electra took a step back. "No for real, why are you smiling? It's creeping me the heck out."

"Oh, no reason." I walked forward, grabbing the Hero by the shoulders. "You're just exactly the thing I was looking for."

"But I'm a person."

"Details."

CHAPTER 21

A Computer Is Just a Rock People Tricked Into Believing It Could Think

They hurt people."

"Yes." I nodded at Electra's words. "More importantly, they fucked with me."

The blonde raised an eyebrow. "I feel like you're missing the point here."

"You're the one who's playing dress-up." I shrugged. "Wasn't this world supposed to be some fun, fantasy, light novel romp?"

She grimaced. "Yeah, well…"

"Yeah," I said. "Well."

Electra glanced off to the side, not saying anything. I leaned back against the wall of my little warehouse. Things were moving again; off by the far wall, the sound of hammering emanated from my forge. We'd figured out steel, making nooks in the wall of the forge for the process. The problem was heat. The forge and warehouse were both made from weathered stone and clay bricks, and I was churning out cheap steel weapons nearly as fast as my people could haul up metal from my demons on the coast.

Really, it was only a matter of time until something cracked.

"I was wrong."

I blinked, turning back towards the Hero. "What was that?" I felt a smirk tugging at the corner of my lips, but I held it back.

It was unbecoming for a villain to gloat *before* she won.

Electra ran a hand through her spiky blond hair. "Thought this would just be an adventure, you know? We'd get our protagonist cheats, beat some demon king, and make it home just in time to enjoy retirement with a bunch of cute…"

I raised an eyebrow. "A bunch of cute *what now?*" Electra's cheeks reddened. "Actually, on second thought, don't tell me. I don't think my opinion of you can go any lower."

She snorted. "Says the girl who's already gotten her first waifu."

"What are you even talking about?"

"Um, Rel? She cleans up pretty nice, doesn't she." Electra chuckled. "Though I gotta admit, I didn't think that scruffy little girl would turn into the loyal kuudere type."

I blinked. "You knew she was a girl?"

Electra blinked. "It was obvious." She shrugged. "Delicate features, timid, one of the first encounters and she followed you around like a puppy?" She paused, narrowing her eyes at me. "Wait, you *didn't* figure it out?"

I crossed my arms. "I feel like we have more important things to talk about."

"You didn't know!" Electra laughed. "Oh man, and here you were going on and on about how you had it all figured out and you didn't even notice?" She snickered at my glare. "Did she end up *telling* you that—"

"Please, keep talking." I flexed my fingers, dark crackling in the palm of my hand. "Just let it all out, you know, before I take your mouth away."

"Woah, woah!" Electra waved her hands in front of her. "Don't go throwing around magic you don't understand."

I shook my hand out, dismissing the spell. "Oh, believe me, I know exactly what that one does."

Her eyes flicked to the side. "What does it do?"

"Turns someone into a demon." I reached out, combing my hand through Blue's mane. I'd given him the mental command to hide after we'd been attacked, and since then he'd never strayed far from my side. "How do you think I got this good boy?" Blue let loose a rumbling purr.

"H-he was a person?!"

I waved a hand. "He was a gang leader who threatened to kill and rape me, potentially in that order. You'll forgive me if I chose to defend myself instead."

Electra paused. "Oh…"

"Yes, oh." I rolled my eyes. "And here *you* were saying you'd figured out that this world wasn't just some story where you were the main character."

She let out a low breath. "Yeah, sorry, it's just…" She shrugged. "You know how it is. I think I had to go through like, half a year of force and restraint training before I was even let out on patrol." She shot me a wary glance. "Please don't demonify me though."

"Demon-itize."

"What, really?"

"You expected anything else?" I sighed. "Besides, it's not like I have the mana to finish the spell." I looked over to my forge, where my two foundry imps were hammering away. "Each demon I have takes mana to maintain. Right now, I'm barely breaking even, and that's *after* dumping all of my stat points into attunement and soul."

"Really? And here I thought you had the real cheat skill."

I shrugged. "It turns out I have a soft cap. Which is why I'll be relying on you for this next bit."

"Right." Electra crossed her arms, digging her heels into the dirt floor. "The Guild. What do you have planned?"

"They'll be *expecting* me to do something." I gave a wan smile. "So, I'm going to be a good little cog in the machine, making their weapons and staying down here in the dirt where I belong." No matter how much it stung. "I want you to join the Guild."

She grimaced. "I don't…think that will work out."

My head snapped up. "What?"

Electra shrugged helplessly. "C'mon, Em'. I'm not good at the whole infiltration thing. If I end up joining up, I'll probably end up fighting my whole team because they decided to extort some village." An ugly frown passed over her face at that.

I decided that I probably didn't want to know. "You're not…that bad?"

"You called me 'as subtle as a thunderclap' on national television."

I paused, finger raised, before I lowered it. It only took me a second to remember what she was talking about.

To be fair, I'd also only ever taken over a national television station the one time.

"They were still recording?"

Electra nodded. "Got the whole thing, including the part where you threw me through the weather map."

"Right into Hurricane Ivanka," I licked my lips, "where you promptly overloaded the whole studio."

"Woulda been a good idea, too, if I hadn't knocked all the dumb lights out." She frowned, crossing her arms. "Then you got away in the dark before the rest of my team could show up. You know, after you finished…whatever nefarious thing you'd been doing."

Well, what I'd been doing was seeding worms into a couple of banks (and maybe a bit of the stock market) while I made a fool of myself on national television. But it wasn't like I was going to tell her that. Imperial Investments was *still* making money.

Instead, I patted her on the shoulder. "You couldn't have known I had a night vision visor."

She gave me a withering look. "Techies *always* have night vision."

Well, she wasn't wrong.

Electra groaned at the memory. "The internet still calls me Thunderclap Barbie, you know!"

"Ouch." I coughed into my fist. "So, I guess that means you starting up a rival gang isn't in the cards either?"

Electra sighed before straightening up again. "I mean, I don't even know how *you* managed to make a gang so quickly."

I quirked my lip. "More easily than you'd think." I waved off her questioning look. "Okay, then I have an idea, just…" I glanced to the side. "Well, some people aren't going to like it."

Electra grinned. "Worried about *someone's* feelings?"

"Certainly not *yours*."

She just laughed, pushing me on the shoulder. "Whatever, Em'. Just go get it cleared with your waifu so you can tell me what the plan is."

"You're the type of person who listens to anime girl sounds over EDM, aren't you?"

"Guilty!"

I grunted, stepping out of her annoying long reach. "Just don't break anything while I figure out what we're doing." I took a step towards my little alcove when Electra cleared her throat. "What?"

She cast an eye towards my little generator in the corner. "Think I could, you know, get some spare volts?"

I cocked an eyebrow. "Is that what the kids are calling it these days?"

"You know what I mean." She socked me in the shoulder. "I've been running on zero electricity since we fried c'thalamari."

"Hmm, I don't know. Last time I offered, someone decided she'd rather run across the island on her own with her new *cheat protagonist powers.*"

At least she had the grace to look bashful. "C'mon, Empress, cut a girl some slack?"

"Tell you what." I tapped her crude breastplate. "Be a good girl, and maybe I'll let you play with my toys." Then I spun, leaving her standing in the middle of the room. "Go socialize with my 'gang' instead. If a single *gear* on my generator is out of place when I'm finished, I'll know."

She huffed, but a second later I heard her open the side door and step out into the street outside.

For my part, I pushed open the door to my 'room' where Rel was lying on my bed. "How are you feeling?"

She gave a weak smile. "Better."

When I'd first checked Rel over a day ago, she'd seemed fine, but some of the bastards from the Guild had kicked her a few times in the stomach before they got bored and moved on to giving Dee and Dum another set of matching bruises. The boys were fine and were itching for revenge almost as much as I was.

But Rel had started to show signs of internal bleeding. Back on Earth, I had my Reaves Corp automated surgery robot for that sort of thing. Here, I'd blown through a chunk of funds on a midgrade healing potion, threatened an apothecary within an inch of his life for instructions on how to use it, and...well, let's just say that draining things by hand is never fun.

I'll spare you the gory details.

I sat down on the corner of the bed, squeezing her wrist. "That's good to hear." I let out a sigh. "I let you get hurt." Not even a week after I'd promised to keep her safe.

Rel just smiled. "You've done more for me than anyone else in this city, Lady Via."

I blew out a breath. "Just another sign of how much work I have left to do." I let go of her wrist, standing up. "We'll get even with them, don't worry."

A complicated expression flickered across Rel's face. "You and that… Electra?"

I nodded. "Yes, I have a plan, but I'll need you to do something for me. If you agree, we're going to have to double down on the 'angered gang leader' angle. I'm going to *pretend* to replace you and leave you out in the cold. Hopefully, the Guild will bite. And when they do, I want you to give away the farm."

She blinked. "Give away…what now?"

"Sorry." I shook my head. "I'm distracted, too many different things pulling my attention. I mean, when they offer you the chance to take over my little 'empire' for them, you're going to accept."

"W-what?"

"I know it's a step up from playing double agent." I leaned over, taking her hand in mind. "Do you understand what I'm going for here? It's going to be a bit of a show, a bit of a song and dance, where I act like Electra is everything I want in a second in command. And then I need you to 'betray' me for it."

She nodded slowly, working out the pieces in her head. I wasn't sure if it was part of her class or based on where she'd put her own stat points, but Rel had grown much more contemplative over the past few weeks, much more easily able to follow my plans.

"You were already going to treat me poorly, Mistress."

I frowned. "Yeah, but I was still going to keep you on." Even if I was 'mad' at her, keeping her close at hand would only make her a more tempting target. I sighed. "I'm breaking my promise again. And I'm sorry."

She nodded again. "Why me?"

I let out a soft breath. "Because I'll be putting a knife at my back and wrapping someone's fingers around the hilt. You're the only person I trust not to stab me."

Rel looked at me, really looked, eyes flashing in the low light. I was taking a gamble here, and I knew it. But I was willing to bet her desire to get even would tip the scales in my favor.

After a moment, Rel huffed, slumping in the bed. But she didn't let go of my hand. "I don't like her."

I laughed. "That's fine. I don't really like Electra either."

She glanced at me out of the corner of her eye. "You acted like you were her friend. With all of that…stuff."

"You could hear us, huh?" I shook my head. "We were enemies before. Now…we're just the only two people from our world. It gets hard, not talking about all the little things we used to take for granted."

"Like…the internet?"

"Yeah. Like the internet." I shook my head. "It's just, there are all these things that have no crossover, no basis, no frame of reference between this world and our own."

Rel hummed looking down at her hands. After a moment, she nodded. "Okay, I'll do it. On one condition."

I blinked. "Name it." Now, where had the nervous cobbler's apprentice gone and come back a confident woman, of all things?

"I want you to explain the internet to me."

"Explain the…" I started to shake my head, but her expression was serious. I took a deep breath. "Right well. The internet is…where even to start? Computers, I guess." I laughed. "The closest comparison I could make to a computer in this world would be the system, but computers don't affect reality directly; instead, they do things for us, like thinking, communication, chess, do you have chess here? Never mind, it's not important.

"The *internet*, on the other hand, is all of the connected computers in the entire world. And we do have a lot of computers. They're just rocks, after all, and metal." I smirked. "Rocks we tricked into believing they could think."

Rel blinked wordlessly.

"But in practice, the internet is nothing more or less than the sum total of all current human knowledge on my world, stored in the cloud, in server farms, in your pocket, and nowhere at all. Accessible from anywhere, to anyone. But it's more than that, it's impossible to comprehend if you haven't seen it, even today things still happen, advances are still made that blow my mind.

"People having conversations with hundreds of people all over the world all at once, livestreams, sensation captures, Insta-thots, Tru-VR, bitcoin, bell buttons, millions upon billions of exabytes of data, growing with every second. It's—I have nothing in this world to compare it to, no frame of reference at all, it's—"

I stopped, as it hit me like a bolt of lightning.

"It's an *out-of-context problem*."

I stood.

"…Lady Via?"

"Of course! How could I be so *stupid?*" I started pacing rapidly. "Here I was trying to jump-start the industrial revolution, like it would get me any closer to my goals as long as I left the status quo intact. Of *course* there's rank protectionism. Even if they don't understand what I'm doing, they can still see the impacts, extrapolate the effects, clamp down on things they *don't want.* Feudalism at its finest, amiright?"

I grinned. "I have to give them something they have no idea how to react to. A complete out-of-context problem."

I turned back to Rel, holding out my hand. "Forget explaining the internet, Relia. If you help me with this, I'll *show* it to you."

Her eyes were wide, lips slightly parted, as if surprised by my tirade. I guess I'd gone more than a bit off the rails there.

But she still grasped my hand without a second thought.

CHAPTER 22

I Dreamed a Dream

Rel stepped off her X-abite onto the massive cloud.

It felt just like she always hoped they would, all soft as silk and feathers and all of the other soft things Ma used to tell her about growing up.

"Bitabit!" The toothy X whipped off through the sky, joining the massive flocks of X-abites soaring through the clouds. If Rel squinted, she could see the books and scrolls in their pockets. It looked like lots of people were requesting knowledge today.

Relia flicked her pocket watch out; the hands were pointing to 'late.' She frowned. "I'm late. I'm late." She started moving, jogging forward past the towering piles of knowledge off to either side. On a normal day, she would have liked to explore them but for now she was late for a very important date. So, she had to hurry.

Rel's feet sank into the fluffy surface of the cloud as she ran, and she felt herself slowly begin to sink deeper, little tidbits poked out of the cloud. "Did you know the average velocity of an unladen swallow?" "What do you do with a drunken sailor?" "Ten tips to keep your man satisfied."

"Guh!" Rel scrambled against the cloud as the knowledge grabbed onto her, yanking her from her walk. She felt herself start to panic when the X-abites swooped around again, looking for new prey. If she didn't project enough confidence, they'd eat her too, just like the killer hummingbirds.

Rel ducked under a copy of a shipping manifest as the sound of "bitabitabitabitabitabit!" passed by overhead in an endless stream. After a moment, they were gone and Rel peeked out from beneath her cover. The sky was clear. She let out a sigh.

"Are ya winning, son?"

"Eeeeeee!" Rel jumped out of the cloud as the Insta-thought popped into being behind her. "Gods! Don't do that!" She swept her hand through the pillar of thought, dispersing it back into mist. "I don't have time for that today." She started jogging again, this time ignoring all of the libraries and towers of sorcery that lined her path through the cloud. She had one very specific tower she was interested in, and the rest could go hang.

Of course, the Insta-thoughts were more insidious. Now that one had distracted her, they wouldn't stop popping up and demanding her attention.

"Lady Via's hair is very nice."

"Wow, I can't believe she made a special outfit just for me."

"I wish Electra didn't come back."

"Mistress smells so nice."

Rel held back a blush. Th-these thoughts were lewd! Too impure! She was just trying to get to her date—her *appointment*! With a huff, Rel concentrated. She pushed her hands out. "Begone, thoughts!" The cloudy pillars vanished in the morning light.

"I never thought that Cutting Words would be so useful." Rel shook her head, pushing the distraction aside. "I'm late."

Again she tried to run, this time into the stream district. The water ran through channels in the cloud before falling to the ground as rain. The thinner ones she could jump over, but some of them were really big streams. Like, huge streams!

Rel's foot accidentally landed in one as she tried to jump over.

"Hey! Watch where you're going!"

"I'm sorry!" Rel jumped out of the livestream. "I didn't mean to, I'm just l-late."

The stream clicked its tongue. "Did you get lost again, girl? Don't forget to follow me, I'll show you where to go!"

"Oh, right!" Rel ducked her head. "S-sorry."

"Yeah, just hit the bell on your way, so the rest of the streams know that you're following me. Then they won't get in the way."

"Thanks."

The livestream smiled. "Don't worry about it! Hey, she's waiting for you, after all."

Rel nodded, hitting the bell beneath the stream. It rang and the cloud shifted, making it so that she could easily keep track of the stream she was following. It led her closer to the central tower, right in the middle of the cloud.

Right where Lady Via would be waiting.

The last stop was the ferry. Rel reached into her pocket and handed a few coins to the ferryman. "I need to get across the last stream."

The ferryman looked at the money she gave him. "That's too much."

Rel blinked. "Huh?"

"Way, *way* too much, lady. I mean, c'mon. It's called *bitcoin*." He took out his scythe, cutting the coins up into tiny little bits. "Honestly, talk about not even knowing the value of your own currency." He dumped the pile of bitcoins back into her hand, keeping just a single bit for himself. "City kids, amiright?"

Rel just huffed, stuffing the coins back into her pocket. "Well, maybe I'd know if people bothered to explain things to me."

"That's the point, lady, it's all out of context. You need to figure out what's going on out of the context!"

"The...context?" Rel asked.

"Yeah! Like your'a taking the pieces and putting 'em together and—HEY!" Rel jumped as the ferryman yelled. "I'm boating here!"

The stream, which had started to shift, returned to its normal form. "Excuse me? Last I checked, I'm the livestream, you're just some guy on a boat."

"I'm just here, day in day, out, trying to do my job." The ferryman shook his fist, big black sleeves billowing out around him. "Then some livestream comes in and tries to tell me how to live my life? Kid, I've been here while you were still a bunch of precipitation on ya daddy's nuts."

The livestream sighed. "Okay, boomer."

"And for the last time, my name isn't Boomer, it's Boomson!"

The livestream rolled its eyes. "Don't you have a passenger or something?"

Boomson shook his head, muttering as he finished rowing Rel across the live stream. "Sheesh, you seein' this? Just…don't grow up to be like him, okay? Do somethin' with your life, lady."

Rel paused, one foot out of the boat. "I will, Boomson."

"Feh, just call me Boomer." The ferryman waved a hand. "Everyone else does."

"Okay…Boomer?"

"Yeah! Just like that!" He grinned at her. "Now you're starting to catch my memeing, lady."

"Your…meaning?"

"Yeah, that's what I said!"

"Okay, Boomer." She waved. "See you on the way back."

"Yeah, you do that."

Rel turned and jogged up to the tower's steps, only to come to a stop right in front of the doorway. "Oh. You're here."

Electra looked up from the captured sensation in her hand. The little sphere looked like a bubble of froth on the waves, giggles emerging from it. "Oh, hey! You finally made it."

Rel held back a glare. "How did you get here before me?"

"Oh, you must'a taken the X-abites, right?" Electra shook her head. "Classic rookie mistake, you know the fastest way here is to go nowhere."

Rel blinked, "Nowhere?"

"Yeah, just like Empress said. It's nowhere and everywhere. So just go nowhere, and then you're everywhere."

"That…" Rel frowned. "That's why I'm late?"

"I wouldn't worry about it." Electra grinned, wiggling her eyebrows. "She's waiting for you at the top of the tower, after all."

Rel paused on the stairs. "I don't like you."

"What?" Electra blinked. "Why? I'm awesome."

"Yeah." Rel bit her lip. "That's why."

Electra just tilted her head. "Uh, okay, I guess? I respect your decision and I hope we can still work together."

"…Sure." Rel turned and started running again.

The tower in the center, unlike the rest of the buildings in the cloud, was made of pure glass. Her footsteps seemed to chime as she ran up the stairs. From the outside, it looked like a scintillating mirror, impossible to see into, inscrutable even.

But from within, Rel's vision was clear. She could see what Lady Via had seen when building the internet for her. The livestreams stretching outward from the center, connecting people to repositories of knowledge. X-abite nests, more and more being built every day. Rel didn't understand it, but here, now, she could still see that it was beautiful.

Slowly, she emerged up onto the top of the tower. "Lady Via?"

From the parapet, Via turned, jet-black hair billowing in the breeze. The woman smiled, wiping her forehead. "Rel, perfect. I just finished." She reached out, snagging Rel's wrist. "Stand right here for me."

Rel complied without thinking. "You're…not mad that I'm late?"

"Well, from a certain point of view, you arrived right on time." Via gave her that sly smile once again, waving her hand towards the cloud. "What do you think? I told you I'd show you, after all."

"It's amazing." Rel shifted, half leaning into Via, half just trying to stop from collapsing back into herself. Via didn't like it when she slouched. "It's just…why did you do all of this?"

Via raised a single, aquiline (thank you, Cutting Words) eyebrow. "What do you mean? Who else would I make it for?"

Rel glanced to the side. "Electra?"

Via laughed. "Oh, good one. I'll have to remember that for next time. She'll hate it."

Rel didn't really, or Relly, understand, but she just nodded along anyway. "But still, why me? I'm just…"

Via hummed, squeezing Rel's hand. "Let me guess, you've never had anyone do something for you before? You've gone through your whole life ignored, just one more face in a crowd, no one special, no one worth remembering? And now you're wondering why someone like me is taking so much of my time for…well, someone like you?"

Rel nodded wordlessly.

"Yeah." Via quirked her lip. "That's why."

"What?"

Via checked her watch, clicking her tongue. "I'd explain more, but we're out of time, Relia."

Rel blinked. "What do you mean, out of time?"

"It's time for you to wake up." Via pointed to the sky. "All of this was just a dream after all."

Rel felt her vision tilt as her gaze tracked Via's finger. Everything flipped on its axis and suddenly she was upside down looking at a rock. No not just a rock, every single rock, of every shape and size in the entire world.

"This is all just a dream," Via repeated, "that we tricked out of a rock." She smiled gently. "And it's time to wake up, Rel."

"Wake up Rel."

"Rel, wake up."

Rel's eyes snapped open. She was lying on her back on Via's straw mattress in the alcove. Lady Via was standing over her, already dressed. Rel blinked once, hearing the ding of a system message.

"Are you ready to go?" Via asked. "Last chance to say no; after this, I'll be pretending that I hate you until the Guild makes their move." She held out a hand.

Rel bit her lip. She glanced down at her new skill, eyes widening as she read the description.

Then, without hesitation, she reached out and grasped Via's hand. "I'll do whatever you need. M'lady."

"God, I should have gotten you a fedora."

Rel didn't understand, but that was fine. She had a skill that would help her fill in the gaps, until the day that Via could finally show her the internet.

Dream Sequence

LvL EX

You see the dreams of your lady, and you know the steps you need to take in order to bring that dream closer to reality.

Don't trip.

CHAPTER 23

Startup Capital

Y ou're late."

I examined my nails. "That's the problem with extorting people: you get what you pay for."

Delia shot me a deep glare. Or maybe that was just her face. "This order was well within your capabilities."

"How do you know what my capabilities are? You haven't set foot in a forge a day in your life." I shook my head. "Even with my process, it takes longer to make swords than daggers, and that's why you'll pay double the ridiculous price you tried to shove down my throat last time."

If anything, her face only grew more pinched. "How about I pay you in a foot of steel down your throat instead."

"Go ahead." I shrugged. "Then you've torpedoed your relationships with the smithing guild, gotten one shipment of weapons, and killed the only one who can provide you with more at such a cheap price." I stared at her dead on. "Even now, you'd still be getting nearly *twice* as many quality weapons as you would from a smith, in a fraction of the time."

"That was not our agreement." Delia leaned forward, hand resting on the hilt of her blade. "Or do I need to remind you why *we* make the rules in Silverwall?"

"I mean, if you want me to give you a bunch of metal bars that snap off at the hilt, I could do it at the price you were offering." I spread my arms. "Or you can try to find literally anyone else in this city that can do what I can do; oh wait, you can't." I leaned forward as well, glaring up into her face.

"Or you can tell your superiors why you burned a new supplier less than two weeks after you brought them on board."

She met my eyes for a long moment, fingers clenching around the shaft of her spear. Hell, for a second, I thought she was actually going to go through with it and try to stab me. Then she snorted, leaned back and crossed her arms. "I'll pay you half again as much as we agreed on, and if you ask for more, I'll kill you and take over your operation myself."

"Deal." I grinned. "And feel free to try. You need someone who knows what they're doing."

"You're not *nearly* as valuable as you seem to think, *Empress*."

I shrugged. "You're right, I do chronically undervalue myself." I smiled sweetly up at the glaring woman. "Maybe you should get me my money before I change my mind."

I could practically hear her teeth grinding together as she handed over a pouch of gold coins. I made a show of counting them, but really, I would have been satisfied with only a quarter more than my new asking price.

The real prize was how she glowered at me from beneath her crimson bangs. Two stooges carried the crate of weapons from the dusty storage room in the guild, doing their best not to look at Delia.

I'd made her look bad, and if I knew one thing about women like her, it's that she would *kill* for the chance to return the favor. If I was lucky, she'd reach out to Rel later today.

Well, maybe not today, there were still a few more pieces to put into place.

I stood, brushing off my suit. "I'll be on my way, then. See you in a month!" Monthly shipments were what we'd agreed on, after all. With the amount of iron I'd been hauling in from the ocean, I could *probably* meet that next date, but sooner or later the bounty of the deeps would run so dry that not even my demons could find another rusted nail.

I just had to make sure to cut my losses before then.

Delia waved a hand, and another Adventurer stepped up to escort me back out of the building. Storage room aside, the rest of the guild was practically palatial, with wide hallways, vaulted ceilings, and practically everything covered in silver filigree. In fact, if I didn't know better, I would have thought the place was the duchess's mansion or something. I wonder how her estates in the inner city compared.

I gave my escort a cheery wave as I stepped outside into the sunlight. The streets of Silverwall were bustling in the afternoon. Here, closer to the center of the town, streets were paved with cobblestones, and I don't think I saw more than a single beggar a block. Beyond that, well, it looked more or less like you'd expect a medieval town would, albeit with more emphasis on silver decorations the closer to the inner districts you went.

I guess the city lived up to its name.

"Ready to go, boys?" I asked Dee and Dum.

They sidled out of the nearby alleyway, Dum in the lead. "Sure thing, boss." They didn't even look out of place in the nice part of town because of their uniforms. Really, between the three of us, *I* was the one getting looks as we walked down the street.

I suppose most noble ladies would prefer manservants suited to their tastes. I snorted.

"Something funny?" Dee asked.

I patted him on the arm. "Just thinking about the future. Now, you said you found an enchanter nearby?"

"Yeah, right up here, boss."

The boys split the crowd for me, leading the way towards the shop district, off to see the wizard, as it were.

You see, the problem with promising someone the internet before the industrial revolution is because of all the *reasons* the industrial revolution came first. In fact, I'd go so far as to say that keeping that promise of mine was more or less impossible.

So, I was going to cheat outrageously.

The brass bell above the door gave a despondent little clang as I stepped into the enchanter's shop. Inside, I paused for a moment, looking around. "This is the best you could find?"

Dee shrugged. Dum rubbed the back of his head. "Said you was looking for cheap, boss."

I sighed. "I guess I am."

The place was a hole in the wall, barely more than a dusty hallway with a counter set in the back.

You'd think an enchanter would be able to rig themselves up a magic Roomba.

"Hello?" I walked up to the counter. "Anybody in?"

There was a muffled thud from the back room. "Coming! Coming!" A moment later, a young man stumbled out of a back room as he half hopped into the other leg of his pants. "What, ah, what can I help you with, my lady?"

I looked him up and down. Amusingly, the 'enchanter' was shorter and stockier than Rel, with foggy spectacles perched on the bridge of his nose beneath a mop of muddy brown hair. Really, though, the thing that stood out most was his rumpled clothes: a simple jerkin and a pair of trousers. "I was hoping to order a custom set of enchantments."

"Well look no further!" The young man leaned forward, putting both hands on his dusty counter. "Maarin's Magical Emporium is more than capable of servicing all of your enchanting needs! Why, just let me know what you're looking for and I'll be able to whip it up in a jiffy at, uh, at *half* the price you'd get anywhere else!"

I hummed. "Been a slow couple of weeks, huh?"

His smile froze on his face. Maarin raised a finger, but before he could speak, his stomach let out a loud growl. Slowly, he lowered his hand. "It's hard, competing with the Enchanter's Guild."

My eyes narrowed. Someone else on the fringe of things, hmm? That was exactly what I'd been looking for when I'd sent the boys looking for the shop. Granted, I was hoping for something more along the lines of 'eccentric maverick' as opposed to 'baby's first startup', but at some point, you take what you can get.

"I *might* be interested in employing you." I lifted up the pouch of money I'd just gotten from Delia, letting it clink in my hands. "But first, I'd like to hear a bit about how enchanting works. Shouldn't you only really have one or two skills like the rest of us?"

"Ah!" He grinned. "That's where Wizards differ from most other classes! Instead of skills, we unlock disciplines. I've unlocked several different disciplines of enchantment with my class. Really, you won't find a more versatile mage in the entire city."

I nodded. "So, you can do a bit of everything?"

"Oh, yes!" He waved a hand. "While the so-called *masters* of the Guild tend to overspecialize, I guarantee that if you let me know what you want, I can make almost any enchantment."

Well, what it really sounded like was that he'd gone wide instead of tall with his training, and probably gotten himself kicked out of the Guild for trying to poach secrets. Still, all *I* needed to know was if he was indeed versatile enough to accomplish what I wanted. Rome wasn't built in a day.

But I'd be willing to aim for a week.

"I need an enchantment that can send a voice from one object to another." I paused, thinking back to all the silver I'd seen. This was a mining city, after all, it just didn't have very good iron deposits… "Or better yet, one that can send an image reflected in one mirror to another, with sound included."

"Ah yes, sensory-linked enchantments!" Maarin's shoulders slumped a bit in what looked like relief. "I could lay an enchantment on two mirrors right now if you wanted." I frowned, was this something that already existed? Luckily, Maarin's next words laid those fears to rest. "Though, uh, their effective range will be about the size of a house— you won't get much better from any enchanter either!"

"Distance is the limiting factor?"

Maarin nodded eagerly. "It takes more power to boost spells like that, especially since they're always running. They make excellent gifts, but really, if you want to communicate with someone long distances, may I recommend a courier stone enchantment?" He reached under the counter, laying a thin stone rod on the table. "Guaranteed to deliver a message to its linked receptacle and back again! In addition, it's—"

"What if I wanted to link more than one mirror?"

This time, Maarin slumped for a very different reason. "Ah, well, I suppose some of the masters at the Guild could put together an enchantment that linked three, though it would, uh, shrink the image on each corresponding mirror. Anything more than that though, well, the magical bindings become geometrically more complicated the more objects that are interconnected. Oh, uh, if you wanted two mirrors linked to one, I could probably manage that, but it wouldn't last as long, you see, because the one mirror would be consuming energy from the enchantment to send two images instead of one."

I hummed, picking up the stone rod. "So they're always broadcasting?"

"Uh, broadcasting?"

"Sending, they're always sending."

"Yes." Maarin nodded. "That's what you pay for a two-way connection in most cases. It's not like scrying, which is really more of a form of astral projection—"

"That's even better, honestly." I waved a hand, "So, Maarin, you say you're a versatile enchanter, yes?"

He nodded. "Of course!"

I set the stone rod on the counter with a sharp click. "What if I wanted you to make a mirror with a *name* that sent an image to a stone rod, like one of these." I twirled it in my fingers. "And that rod knew the names of, say, the two other mirrors connected just to *it*, and could send that image to the right mirror."

Imitation is the finest form of flattery, after all. Little magic 'cell towers' would fix the range issue as well.

"Just connect them all to a keystone object?" Maarin thought about it for a moment before shaking his head. "But the mirrors always send the message, miss. It's not so simple as just having a central object, even if that does simplify the enchantments by having a central fixture."

"So?" I shrugged. "Have the mirrors always send their images to the stick, hell, have an output mirror, or a scroll, or a crystal ball, that the images are always being sent to. It doesn't matter if it's an unintelligible mess if no one's watching it, so long as you can start sending that image to the right mirror on the other side when you want to. Just switch the output."

He frowned deeply, eyes blinking slowly in thought. "Maybe?" He shook his head. "I…don't want to turn down business, but I'm sure it's probably impossible, miss. In fact, I'm sure my old ma—I mean, an enchanter from the Guild would be able to tell you exactly *why* it wouldn't work, but, uh."

"But do you think you can maybe do it?"

"Maybe?" Maarin shrugged.

I pulled out a gold coin, placing it on the counter. Maarin's eyes snapped to it. "How about this. I pay you, no strings attached, to see what you can do with the idea. If it doesn't work out, well…"—I shrugged—"then at least we know."

Maarin nodded slowly. "But, uh, if it does work out?"

I smiled. "Then there will be a great deal more gold to go along with this one."

CHAPTER 24

Tweedle Dee and Tweedle Dum

Boss Lady made sure to hand out the pay herself.

Dee and Dum didn't mind it; she was better at numbers and didn't get mad at anyone when she got her math wrong. Not that the Boss ever got 'er math wrong.

"Here you go, boys." She smiled that smile of hers, handing the two of them slightly larger than average pouches. "You've done a good job keeping the salvage operation running, so here's a bonus."

Dee grinned, elbowing his brother. "Ain't nobody gave us bonuses before."

Boss shrugged. "Well, maybe they just didn't appreciate you enough."

"Well, crud." Dum rubbed the back of his head. "Thanks, boss, we try."

She laughed. "I noticed." She patted him on the shoulder. "I'm going to need you to keep an eye on things for a bit longer. I have work to do in the city.

"Would be easier if you left Rel in charge," Dum muttered. "That new 'Lectra lady…"

Boss laughed. "She's good at her job, isn't she?"

"Uh, no, boss, she isn't. Nobody really likes her." Dee scratched his scalp. "Too pushy."

"Rude."

"Thinks she knows better than everyone."

"Boys, boys." Boss grinned. "You misunderstand me. Being bad at her job *is* her job!"

"Oh…" Dee and Dum shared a glance. "Well, she is pretty bad at her job. Good at her job?" Dee shrugged. "But why d'ya need someone who's bad at stuff?"

Boss smiled, leaning back in her chair. They were the only ones in the warehouse right now, so Dee figured there was a pretty good chance Boss Lady would take the time to explain.

That was the other thing they liked about her.

"Because I can't exactly bait the Guild into replacing me if I look super popular." Boss waved a hand. She did it a lot. Dum thought she was maybe brushing away the extra thoughts always flying 'round her head. Boss had way more than most people, felt like. "Naturally, I won't be doing anything that makes my lovely little employees *too* upset with me, but if there's someone to act as a lightning rod for everyone's anger…" She did the scary chuckle.

"Must be a good plan, then." She only ever did the scary chuckle when it was a good plan.

"Indeed." With a sigh, she stretched, pushing her hands up over her head.

Dum held back a chuckle, and Dee elbowed him in the side.

"Hmm, something wrong boys?"

Even stretching like that, Boss's arms barely came up to their chins.

"Nothing, boss," they said in unison.

She gave them a sharp look before waving her hand again. "Well, whatever. If it's not important you can keep it to yourselves. Now, if you could send in everyone else to get their pay." She turned. "Blue, Tock, my ledger!"

Dee and Dum held back a shiver as Boss Lady's little robot came over riding on Blue's back. The spider bot grasped a sheaf of parchments in its forelimbs, the very same limbs that had almost put Dum's eyes out.

Boss cooed over the little robot like it was a baby bird, stroking its metal carapace and scratching Dee and Dum's *old* boss under the chin.

Boss was scary and she knew it.

That was a good thing though. Bosses who knew they were scary didn't go outta their way to prove it and suchlike. This was known. Last thing you wanted was a boss that had to go out of their way to intimidate people. Usually wound up dead too.

Or turned into giant lizard demons, as it were.

"What should we do after?" Dee asked as Boss sorted through her papers.

"Whatever you like." She tapped her chin. "It'll probably take an hour to pay everyone, we've gotten so many new recruits. There are a few I'll have to talk to…personally."

Dee shivered.

"Just be back in an hour or so, I need to go back into the Merchant Quarter."

"We'll be back, boss."

She nodded distractedly, and the two hulking men made their way to the front doors of the warehouse.

It had changed a lot in the last few weeks. Now, with more and more people from the old docks streaming into the Imperium, they had more than enough hands to do work and more than enough building materials in the old warehouses.

The dirt floor had been replaced with wood, and outside, there were two completed bunkhouses with people working on a third. Boss's demons took care of the more specialized labor, like diving for metal or cutting stone into the right shapes, but there was a retired mason whose family business went down with the rest of the docks, and a shipwright who still had his tools.

It was enough to get things moving, with enough elbow grease, as the Boss said it.

"Think she'll tell us what elbow grease is if we ask?" Dee asked.

Dum shrugged. "Dunno. She'll probably find more if we run out though."

Dee flexed his elbow, popping it. "Feels like I could use some more already."

"Knockin' heads is a full-time job." Dum nodded sagely.

"The gods' own truth."

Dee pushed the main doors of the warehouse open, an action that was a lot easier after the rollers had been changed for fresh ones. Meanwhile, Dum put his hands to his mouth. "PAYDAY! GET IN LINE!"

"Jesus fuck!" There was a clatter behind them. "I almost fell out of my chair, Dum!"

"Oh, sorry boss!"

"Note to self, make a fucking dinner bell for you assholes," she muttered.

Dee and Dum shared a glance before shrugging. They stepped to the side, letting everyone trickle into the warehouse to get paid. Boss did it in the evenings, after the day's haul had come in from the ocean, and those creepy forge imps of hers were starting on the next batch of weapons. They had another shipment due for the Guild tomorrow; Boss said she'd deliver it the day after.

Probably made sense to Boss.

Dee and Dum made sure to nod to Rel as the girl came in. They were the only ones that knew the secret. Well, them and that blond girl, but Boss had her off running errands somewhere else.

"Hang in there."

Rel nodded back, clasping Dum's hand. "Thanks."

Dee and Dum smiled. Girl was a good person to work for, almost as good as Boss. But they had some time to kill and some coin to spend. Really, in this part of town, there was only one thing to do.

"Mama's?" Dee asked.

"Mama's," Dum said.

The two of them started down the street, back towards the center of town. There were plenty of people on the streets, like usual. They also got out of the way, like usual. Dee and Dum barely noticed it.

"What do you think we should do?" Dum asked after a few minutes of walking.

"Ain't selling out the Boss." Dee shoved his hands into the pockets of his nice black pants. He loved the pants. "Ain't never had big enough pockets before."

Dum grunted for a second scratching the back of his neck. "The Guild'll pay a lot of money."

Dee nodded. "Lot more than we ever got paid, right?"

"Yeah."

The two of them walked in silence for a little longer.

"Boss pays a lot too," Dee said.

Dum nodded. "Boss is good people." But they grew up on the docks, and money was money.

"You know, Boss's been talking about, uh, returns on investment." Dee kicked at the dirt. "Got me thinking."

"Thinking?"

"Yeah."

"Huh."

Dee shrugged. "It's like this. Guild'll pay a lot of money, but only once. Then whatta we do when the money runs out?"

Dum opened his mouth, then closed it. "Dunno."

"Exactly!" Dee slammed his fist into his palm. Several nearby people quickly ducked off the street. "But Boss pays us every week. All we gotta do when we run outta money is wait for next week!"

"I dun' think that's how investments work."

Dee jabbed his brother's shoulder. "You got a better idea?"

"Dunno."

"Look, all I know is that this is the best gig we've got since, well…"

"Yeah."

"Why ruin it? 'Sides, you know Boss is gonna win, right? Not like them Guild chumps are gonna put down enough to take her out."

Dum spat. "Never did respect us. She might win even if we told 'em what she was planning."

"Yeah, and where'll we be then?" Dee asked.

Dum considered that, bouncing his coin purse in his hands. "Yeah."

Dee nodded. Then they shoved open the door to Mama's, stepping inside.

"Boys!" Mama bustled around the counter, grabbing them in a big hug. "How are my two favorite customers?"

"We're good, Mama."

The woman stepped back, looking at them. She was an older woman, with gray in her blond hair. She was almost as big as the boys too, side to side that is, not that it slowed her down any. "Heard you two got yourself a new boss."

"Yeah." Dee nodded.

"Well take a seat, you'll tell me all about it!" She turned. "Sherry, get me two specials—actually, make it three!"

"You got it, Mama!" A little girl behind the counter scampered into the back room, and in a moment the three of them were sitting at a table off to the side of the room. Dee and Dum shared nods with the rest of the patrons. Mama knew how to cook, and she taught it well too.

She ran a tavern, a bit deeper into the old docks than most would have liked, but there was one big difference between this tavern and any other in Silverwall.

It was staffed entirely by orphans.

Mama was pretty old now, but Dee and Dum had never known a time she didn't work at her rickety old tavern with mismatched chairs and the big brick hearth. She took in the kids she could find, teaching them how to cook, how to clean, using all of the money she made to keep everyone fed. She even did her best to find places for them to go, when they got old enough.

After all, everyone in the docks knew Mama.

"I never wanted that life for you two." The woman gave a small frown, patting her old green dress. "I told you that you coulda signed up with the guard. Eloncio's a vice-captain now!"

Dum shrugged. "We're good at what we're good at."

Mama sighed, patting him on the hand. "You're good at a lot of things, boys. Same as all the kids who worked here."

"Sure thing, Mama." Dee rubbed the back of his head.

She clicked her tongue. "Well, is she treating you better than the last one? That blue-haired boy never did strike me the right way!"

Dum gave a toothy grin. "Well, Boss struck him the right way."

Dee nodded. "She's a good boss. We're gonna stick with her for a while." He pulled out his coin purse. "She paid us a bonus; we wanted to help out some."

Mama bit her lip, amber eyes dipping to the full purse. "Boys, you know I'd never ask you to do that."

"We wanna help." Dum took out his own coin purse, putting a handful of silver coins on the table. "'Sides, she pays us every week."

The woman sighed before taking the money and secreting it away into one of her frilly sleeves. "Thank you, boys. Things haven't been easy since the Tarnished started pushing in 'round here, to say nothing of the Guild."

"You helped us," Dee said. "Only makes sense we help you back."

She laughed. "Well, aren't you boys just the sweetest. Stick with the people who stick with you, I always say."

Dee elbowed his brother. Dum grunted, looking away. "Yeah, yeah, you were right."

Mama raised an eyebrow.

"Dum was being dumb, s'all."

She gave a little laugh, slapping them both on the shoulder. "Now boys, be nice to each other."

Both the big men smiled. "Yes, Mama!"

CHAPTER 25

Making Connections

I'm pretty sure I can do it, but…"

I raised an eye at Maarin. I was starting to have second thoughts about hiring him to make my cell phone network. "You must really want more of my gold."

He coughed, hunching slightly into his jerkin. "Be—be that as it may, there's only so much I can do with the resources I have."

I folded my arms. "So what *do* you have then?"

"I'm glad you asked!" Maarin quickly bustled into the back of his hole in the wall shop.

I sighed, glancing over my shoulder. Dee and Dum were with me again. I would have preferred Rel for company, but, well…that's the problem with making your own plans. You have to carry them out.

"Think he actually has anything?" I asked.

Dee shrugged. "Dunno, boss."

"We could *make* him have something." Dum cracked his knuckles.

From the corner of my eye, I saw Maarin half stumble on his way back to the front. I gave a little grin. "Now, boys." It was my villain grin, and believe me, I'd practiced. "We only do that to people who disappoint us. You wouldn't disappoint us, would you, Maarin?"

The young man paled slightly, setting down several wooden rods on the counter with trembling hands. "N-not at all, miss. Uh, in fact, I've already managed to make a simple prototype that does almost exactly what you wanted!"

"Then what was all this about needing more money?"

"I never said I needed more money…per se…" He waved his hands in front of him. "But if you want the enchantments to cover large distances, I'm going to need better reagents."

I hummed, looking at the assemblage on the table. He had four wooden dowels, two long and two short. One of each was sitting in a small wooden plank with holes carved into it. He set two more medium-length rods off to the side. "Did you carve the wood yourself?"

He gave a wary nod. "One must…as an enchanter. Working the materials is what puts our mana into it." He paused a moment before handing me one of the short dowels. "If you would?"

I tilted my head, holding the rod up. "Testing, testing."

"*Testing, testing,*" went the long dowel in Maarin's hands.

Maarin blinked. "Testing?"

"*Testing?*" the rod transmitted back.

"Excellent!" I grinned. "It works."

He let out a relieved breath. "Of—of course it works! I managed to link each of the rods to each other, that was the easy part." He swapped out the long dowel in the wooden plank for one of the medium ones, then picked up the second medium dowel. "The harder bit was setting up the enchantment on the linking board," he said into his device.

The rod in my hand buzzed. "*The harder bit was setting up the enchantment on the linking board.*"

My grin grew even wider. "So how does it work?"

"As you can see, it begins here." He tapped his dowel into his hand and the sound reverberated into mine. "The enchantment on each rod captures the sound, sending it to the matching rod just like you suggested." He pointed at the other dowel in the board. "It's the board that has the enchantment to transfer the sound from one set of rods to the other. And then it replicates the sound in the final rod, just like I've, uh, demonstrated."

"What's the range?"

Maarin glanced off to the side. "About as far wide as my shop?"

I hummed. Not a good start, but now that we had a proof of concept, we could work from there. "Any thought to my enchantment relays to make it go longer range?"

"Yes…a few." He shrugged his shoulders. "That's what I needed to talk to you about more reagents for. That sort of enchantment isn't quite something I can do with leftover pieces of wood and some glass."

I raised an eyebrow. "There's glass in this mess?"

He flipped over the 'linking board,' showing where he'd set a small piece of foggy glass into the other side. "Glass or some other reflective surface is necessary for the reflection of the sound," he said. "Without that, it would be difficult for even a master enchanter to make the rods do more than buzz."

I clicked my tongue. Of course, there would be a material cost to magic as well. So much for cheating outrageously.

I was still going to cheat *normally*, of course.

"I also noticed you switched the rods out manually. Is there no way to make the rods automatically connect, either with a verbal or manual cue on the user's end?"

He blinked, looking up at me. I held back a sigh. Come on, this was just simple cell phone protocol stuff. I hadn't even started bringing in the browser features yet.

"No."

I raised an eyebrow. "Are you sure about that?"

"I'm very sure," he said.

"So, you're telling me, that if I took this little idea to the Enchanter's Guild, they'd tell me it was impossible as well?" I leaned forward. Behind me, Dee and Dum leaned forward too.

I could tell by how the floorboards creaked.

Maarin swallowed before rallying. "I'm telling you that if you took this idea to the Enchanter's Guild they'd laugh you out of town." He frowned. "If you took *this* to the Guild, they'd rip it out of your hands and *run* you out of town."

I looked at him for a moment more before leaning back with a smile. "Good to know." I ran a hand through my hair, reassessing. "Guess we're going full grapevine, then."

He blinked at the non sequitur. "Grape…vine?"

I chuckled. "Don't worry about it." Demons were useful for all kinds of things. "I'm guessing you haven't been able to make a recording feature yet either?"

He shrugged. "Not really? With better materials, I could manage something, but it would be tricky."

"Don't worry about it." I waved a hand. "Instead, if I got you some… copper *wire*, could you make the linking enchantment use that instead of another piece of wood?"

Maarin blinked before frowning down at his proof of concept. "How much wire?"

"Probably two or three feet?"

"How are you going to get three feet of spooled-out copper?" He looked up at me, eyes wide. "Most smiths don't even bother making that type of material."

I patted him on the cheek. "How's about you let me worry about that as well."

"Uh, right, yes." He took a step back, glancing away. Behind me, Dum chuckled.

I elbowed him in the gut.

Dee chuckled instead.

"I could do it!" Maarin missed the rest of our byplay. "It would actually be easier than using the glass if the wire was burnished. But what are you thinking to do with it?"

"Imagine this." I stood the dowels up in a row. "Put these on a wall, with a hoop of wire hanging over one. When you want to connect it to another rod, you just loop a piece of wire over that one, and when the person is done, you take the wire back down. Easy peasy."

He blinked dumbly, mouth opening and closing a few times in quick succession. "Th-that's—"

"Stop, you're making me blush." I took a step back from the counter. Really, I'd feel prouder of my 'brilliance' if I'd managed to come up with the idea on my own, instead of ripping it off. Standing on the shoulders of giants was all well and good, but fall off and you have to shank a few of them in the back of the knee to get back to where you started. "Can it be done?"

"Yes…yes, it can! Uh, but…" He paused. "Who's going to move the wires?"

"Remember how I keep telling you to let me worry about these things?"

"Yes?"

"You do that."

"Oh. Uh." Maarin scratched his ear. "Alright."

"Perfect." I smiled. "Just…one more thing. I'll need you to add something that will send a buzz to our little wall of connections so that the operator knows when someone wants a connection. Oh, and while you're at it, make it so the conversation can be listened to, that way the operator knows when to take the wire back down."

"I…think I can manage something like that?"

"Think of it this way." I drew a few lines into his dusty countertop. "One device is sending a sound to a…crystal ball or something, then the crystal ball sends it one to the other device. Simple, easy."

"Does the part in the middle need to…send anything?" He asked slowly.

"Not at all." I affected a much put-upon sigh. "It's just the only good way to make sure someone knows when to take the copper wire back down. After all, even *I* can only manage to get so many of those."

I was also…going to have to put a lot of points into Attunement and Soul to get enough mana for all of the demons I was going to need.

There had to be a gossip demon, right?

Right.

"That's…very complicated."

"Maarin."

"Of course, of course, my lady." Maarin scratched his cheek. "I will not worry about it."

I smiled. "First, focus on the distance problem. Get me a few sets of linked mirrors that can communicate across a city, and we'll deal with the rest in time."

Maarin nodded. "I understand. I'll focus my efforts there."

I crossed my arms. "So, what did you need me to get for you?"

"Oh, yes. To begin with…" Maarin scrambled around under his counter before pulling out a rough map on parchment. "It's for the connections that you wanted. I need something I can trick the enchantment into believing is the same object; that way we can have one enchantment that functions through multiple reception enchantments without the entire apparatus breaking…I think…" The last bit was muttered, so I ignored it for the time being.

"And this is the part where you tell me what you need, Maarin." I rolled my eyes. "Enough beating around the bush. What is it? Blood diamonds? The tears of the fae? A virginity other than your own?"

"I…that's—" He sputtered for a second before looking away. "It's actually…hummingbird feathers."

I nodded, looking at his map. "Okay…" He didn't say anything. "That's it? *Hummingbird feathers?*"

"Yes…"

"And you can't go to the Guild for this because?" I held up a hand. "No, stupid question. I wouldn't want them to know what I was doing, anyway. Much better as a fait accompli." I snagged the map out from under his hand. "How many?"

"As many as you…can get back within one piece?" he managed.

I held back a snort. "I won't damage your precious hummingbird feathers, Maarin." I moved towards the door of the shop before pausing, one niggling thought at the back of my head. "By the way, how big are the hummingbirds around here again?"

He made a hummingbird-sized circle with his fingers.

Well, good. It would have been rather embarrassing to realize the hummingbirds in this world were the size of an SUV or something. Especially after laughing at him about it. I tapped Dum on the shoulder. "Go get Electra, tell her to meet me at the Miner's Gate."

"Sure thing, boss."

Dum wasn't worried either, so really, how bad could it be?

I left quickly, Dee behind me as Dum split off for the docks. The two of us were stopped by a procession on the main thoroughfare, where a small group of people in silver plate armor were riding into the city. The crowd blocked us from passing.

I leaned over towards Dee as a group of guardsmen—their armor noticeably *less* shiny—came up to greet the new arrivals. "So, who are these guys?"

"They're the Watch," Dee said.

"The Watch?"

Dee shrugged. "Big important people, never really heard much about 'em. 'Cept that they got a fancy tower on the North Coast."

I shrugged. "None of our…"

I paused when the leader of the Watch pulled something out from under his cloak, showing it to the guardsmen.

"Boss?"

"The fuck are they doing with my armor?!"

CHAPTER 26

Rel Event

They found her after Lady Via left the city, just like Rel's mistress said they would.

Well, Lady Via had said as much after complaining that people had stolen her armor and whining about the unfairness of it all. But Mistress always made sure to give Rel all the information she needed, even when she was upset.

So, to put it simply, Rel was entirely unsurprised when a Guildie came up to her while she was overseeing a work crew.

"Seems like a waste of your skills."

Rel paused, hand dropping to the row of daggers strapped to her hip. She'd gotten a knife fighting skill as well recently. It would be a shame to get blood on her suit, but she was never against a few easy levels.

"I don't know what you mean."

The young woman in armor, a <Warrior lvl 8>, waved towards the group of people working on the new dormitory building. "They got a rare class like you doin' scutt work."

Rel said nothing.

The woman ran a hand through her short blond hair. "What, you can't tell me you're not pissed off! I know I would be."

The woman was short, almost as short as Lady Via. And even though she tried to dress up like she was from the docks, her cloak was new, and the dirt stains obviously rubbed on. There was more to poverty than *filth*, and if the Guild couldn't see that, Rel wanted no part of their offers.

But she knew the part *she* needed to play.

Feigning irritation might work? Ah, but…being overeager would b-be bad though…

System Messages

Dream Sequence has increased to lvl 3(EX)!

Rel loved and hated *Dream Sequence* in turns. On one hand, whenever she was out of her depth, the skill tossed her a lifeline. How to move forward. How to bring Mistress's dreams into reality.

But on the other hand, did it really have to sound like her from before Mistress made her more confident!?

Rel huffed, crossing her arms. Feign irritation nothing. "Lady Via makes me go where she needs me."

The warrior girl laughed, putting a hand in front of her mouth. "Oh, and she really needs *you* of all people to make sure this building goes up?" She shook a hand. "Jeez, *Empress* must be really short on competent people. Oh, wait."

Rel let herself twitch in frustration.

"It's not like she took all the people she trusted with her out of the city or anything. Even those two oafs that follow her around everywhere."

Rel looked away. "So?"

"I'm just saying…you've been around since the beginning, haven't you? It seems weird that you'd be on the outs. 'Specially over that new girl." The warrior pulled a face. "She's an idiot."

Rel clenched a fist in the fabric of her sleeve. "She'll get what's coming to her sooner or later."

"Yeah, well, maybe." The girl shrugged. "But hey, if good things happened to good people, we wouldn't all be stuck here, would we?"

You're not stuck anywhere. Rel bit her tongue. She hated when people lied about being in this together. They were always the people who chose the wrong fights, as if being poor meant that Rel should choose to go against her best interest, just because the Guild dangled something shiny in front of her face.

"What do you want, anyway." Rel shoved her hands into her pockets. "In case you couldn't tell, I'm…*busy* here."

"Suuuuure!" The girl gave a little twirl, coming to lean against the wall of another run-down building. It hadn't rained in the last few days, so the dirt road beneath their feet was hard and cracked. Across the street, members of Empress's gang continued to lay out stones for the building's foundation. "I just…wanted to make an offer, 's all. From the people who all *know* you do a better job than that Electra bitch."

Rel gave a little jump. No way they'd managed to infiltrate so quickly…

S-she's lying…

Rel took a moment to gather herself, letting out a slow breath. "I don't know what you're talking about." She shouldn't be too eager.

"But don't you want to at least hear what we have to say?" the girl asked. "We *all* know you could do a better job around here than Electra. And if Empress doesn't see it, well…" She shrugged.

Rel turned. "Well, what?"

"Then you've gotta show her, don'cha?"

It was…ambiguous on purpose, wasn't it? Rel chewed on the words. They were still feeling her out, trying to figure out just how mad she was with Empress. Maybe they were still deciding if they would keep her after knocking Empress off, like Lady Via said.

She took a deep breath.

"Maybe I'll listen to what you have to say." She glared at the girl. "But you better not be wasting my time."

"'Course not!" The girl skipped forward, pressing a thin piece of parchment into Rel's hand. "Don't let anyone catch you with that though!"

They won't help if w-w-we get caught, huh?

No, Rel thought, they probably wouldn't. She shoved the piece of parchment into her pocket. "Got it. Now, go get another cart of stone."

"E-eh?" The girl paused midstep.

Rel raised an eyebrow, doing her best to copy Lady Via's expression. "Don't you think it would look suspicious if you just talked to me and left?"

"Well, that's—"

"What, don't want to be taking orders from me either?" Rel crossed her arms. "I see how it is."

"Ugh, what a fucking pain." The girl tossed her hair. "Whatever, I'll be back with a cart. You better not stand us up."

The 'we' got lost pretty quick there, Rel noticed. "I'll be there." She slid a hand into her pocket, rubbing a finger over the rough parchment. The Guild made contact. Now she needed to be the bait that would reel them in for Mistress to catch.

D-don't mess up!

She wouldn't.

The moon was out tonight.

The piece of parchment had a location and time. It was another building in the docks, still deep enough to be considered part of it, but far closer to the center of the city. Parts of the town that had been converted into a merchant district without much fuss.

Rel knew because her Da used to complain about it when he was in his cups. Talking about all them blue bloods…

Rel shook her head. Now wasn't the time to get distracted.

She rapped on the rough wooden door twice. After a few moments, the door opened. Rel saw the warrior girl again, still in her bad cloak with the fake stains. Of course, she wasn't the only one in the building.

"What's the Guild doing here?"

There was another warrior sitting at the table, *level 11*. It made Rel suck in a breath.

The woman smiled at that reaction. "I thought it would make sense to be here," she said, idly playing with the gold tassel hanging over her shoulder. "Your little gang is my investment after all. Suffice it to say you aren't the only one…displeased with the current state of affairs."

Act surprised, already!

Rel spun, glaring at the first warrior. "I thought you said there were other people in the docks that cared!"

"Oops?" The girl shrugged, tossing her cloak into the corner, revealing a much better set of armor than anyone from the docks would be able to afford. "I mean, I wasn't really lying, was I?" She smirked. "You showed up, didn't cha?"

Rel took a deep breath, trying to appear like she was getting her anger under control, even as two other people came out of the corners of the room. A rogue and an archer both moving to stand next to the younger warrior. They were clearly her party.

The archer pushed the door shut behind them.

Rel glanced around. It was a small building, only one story. There was a door leading to another room, full of empty barrels. But other than that, there was nothing but a rough-hewn table with a lantern on it.

Rel drew herself up to her full height. "Is this the part where you kill me? 'Cause I dun' die easy."

The woman just laughed. "Oh, that's precious." She waved a hand. "Take a seat, Relia."

Rel stiffened for a moment before moving to take a seat across from the woman.

"How do you know my name?"

"We know a lot about you," the woman said. "We know that your father is a waste of space, we know that you've been through quite a few different apprenticeships." Her smile grew sharp. "We know that you're always looking for a better deal."

That was so far off base it wasn't even funny. Rel switched jobs because she didn't like the idea of paying to be a scrivener with her *body*. But then, that wasn't something Rel expected a person with *power* to ever understand.

There was only one person who ever had.

Rel waited a moment and then nodded. "Okay, and who are you?"

"I am Lady Delia, Guild Knight."

Rel nodded again. The Guild liked to arrange their ranks like some kind of fake nobility. At the bottom were Recruits, or 'shield bearers.' Then it went Captain, Knight, Marcher, and Lord Marshal. Technically, this Delia lady was supposed to be a *Sira* or something. But then, Guildies loved putting on airs and acting better than the rest.

S-she's used to getting her way…

And she thought Rel was looking for a better deal.

She ducked her head for a moment as if she was bowing.

"E-empress has a new project she's working on," Rel said.

Delia raised an immaculate eyebrow. "Oh?"

"I don't know what's going on with it yet, but if you give me some time, I can figure out that one too." She looked up, meeting the other woman's gaze. "That's what you want, right? Someone else to…help move things along."

"Hmm, perhaps."

Rel didn't let the ambivalent reply faze her. She had a feeling of surety growing in her chest as if she knew this was what she needed to say. "I hear things, even if I'm on the outs. Empress has been slowing down production on purpose."

An ugly glower crossed Delia's face. "I knew it. That bitch." She tossed her hair, rising. "Well, you've certainly proved you know how to play the game, haven't you, Relia?"

Rel ducked her head again, covering a glare of her own. "Yes, Sira."

The woman huffed, walking around the table. But she didn't make any issue about not being called *Lady Delia*. Which was good, because as far as Rel was concerned, she only had *one* lady. There would be no room for another.

"Vire."

The warrior snapped off a salute. "Yes, my lady!"

"Your party will help little Rel get everything into position." Delia smiled. "Erak should be helpful figuring out that *new* project of hers." The woman gave Rel a sharp look. "It had better be something important, if you're going to spend time on it."

"It is." Rel could say that without restraint. "The whole thing with her foundry, it was just to get money and resources for this next project. Whatever it is, it's big."

Delia sniffed. "Well, if you say so." She breezed past them, golden tassel swaying from her shoulder. "I'll leave you to work out the details then. Move quickly."

"Yes, my lady!" Vira gave another grin before coming over to Rel as the door shut behind the *Knight*. "Looks like you made a good impression on her, huh, Relia?"

Rel put on a smile. "Call me Rel." She held out a hand. "We're gonna be working together, after all."

"That's what I like to hear!" Vira snagged Rel's hand, holding it for just a bit too long. "Last Rare Classer we ran into ran off with your old boss." She pulled Rel half a step closer. "But we'll…get to know each other, won't we?"

Rel's smile went wooden. Behind the short warrior's shoulder, she saw the archer sending her a venomous glare, thumbing the arrows in her quiver.

How was she going to get out of *this* mess?

M-maybe try…flirting b-back?

CHAPTER 27

A Bird in the Hand

God, will you stop pouting already?"

I huffed, slapping away a low branch. "I'm not pouting."

"Suuure you're not." Electra rolled her eyes. "And I'm having a grand old time slogging through this stupid jungle."

We were, of course, trekking once more through the jungle beyond Silverwall.

"How are the mosquitoes treating you, by the way?"

Electra just snorted, and I turned back towards the dense foliage, definitely *not* pouting.

Maarin had given us a location where hummingbirds usually nested, and I'd taken Electra with me out of the city. Dee and Dum were up on the coast, making sure we had a nice big stockpile of metal for the next few orders. Wouldn't do for the fox to be in the henhouse while the chickens were plotting a coup.

Pardon the pun.

"You're acting like a little kid, Em'."

I rolled my eyes. "Like all the little girls who buy Halloween versions of your leotard and prance around in it."

She blushed lightly, rubbing the back of her head. Her hair had grown out a bit, and that plus the humidity made it tend to be more frizzy than spiky these days. "That's—look, I had a talk with my agent about the whole costume thing, alright?"

"I'm sure your fanboys were devastated by the loss of your thighs."

"Hey man, these thighs *do* save lives."

I snorted. "I'm sure." I ducked under a branch, letting Electra stumble as she got a faceful of leaves.

"Hey! We're on the same side here, aren't we?"

"Hmm?" I turned back to look at her as if butter wouldn't melt in my mouth. "What was that?"

She glared, tugging the thick fronds out of her hair. "Whatever." She huffed. "This is the thanks I get for running your little criminal empire for you? Maybe I won't work so hard next week."

I choked, holding back a laugh.

Electra's eyes narrowed. "What?"

"N-nothing!" I waved a hand. "I-I'm sure you'll manage things perfectly, no matter how much or little effort you decide to put in. Your… efforts have been…*exemplary.*"

She glared at me for a moment longer, as if looking for the trap in my words. Of course, she missed the fact that the *entire thing* was the trap. Oh man, the look on Wonder Man's face when he got to the center of my Doom Fortress and the entire thing turned out to be just a giant Doom For*trap*… Good times.

But I digress.

"Thanks, I guess."

"No, no, thank you!" I smiled. "I mean it, I wouldn't have been able to pull off my plans without your assistance."

We kept walking, and I affected not to notice the suspicious glances at me from the corner of my eye. She wouldn't figure me out.

She never had before.

The only thing I was worried about was if Rel could hold everything together while we were gone. I knew this would be a prime chance for the Guild to reach out and contact her. I needed the Guild to try their coup d'état sooner rather than later.

Especially because the city now had my armor.

Speaking of. "We will need to get it back though."

"Your suit?" Electra shrugged. "Well, yeah. Honestly, I'm surprised you didn't call this whole thing off to go charging the palace or something."

"None of us have even been allowed through the inner wall," I said. "There's no way some half-baked attack would work."

Silverwall was divided in many ways, not the least of which was that the poor sections of the city lay along the north and east walls. Those areas were where the miners lived, and the sailors lived no longer. The main thoroughfare through the city split it in half. Beyond that, even, there was a second wall cutting off the middle of the city from the rest.

That wall was capped with silver on the crenelations, no less. It was probably Silverwall's titular namesake. The gates were always manned, and there was no Miner's Gate into the inner city.

"What's your play, then?"

I sighed. "For now? The exact same as I always do. Amass power, take over the underworld, topple the Guild. Then I'll have enough resources to launch an attack." I allowed myself a small smile. "It fits in rather neatly, doesn't it?"

"Is that how you do all your planning?" Electra waved a hand nebulously. "Just, get stuff so that you can do…*something* in the future?"

"Were you expecting something different?"

"Well, yeah?" She shrugged. "I mean, your schemes back on Earth were always so…one thousand steps or something, right?"

I tilted my head. "Is that what they looked like?"

"Yeah?"

"Well." I chuckled. "You know you're watching a professional when they make it look effortless." In reality, things back on Earth had been *more* ad hoc than my 'schemes' on this world. Here, I had a clear end goal, I had only minor opposition, and I was allowed to operate freely with the knowledge that the system didn't know how to counter.

Electra just snorted. "Suuuure."

I just shrugged. "There's a reason I was the last one left."

Electra paused at that. I stopped a step later, turning to look at her over my shoulder. "What?"

"What was it like? Being the last big Supervillain?" She rubbed the back of her head. "I mean, sure, people would pop up, using laser vision to rob a bank or something, but you, you were the only one who *still* tried to take over the world, or whatever. Like, you could have swapped sides and made mad bank with your inventions just because of the *clout*."

I turned away. "And here you were saying that I wasn't actually big news."

"Oh, c'mon, Empress, that was just talk."

I smiled. "It always is. Now, let's keep moving. I want to get back to Silverwall by the end of the day."

"Huh? But you didn't—"

I started walking. "Are you coming?"

She huffed, jogging to catch up with me. "If you didn't want to talk about it, you just had to say so."

"So," I said. She gave me a dry look. I sighed. "Look, did you think it was fun? Being alone against the world? Being the only one left with any ambition among a bunch of two-bit thugs and wannabe Capones?"

"You made it look pretty fun, not gonna lie."

I sighed. "Oh, the things we could have done together. Ruled the galaxy as father and son." Electra gave me an odd look. "Don't tell me you haven't seen those movies!"

"What movies?"

I turned to stare at her. "You know what, never mind. I probably would have just stuck you in a capacitor. I need minions I can talk to."

She gave a laugh. "Oh, that's why you keep the boys around, huh?"

"They're excellent conversationalists."

Electra rolled her eyes. "Hey, don't change the conversation now. I'm serious, you think we didn't talk about you, what made you come back each time we beat you? Hell, *I* always wondered what made you come back each time *you* won. "

I worried my lip, casting my gaze up towards the dense green canopy. "Because…I'd already changed sides once, and I'd be damned if I came back after that."

Electra blinked.

"I used to work for Aegis, you know?" I glanced at her from the corner of my eye. "*The* Hero organization. Of course, I signed up. I got a job there too, for a while." I smiled. "Then I met Marvelous."

Electra pulled a face. "Oh, yeah. She was kinda stuck up, wasn't she?"

I shrugged. "Sure, we can go with that."

"So that's it?" Electra asked. "You were on our side once, so that means you could never come back, even if you could have made a fresh start for yourself? Hell, you could have just hung up the cape, I know you know that we couldn't have come after you."

"I'm sure it started that way." I shrugged. "But then, at some point, it stopped being about that."

"What was it about then?"

I smiled. "Winning."

She followed after me, a difficult expression on her face.

I laughed. "Why so serious? It's not like I'm some martyr who was forced down this road every step of the way. I made my choices, I decided what was important to me…and what wasn't."

"I guess that makes sense why Marvelous got transferred, huh?"

"Oh, no."

"No?"

My smile grew slightly. "I made her ask for it herself."

Electra didn't say anything.

Which, if we were being brutally honest in this moment, was my preferred state of affairs.

In due time, we made it deep enough into the jungle to find one of the clearings. Really, it was the glinting of bright feathers in the sunlight that drew my gaze. Electra and I moved to the edge of a small open area in the jungle. There was a break in the trees, and there was a whole group of hummingbirds nesting in the eaves of a smaller palm tree closer to the center.

"That's a weird clearing."

I nodded, looking down at the carpet of wildflowers that grew denser in the clearing itself. "Probably has something to do with the birds themselves. Hummingbirds are pollinators, after all."

"What, do they kill the trees?"

I shrugged. "It wouldn't be the weirdest thing we've seen since landing here, would it?"

"No."

We stayed for a moment longer. The birds themselves were still sleeping. It was only a little bit past sunrise, and it seemed like they were still in their early morning torpor, or whatever the equivalent was. After a moment, Electra nudged me in the side. "Well?"

I sighed. "How about—"

We both paused at a low growl.

Behind us, an emerald green cat was padding out of the shadows, thick mane of fur bristling in an obvious threat display.

<Moss Pouncer lvl 9>

Electra took a step forward, fingers sparking.

What, you thought I wouldn't give her a few hours with my generator before heading into hostile territory? I was petty, not *stupid*.

Still, it wouldn't do to let her have all the fun.

I snapped my fingers.

Blue launched out of the underbrush like a shot. My demon caught the pouncer in the side, biting deep into the creature's neck even as both pairs of forelimbs clawed deep into its sides.

The cat yowled, twisting and jerking as it tried to get free.

"Toss it."

At my command, Blue reared up, jerking his head to throw the pouncer into the air. It tumbled past us, into the clearing, leaving a trail of blood.

Blue loped after it, sliding to a stop at my side. I reached over, ruffling the blue hair along his spine. "Who's a good boy? Who's a good booooy?"

Electra snorted. "And here I thought villains were all cat people."

"Villains are people who make do." I rose. In the clearing, the pouncer got back to its feet as well, stumbling because of the blood loss through a low haze of pollen. At my side, Blue crouched, awaiting my command.

Then a hummingbird landed on the cat's flank.

The beast froze. The hummingbird pecked once.

It turned, claws lashing out into the air, but the bird was gone. In its place, a chromatic storm of wings descended on the pouncer, drawing thin pinpricks of blood along its sides. The cat swung once, twice, both times hitting nothing but air. Then the flock pulled back, flying up to rest in their tree.

The great cat's sides heaved, but the wounds were superficial at most. They must be waiting to make another pass.

At least that's what I thought until it let out a low whimper and fell to the ground.

Blood, tinged with the slightest hint of purple, leaked from its wounds. It soaked into the soil, and the flowers bloomed.

"Ah." I nodded. "*That's* why Maarin was so worried."

Of course the hummingbirds were venomous.

CHAPTER 28

Two in the Bush

I categorically refuse!"

I raised an eyebrow at Electra. "Honestly, I'm surprised."

Electra snorted. "What, that I *won't* charge into the poison hummingbird clearing for you?"

"No, that you know what 'categorically' means. SMH." I shook my head.

"Bitch." Electra punched me in the shoulder. "I'm still not running into the murder swarm for you."

We'd pulled a bit back from the clearing, especially once the lovely little *venomous hummingbirds* started to feed. Actually, that was the other thing.

"Also, they're venomous, not poisonous." I gave a little giggle. "I guess your word-a-day calendar only went so far."

She rolled her eyes. "Tomayto, tomahto."

I patted her on the cheek. "You're right, let's call the whole thing off."

I turned back to the clearing as Electra huffed. The birds were eating now, but they weren't going after the corpse. Instead, they were behaving much more like, well, actual hummingbirds.

The tiny things streaked around from flower to flower, pausing only long enough to drink. I noticed that the swarm—and really, that's what it was—was going around the whole glade, but they were much more interested in the blooming ones than the rest of their little glade.

"Huh, so it's a symbiotic relationship."

Electra glanced at me. "What?"

I waved a hand. "The flowers probably have poisonous nectar or something like that. The hummingbirds drink the nectar, get the venom, and use it to kill anything that comes into the glade. The blood waters the flowers, the hummingbirds get more poisonous nectar. Everyone wins."

"Okay, little miss '*venomous* and *poisonous* are different.'"

"*That's* your take? *Madre de Dios.*" I rubbed a hand over my face. "Poisonous means if you bite it, you die. Venomous means if *it* bites *you*, you die. Get the picture, or do I need to make it into a nursery rhyme?"

Electra pulled a face. "Why did I decide to work with you again?"

"Good question." I turned back to the clearing. "*Anywho,* it's actually kind of interesting to see a *swarm* of hummingbirds. I thought they were more territorial."

"Because you're a zoologist now?" Electra asked.

"Saw a ViewTube video once." I waved my hand. "I guess that there are enough flowers for—no, wait." I narrowed my eyes as a pair of the birds started jostling around a particular patch of flowers.

Specifically, ones that had just bloomed.

Then one bird skewered the other, sending a cute little feathery ball of fluff to the ground with a piteous chirp.

"Aww, that one got stabbed." From the corner of my eye, I saw Electra pouting at the birds. "Think we can grab that one after they all go to sleep?"

"And here I thought you liked cute things." I rolled my eyes. "Are you going to be the one picking them up?"

Electra paused. "Well, don't you have demons for that?"

I snorted. "My demons are actually useful, unlike some people in this relationship."

Electra shot me a sharp glare before huffing. She crossed her arms, looking back towards the clearing. At this point, several of the birds had spread out along the rest of the glen, taking nectar from the other flowers that hadn't been so…liberally watered.

"You're the one who needs the flowers," she said.

I huffed. "And you're the one who needs my generator." I looked over at her. "Or are you just going to leave a poor, defenseless damsel to fend for herself?"

Electra let out a sharp laugh. "Okay, but for real though, what's the plan?" She pointed towards the swarm. "Because, like, again, I am not going into *that*."

I hummed, tapping a finger against my chin. On one hand, there was a whole clearing full of venomous hummingbirds that fed the blood of other animals to poisonous flowers, and we were supposed to gather the feathers of said venomous birds in the aforementioned poisonous clearing for my project. Common sense said that it would fall to me to take the risk.

But common sense also said that 'villains are all dicks.'

"What was that new skill of yours again?" I asked. "Something to do with reflexive lightning or somesuch?"

Electra grinned. "It's called Lightning Reflexes."

I nodded. Right, she'd mentioned that before. My own skills were slow to come, though I had picked up a few levels just in the act of running my burgeoning empire. On the other hand, Lightning Reflexes. If it was anything as close to as punny as the rest of the skills in this world, it would likely prove to be quite helpful in the current situation.

"Hold your breath."

Electra turned to look at me, eyebrow raised. I took a step forward, Blue coming up on her other side, and I gave her a shove. She tripped over my cute little demon lizard, falling into the clearing, ass over teakettle.

At once, the swarm of deadly, killer—but *also* very cute—hummingbirds rose back into the air, their wings beating a sharp staccato.

As one, the flock of birds dived towards Electra, beaks first, like little streaks of light.

A predictable burst of lightning was the result.

The birds were thrown backwards, scorched, several dozen landing on the ground right away from the first wave, while the rest spiraled around disoriented. Of course, I wasn't about to leave Electra to fend for herself, even if I was using her as bait.

I whistled.

General Tock, who'd been shadowing us from the tree line, rushed forward into the clearing. His metal body was proof against the venom, the poison, and any combination thereof, which made him the perfect follow-up for my Electra bomb. Oh, sorry, I meant *electric* bomb.

My little robot lived up to his name by leading a charge into the clearing as I watched, one hand idly scratching Blue's mane. General Tock's fabricator and disassembler in his mouth fired up, launching a small ray of heat that sent several birds spiraling backwards, beating frantically at their wings.

They were too small to get picked out of the air, and Tock only managed one or two, but the new threat threw the whole flock into disarray long enough for Electra's skill to come back up.

She threw out a Buzzer Bolt or two straight through the swarm, clipping a few birds. Then, when the swarm of hummingbirds dived again, she erupted into electricity for the second time, sending several more plummeting to the ground.

She even threw in a few bursts of actual lightning, which grounded through the hummingbirds beautifully.

At that point, the rest of the hummingbirds cut their losses, moving backwards in a much-diminished swarm.

The part of me that was a scientist first and a Supervillain second was interested in the potential quorum-sensing of these birds. What level of appreciation did they have for their situation? By what method did they communicate, and to what extent?

But, of course, I hadn't been more scientist than Supervillain for several years now, so instead, I gave another sharp whistle.

"Get the birds, Tock," I said. "Also, you might want to get out of there, Electra."

The Hero, outfit stained with bits of dust, glared at me. At least she'd managed to keep her mouth shut this time.

She tromped to the edge of the clearing, hands clenched at her sides. "You just pushed me into a clearing full of poisonous hummingbirds!"

I sighed. "I thought I told you: *venomous*." I gave her a droll look. "You'd think being chucked into the middle of them would help you remember…"

"You…you bi—" She cut herself off, settling for a sharp glare. "That's the last time I help you with anything."

"Well, if that's the way you really feel." I shrugged.

Electra continued to glower. "God, you just don't care do you?"

I raised an eyebrow. "I feel as though we've had this discussion several times now." I pointed back towards the clearing, where General Tock was loading the thirty or forty birds into the popped-open storage compartment on his beetle-like back. "Besides, we got what we came for, didn't we?"

"Yeah, but you almost killed me!"

I rolled my eyes. "Please, I wasn't about to let you die."

"Really?" Electra continued to glare as though her face were locked in that expression. "Because from my point of view, you did jack all!"

I gave a little laugh. "Oh, Electra," I said, "I've put people I cared about more than you into situations that were much, *much* more deadly."

She gaped at me for a second.

I smiled. "Be happy I still need you alive, or maybe I wouldn't have warned you to keep your mouth shut."

With that, I spun back to the clearing, taking out the bag I had bought back in the city. General Tock had the goods, so all that remained was making good on our payment. No reason to stay out here any longer than we had to, and I'd need to make sure Electra *did* get checked over for poison inhalation when we made it back.

The idiot would probably forget.

My motto was never taking unnecessary risks. It wasn't my fault if I had a different definition of necessary than the average person.

"Where do you get *off*?" Electra asked. She had a confused expression on her face, though that was nothing new. "Just throwing people under the bus whenever you feel like it, where does it stop? How do you ever get people to trust you?"

I looked over at her. "People trust me," I said, "because I show everyone exactly what I'm about. And I never, ever lie."

Well, not to the people I was working with, in any case. Most villains believed that they were the only ones that mattered and that the opinions and beliefs of the people working for them were less than dust.

Most villains ended up dead or worse, at the hands of Heroes *much* less capable than Electra.

I was not most villains.

Back on Earth, people seem to think that the Heroes stood for something, while villains stood for nothing at all. Or at least, they stood for nothing more than their own selfish gain.

In my experience, it was quite the other way around.

But then, this wasn't the time to be sharing that kind of opinion with Electra.

"Look," I huffed, running a hand through my hair. "You told me the definition of your skill. I took that into consideration and came up with a plan that was guaranteed to work, except for the reticence of some of the people involved." I gave her a look. "One of the other ways I get people to trust me is by being right *every* time. Like I was here."

Electra let out a groan, running a hand through her spiked hair. "You don't get to just decide for other people, Empress."

I laughed. "Isn't that what everyone does?"

"What are you talking about?" She looked honestly bewildered.

"I mean, how many people *really* get to choose for themselves?" I leaned forward. "And how many people never bother to stop and think before choosing for someone else? At the very least, I know that *my* decisions are made with our best interests in mind."

Electra glared; it seemed like she was back to that old standby. "And how the heck was shoving me into a clearing full of poisonous—fine, ugh, *venomous*—birds 'in my best interest'?"

I raised an eyebrow. "Why, Electra, because now we get to get out of the jungle before you're eaten alive." So saying, I reached out, flicking a mosquito off her neck. "Unless you want to stay out in this morass a second longer than you have to?"

Electra raised a finger, still half-mad, then she grumbled. "You… might have a point."

"I always have a point." I smiled up at her. "Besides, it's not like either of us are new to life-threatening situations."

Electra shrugged, looking off into the jungle. "I just have one question," she said. "If you were the one with electric powers instead of me, would you have jumped into that clearing yourself?"

I smiled. "If *I* had electric powers, I would have finished my industrial revolution already." I shrugged at her much-aggrieved expression. "But to answer your question, yes. You of all people should know by now that I never ask someone else to do what I wouldn't be willing to do myself."

Electra let out a low sigh. "Yeah, but the problem with that is…"

I raised an eyebrow, tilting my head. "What?"

Electra looked off to the side.

"No, really, I'm honestly curious."

Electra ran a hand through her hair. "The problem is that the end always justifies the means with you. There is nothing you're not willing to do."

"And did you ever think that maybe there was a reason for that?" I met her gaze head-on. "Did you ever stop to consider that I was willing to go so far because I knew the cost of falling short?"

Electra just looked at me, eyes meeting mine but not really seeing. "What the heck even happened to you?"

"Why are you asking?" I gave a mirthless laugh. "You were there for most of it, weren't you?"

To that, Electra had nothing to say.

CHAPTER 29

Lightning the Way

Empress knew that Electra was watching, of course.

Electra knew she wasn't subtle. Her old team went out of their way to remind her of that every time they went for a stealth mission, and Empress certainly hadn't let it slide.

That said, the Hero still couldn't stop herself from assessing her tiny, vindictive companion in a new light. And not just because Electra had just gotten shoved into a clearing full of venomous hummingbirds yet had walked out unscathed.

She had known Empress for most of her heroic career, from the time she made her debut to their final climactic showdown in the middle of Empress's giant DoomTron 5000 (and no, that name was *never* going to stop being hilarious). Electra thought she had the villainess pegged, but the more time they spent together, the more Empress let her mask slip, giving glimpses of the person beneath.

A person that Electra was realizing that she *didn't* know.

That she'd never known at all.

"Take a picture." Empress's words jolted Electra out of her thoughts. "It'll last longer."

Electra laughed, rubbing the back of her neck. "You'll need to advance the camera first."

"Yeah." Empress rolled her eyes. "That and everything else we need."

For instance, El knew that Empress had a biting humor, but she never realized the woman was as deprecating with herself as she was with everyone else.

"How's that going for you?"

Empress shrugged. "I have no idea what they call silver nitrate here, so mostly I'm just hoping there's a picture demon or something that I'll stumble onto eventually."

That was the other thing. Between the two of them, El was the one with a background in light novels and Isekai stories, but it was Empress that was really getting the mileage out of her cheat skill. Not that Electra hated her own powers, but it was clear that she had a lot of catching up to do.

But none of that was the reason Electra was spending so much time staring at her current companion.

"Which one is the real you?" she asked.

Empress turned to look at her, one immaculately sculpted eyebrow arching oh-so-delicately above her nemesis's olive features. "Whatever do you mean?"

Electra shrugged helplessly. "You flip-flop at the drop of a hat," she said. "One second you're all, 'There are no lines I won't cross!' and the next you're, 'I'd die to give my employees a livable wage.'" She shook her head. "It's just...I have no idea what to expect from you."

"Maybe you should have been paying more attention."

Electra huffed. "Don't give me that! If you don't want to talk about it just say so, Jesus." She crossed her arms. "Excuse me for wanting to know what flips your evil, villainous, megalomania switch."

A second eyebrow rose to join the first. "Evil, villainous...megalomania...switch." Empress nodded slowly. "Got it. Give me a second to write that one down."

Electra sighed. After nearly a day's walk, they were most of the way back to Silverwall. If she hadn't gotten any more answers out of the villain by now, she just wasn't going to, huh? "Sure, sure. It's not like you need any help coming up with new one-liners."

"No." Empress gave her a sharp smirk. "You've given me plenty of practice."

"And don't I know it," Electra grumbled. "But for real, it's heckin' freaky, the way you go from caring middle manager to a quote evil, villainous megalomaniac, unquote."

She jammed her hands into her pockets, ignoring the way Empress stared at her for a few long moments as they trekked back towards the city. Well, at least they got the feathers. Now, Electra liked to think of herself as a pretty self-sufficient kind of girl, but not having a cell phone? Definitely the worst thing no one ever mentioned about getting sucked into an Isekai.

Well, there was that one anime, but no one talked about *that* one.

For obvious reasons.

"Why are you interested all of a sudden?" Empress asked.

Electric glanced over. "Isn't it obvious?" Empress just waved a hand for her to continue. With a sigh, Electra said, "Before, you were always in evil megalomaniac mode. You know, you show up, blow up whatever, we try to stop you. And then we'd all go off and…I don't know, do our own thing in between." She shrugged again. "I guess I never really wondered about what you were like off the clock."

Empress gave that laugh of hers, the one that still sent chills down Electra's spine, and had done so ever since…well, if you were up to date with the Hero scene, you'd know. "There is no off the clock for villains, Electra."

Now it was Electra's turn to raise an eyebrow. "You're still avoiding the question."

"Am I?" the villainess spread her arms, one hand reaching out to ruffle her pet lizard demon's mane. And apparently, that one was the leftovers from the first gang boss to mess with her. If that was how Empress treated her enemies, well, Electra guessed it paid to be her friend. "Why does one of them have to be fake?"

The Hero blinked, taking a second to process that. "Uh, 'cause they're like, polar opposites?"

Empress just smiled.

Electra watched her for a second, eyes narrowed. "No, for real. I've seen you string a guy up by his intestines." It was a moment that had stuck with her, because while Empress had killed people—more people than Electra would ever really be comfortable with—she was never so brutal about it. "And now I'm supposed to believe that in your down-time you went around handing out Christmas gifts to good little boys and girls?"

"Well, there was that one time, with the lump of coal." Empress giggled, tapping her chin with one hand. "But that's hardly germane to the conversation."

Electra rubbed her forehead again, trying to slot this new tidbit of information in along with the rest. It didn't make things any easier.

The woman was *the* villain, essentially the last big player in the entire continental United States. Electra and the rest of Aegis were the Heroes that stopped her. And yet, here she was 'in a new world with your arch enemy who's really hot,' and Empress was the one actually making a difference.

Electra wasn't so blind that she couldn't see that.

She hadn't joined the Heroes to feed her pride either. It was the whole reason she'd been willing to show up at Empress's doorstep, hat in hand, and ask to be put to work.

She just wanted to know why.

Electra opened her mouth when Empress spoke again.

"Did you ever wonder what he did?"

Electra blinked at the non sequitur. "What the who?"

"David M. Elliot." Empress cast her gaze skyward, fingers curling in Blue's mane.

"Uhhh."

Empress coughed. "The intestines guy. And here you were giving me shit about it."

"Oh, uh, yeah! I remembered that." Electra put on a weak grin, stomach twisting guiltily.

"Anyway." Empress gave her a *picture-perfect* Shaft head tilt, and Electra felt her breath catching slightly. God, and here people still called Electra a weeb for trying to make Sentai poses a thing. "Did you ever wonder what. He. Did?"

The air suddenly felt heavy. Electra swallowed, all thoughts of god and anime vanishing like the morning mist. "What did he do?"

"You know, that's funny." Empress mimed laughing. "That's actually really funny because I know for a fact that the information was in your

database, or at least, it was. That's where I found it in the first place."
She shrugged. "Guess they swept it up before the internal audit."

Electra didn't like where this was going. "What did he do, Empress?"
Before, she wouldn't have even questioned it. Of course, Empress, no
matter what her past record was, would eventually snap and hang some
guy up by his intestines in the middle of Times Square. But now, Electra had seen the woman behind the mask. The woman who took in the
tired and the poor, the woman who protected people, the woman who
was doing a better job of being a Hero than Electra was. "What did he
do, that made you come for him?"

Empress shrugged. "Oh, you know, not much. It was just a child
trafficker and molester. A regular Jeffrey Epstein, if you will."

Electra's lips twisted down into a sharp frown. "And you decided
to—" She stopped. Of course, Empress hadn't gone public. At that
point, she was already nearly six months deep into her career as a Supervillain, on a tear through the United States and abroad.

Not to mention that, when she wasn't busy stealing priceless diamonds, or holding entire conglomerates hostage from orbital satellites,
she tended to eviscerate the local crime lords and cartels wherever she
put down roots.

Empress raised an eyebrow. "Yes?"

Electra shook her head. "I realized it was stupid before I even said it."

"*That* would be a first."

Electra huffed. "Every time with you, huh?" She ran a hand through
her hair. "God, and he was a major donor as well."

"Aren't they all?" Empress asked whimsically.

Electra grimaced, but said nothing. She had been on her fair share
of busts in the past before. They weren't always what she thought
they'd be.

"It wasn't just that though, was it?"

Empress stilled. "Hmm?"

Electra turned to face her. "It was personal."

Empress didn't say anything for a long moment. Then she started
walking again.

"You asked me, a little bit ago, which one was the real me." Her lips
pulled back into a sharp grin, the kind she usually wore while revealing

her master plan one second too late for the Heroes to stop her. Half the time, she was even right about that estimation. "What's the difference, between the Empress that goes around handing out presents and kittens and works to build a better, brighter tomorrow for the people under her care, and the Empress that will cheerfully eviscerate men without batting an eye?" She spread her arms, spinning to put Silverwall at her back. They were only a few minutes' walk from the city. "The answer is that there is no difference. This is, as I've said over and over again, exactly who I am."

Her smile vanished. "And I make no apologies for it."

Electra met her nemesis's eyes for a long moment. In a way, it almost hurt.

Electra had spent her whole life trying to live up to her own ideals. She'd fought, and she'd struggled, and she'd risen every step of the way, doing her best to make the world a better place. It hurt because she just now realized that the woman she spent so much of her life fighting had done exactly the same.

Or, well, so close that Electra began to see the differences that led them both to where they were.

And how few these differences really were.

"Alright."

Empress raised an eyebrow. "Alright?"

Electra had always hated the whole 'we're not so different, you and I' thing that superhero comics liked to do. It was overused, it felt cheap, and it was never really true. Except, it wasn't true here either.

Empress and Electra weren't anything close to the same person.

But Electra would bet that, at one point, they'd both been little girls with a picture of Marvelous on their wall. They'd both been little girls who had looked up to the Heroes that made the world a better place.

And it hurt.

But, in her experience, the truth usually did.

"Alright," Electra said again. "What's next?"

"Just like that?" Empress asked.

Electra nodded. "I mean, you answered my question."

Empress gave her a sharp look. The Hero could tell that the other woman didn't really believe her yet, but that was fine. She'd been playing along so far, but they both knew there was a world of difference between working together when your back was against a wall, like during the Ilmorian invasion, and *actually* working together.

That was fine.

Electra had struggled her whole life to get where she was, and she didn't regret—*couldn't* regret—the lives she saved as a Hero.

But being a Hero had never been the end goal. She had chosen to be a Hero because she thought it was the best way to help people. If it wasn't the best way anymore, then she just had to look for a new one.

Even if it came from her worst enemy.

"So, what's the play…" Electra took a deep breath. "Boss?"

CHAPTER 30

Pieces and Places

I returned to Silverwall to find the pieces all falling into place.

A runner handed me a note not a second through the Miner's Gate, shoving it into my hands while he made a flashy grab at my coin purse before darting off.

"What the heck was that?"

I glanced at Electra as the two of us slipped deeper into the city. It only took me a second to read the note before I smiled.

"You want to know what the play is?" I asked.

She stopped, giving me a determined look.

I took the box full of hummingbirds that we'd so painstakingly collected, pushing it into her hands. "Get this to Maarin, I showed you where his shop was before we left."

She blinked before taking the box. "And you?"

I just grinned, shoving the scrap of paper I'd been handed deeper into my pocket. "I have a trap to walk into." I took a step back. "I'll need one of those scrying mirrors as soon as you have a working pair."

Electra blanched. "How the heck am I gonna get one to you?"

"Don't worry." I turned. "I'll send someone by to pick it up."

I heard her huff behind me, but I was already dipping into the nearest alley. I sent Blue off with a quick mental instruction, General Tock still riding on his back. There was no reason for them to get caught up in this, especially not with the Watch in the city. I didn't want them sniping anymore of my tech.

The way back to the old docks was twisting and narrow as always, but now there was something else in the air, a feeling of anticipation. The people who lived here didn't know what was going to happen, only that something was clearly coming.

After all, no matter how hard the Guild tried to hide their members, there was nothing that could make them blend in with the rest of the people who lived here.

Dee and Dum were about five minutes from the warehouse.

"Boss," Dum said. "Been a lot of new faces around here in the past few days." He grimaced, casting an eye over his shoulder. "We need to take another way back." At his side, Dee nodded.

I let out a breath. "How many?"

Dee grimaced. "More than us, boss."

I nodded. That was…unfortunate, but we could handle it. "Have you spoken to Rel?"

Both men shook their heads. This time, I did grimace. The note had been annoyingly vague, the kind of thing that even I could barely make heads or tails of. Maybe she was worried about it getting intercepted by the Guild.

Though, that did beg the question, how the hell did she learn about that meme?

I shook my head. "Nothing for it," I said.

"We don't have time to beat around the bush here, boys. Speed is more important than stealth."

Dee and Dum shared a glance before their expressions firmed. "Whatever you say, boss." Dum put a hand on my shoulder. "Just wanna let you know that we're behind you all the way, no matter nothing."

I smiled. "Thanks." God knew I would need it.

The closer we got to the warehouse, the clearer the tension became. Where normally people weren't scared of me anymore, even going so far as to thank me for helping out their families or giving their son a place to work, now there was an utter lack of people on the street. Anyone who saw my little group vanished almost before I could make them out.

I sucked my lip. Now, I was hoping that the Guild would make a move, but I didn't think that I'd pissed them off so bad they'd jump straight to a coup the moment I was out of the city for a day.

Just goes to show, you should always be careful what you wish for.

The warehouse looked the same as always, but here the tension was even thicker. About half the men and women I'd recruited looked down as I came into sight, refusing to meet my eyes. The other half, the ones that Rel and the Guild hadn't brought in on their little plan, just continued to look around. They were wary, but they had no idea what was going down.

They were the too loyal, or the not loyal enough.

To be fair, I barely had any better idea what was going on. The first hint that something had gone wrong was that Rel didn't greet me the moment I came to a stop in front of my foundry. I'd expected a chance to talk before plans were set in motion. But...

I reached out to open the doors to the warehouse, only for them to be thrown open from the other side, revealing half a dozen Adventurers, Rel, and Delia, the Guild Knight at their head.

...It looked like that wasn't going to be much of an option.

Delia smirked at me, teeth flashing. "What a pleasant surprise; I was just about to go looking to tell you the news!" She twirled her spear once, slamming the butt into the dirt hard enough to send out a whoosh of air. "I'm afraid that the Guild has reevaluated our current working relationship."

My eyes snapped to Rel. I barely had to fake the expression of surprise on my face. She was supposed to delay until after I got back, not go full speed ahead.

"Rel, the fuck are these people doing here?"

She looked down for a moment before gathering herself and meeting my eyes. "Sorry, Via, but there's been a change in management."

I glared. "So, I see." I took a look around, taking in the group of Adventurers, mostly level 10, along with my own 'people' that were spreading around to completely surround me. "When the cat's away, the mice will play, hmm?"

"I'd like to think the only *rodent* here is you," Delia said. "After all, this could have been a mutually beneficial relationship! But someone had to go ruin it."

"Yeah, that someone being your flunkeys." I rested a hand on the pommel of my sword, but the real trick was the mana slowly gathering in my other palm, hidden behind my back. "Or was half market price not good enough for you?"

Delia tsked. "I don't want to talk about prices this and market that." She placed a hand on Rel's shoulder. "Maybe fast talk would have saved you here if we didn't know *exactly* how much money you were putting into your own pocket. But, thanks to our mutual friend here, now we do." A low murmur swept through the rest of my gang.

I grit my teeth, and this time it wasn't feigned. *That* was a wrench in my plans. The last thing I needed was the other guilds, or even the guard, knowing exactly what my profit margin was. If the Guild managed to turn enough of the city against me, they wouldn't even need to run me out of town.

And, if they turned enough of *my* people against me with insinuations like that...

But I couldn't let that thought show on my face. Instead, I turned my glare on Rel. "So, you think you can lie to both sides and come out on top?"

But Delia just laughed. "Please, as if the truth wasn't painfully transparent." She leaned forward. "I wondered why a little bottom feeder like you would be willing to sell at such rock bottom prices, but it's because you're still making *nine* coppers for every one you spend and pocketing seven of those for yourself."

She cast a glance around the rest of my gang. "Has anyone else ever wondered where the rest of that money was going?"

The 'rest,' as she so eloquently put it, was how I had been bankrolling my industrial cum internet revolution. But...from an outside perspective, it probably didn't look that way.

Especially not for people who lived their lives in the slums, at the mercy above one would-be crime lord or another. I doubted that the rest of them had my business acumen.

But there was no way out but through. I made a show straightening myself, even as I finished weaving the spell hidden in my offhand. "Fucking fine, you got me. Didn't have to make such a big damn show about it." I pulled a sullen glare at the woman. "Tell me what you want."

"Why, Via." Delia smiled, wagging a finger. "I don't think you're in a position to give me anything that I want."

I closed my eyes, letting out a deep breath. "It's like that, huh."

Delia shrugged. "Easy come, easy go. Maybe next time you'll learn to play nice." At that, her little band of enforcers started forward, brandishing their weapons, and their higher levels, with cheery and bloodthirsty grins.

The rest of mine who were in on it drew their own clubs and nightsticks. The ones who had actually been caught by surprise let themselves be pushed back without making a fuss. I'd have been upset, but you didn't survive in the ghetto by sticking your neck out. The only two who stood by me were my boys.

That was why I never recruited *henchmen*.

"Boss?" Dee asked. "What's the play?

"Come now." Delia twirled her spear again, leveling it up at us. "We're just here for that two-faced bitch. Step aside, and I'm sure little Relia here would be more than happy to keep you on her payroll."

Rel flinched when Delia reached out, combing a hand through the girl's short-cut hair.

"Or don't." The woman grinned. "Really, either is fine with me."

Dum shifted, moving to cover my back. "Boss?" he asked again.

I glared for a moment more before slumping. Fuck, but this was a rough spot. If not for the note that runner had slipped me, I'd have thought Rel decided to jump ship in truth. As it was, there was nothing for me to do but hope my girl knew what *she* was doing.

Because I'd been taken off the board before I even realized it.

"No reason for you two to go down with me." The words tasted sour in my mouth. I'd never been good at giving up, even when that was the plan. It was made worse by the fact that I didn't even know what the plan was at this point. "Get yourself a fat bonus for turning on me, at least."

Delia laughed. "I like the sound of that. Go on, then. Show us all exactly how loyal you two are."

I flicked my hand out, a bolt of inky black energy lancing towards her face.

Her spear flashed out, shattering my spell. I grimaced. So much for taking one of their pieces off the board.

Delia's smile grew. "Cute," she said. "But a tier one like you is no match for my mage hunter class."

I sighed, lowering my hand, and holding them both out, palms down. "Can you blame a girl for trying?"

Delia hummed, walking forward even as Dee and Dum stepped away, joining the crowd of people who'd turned on me. "You know, I think I can."

Her spear lashed out again, and I *heard* more than felt the impact it made against my skull before everything went black.

I woke to a pounding headache.

My body felt stiff and sore, my swollen cheek pressed against my shoulder.

It was dark, and my face was pressed against something hard. With a cough, my eyes fluttered open. I saw a stone floor, stone walls, and iron bars.

A classic jail cell. The only thing missing was a cot. Instead, they'd given me a moldy pile of straw.

I staggered to my feet, massaging my face and wincing. "That's going to bruise." It was hardly the worst hit I'd ever taken, but it still stung. The cell itself was small enough that even *I* wouldn't be able to stretch out fully lying down. Outside the bars was a rickety wooden chair, and a set of stairs leading up into the darkness. It wasn't a full prison, then.

I quirked my lip. Had they really left me down here unattended? I called on my mana, forming the Summon Demon spell with the ease of long practice.

Then it shattered with the sound of breaking glass.

>> Skill Locked

I blinked at the message, and then down at my hands.

It was only then I noticed the silver shackle clamped around my right wrist. It was a few inches long, inscribed with bright patterns whose meaning I couldn't discern. Those swirls glowed lightly as my mana dissipated against my will before fading back into the rest of the metal.

I groaned. "Of course they'd have something like this."

I tried my other hand, of course, only to get the same result. Looks like Maarin hadn't been lying when he said enchanters could do a lot with the right materials.

With a sigh, I set myself down against the wall, right below the small window set maybe two or three feet out of my reach. It was barred too, of course, but it was nice to know I couldn't have gotten up there even if I wanted to.

The stone was smooth and mortared together, no footholds.

Nothing left to do but—

My head snapped up at the sound of scratching, but no one came down the stairs across from me. I looked up farther, towards the window, just in time to see a familiar muzzle and blue mane peek through the barred window. A grin broke out across my face as Blue dropped the pouch he'd been holding in his teeth before pulling back and vanishing. I caught the pouch out of the air and pulled out a small hand mirror.

On the back, a single glossy hummingbird feather was set into a copper inlay.

CHAPTER 31

Hurry Up and Wait

The phone didn't ring that night.

Or buzz or glow or do…whatever it was going to do when someone was trying to contact me via magic mirror. You get the idea.

It wasn't like there was anything I could do on my end; there was no button to activate the mirror, and my ideas of a demon call center nothing more than a far-off dream. The only demons I had access to were Mr. Burns and Coaline, and they were busy filling out the Guild's next order.

It would be a real shame if we went through all this trouble just for my planned coup to fall through because Rel couldn't provide the necessary weapons to convince the Guild that she really did have control of my operation.

Of course, that left me in the spot of being stuck with nowhere to go. I was completely at the whims of the other players on the board.

"And here I said I'd never wind up in this spot again…" I let my head fall back against the hard stone of my cell.

It was the middle of the day. I had been in this cell for a little over eighteen hours now, by my reckoning, and they had yet to feed me once. Classic interrogation tactic. Luckily, this wasn't the first time I've been hungry. No, as long as they thought these lighter tactics could bear fruit, I would at least be spared the torture.

I…had no illusions about myself and torture.

The heavy clunk of a door opening drew me back to the present. I glanced up towards the staircase coming down towards the cell just in time to see two armored men dragging a familiar face down the stairs.

"Got your friend." One of the men grinned at me. He had a crooked nose, and I made note of that for later. "Looks like you're up the creek now, girl."

I said nothing. Instead, I just waited as the guard opened the cell and tossed Electra inside. She landed with a groan.

"Just got a new batch of weapons too!" the other man said. He twisted, showing off the sword on his belt. "Straight from that 'Devil's Foundry' of yours."

System Messages

Summon Demon has increased to lvl 10!
You've reached lvl 7. 5 stat points awarded

This time, I looked down to hide my smile. Turns out, even if I wasn't focusing on my skills, there were plenty of things I could do to raise their levels while going about my business. I just hadn't thought about it recently; the consequences of having too many important things to do.

But I certainly hadn't been *idle*. Especially not when it came to my demons.

System Messages

Now that your skill has reached lvl 10, it has gained a new passive. Please select one passive ability from the list below.

Demon's Sight -- You can now see through the senses of your demons within a one-kilometer radius

Demon's Might -- Your demons are now much stronger and can take more damage before being banished back to the demon plane

Demons Light -- Your demons have a reduced upkeep cost and draw in mana from the environment instead as long as they remain bound to you

I sucked in a breath before putting it to the side for the moment as I looked over Electra's injuries. She was beat up, but as long as she wasn't bleeding internally, it looked like she'd be okay. Well, probably.

Facial wounds always bleed more than you'd think.

The two Adventurers gave a few more rude remarks before leaving us behind, the door slamming shut behind them a few moments later.

"Hey." I tapped Electra's shoulder. "You still with me?"

"Guh." She rubbed her face. "F-fuck you, Empress. If this is still your plan, it sucks."

I chuckled. Normally I would have dropped her for that remark, but it seems like she was still playing ball. Loyalty deserves a reward, doesn't it? Instead, I sat down, pulling her head into my lap as I gave her a second to recover.

"The best plans usually do." I shrugged. "Though, I don't remember telling you to get caught…"

Electra groaned again. Her hand flopped back down to the stone, silver manacles flashing in the light. Looks like they bound her class the same way they did mine.

But unlike me, Electra had another trick or two up her sleeve. This might work out after all.

"Yeah well, you didn't tell me that your little waifu was planning a coup either." She glared up at me. "Don't you think that would be *need to know* information? Also"—Electra glanced around the cell—"she seems to be doing a pretty dang good job of it…"

"Yes…" I sighed. "I was expecting a bit more time, but what can you do? It's not like I can predict the *day* or anything."

Electra hummed, pushing herself upright. "Did you…" She paused, giving a quick glance around the room.

"I checked." I shrugged. Tapping my ear. For listening devices, I mean. I could see she got the memo. "No way…out…that I could find, of course, who knows?"

She swallowed, rubbing her arms. "Think it's worth it?" She made a talking gesture with her hand.

"I mean." I waved a hand. "You and Wonder Man managed well enough that one time."

"Well, duh." Electra rolled her eyes. "*We* knew what was going down." And they'd used my own listening devices to pass along false information.

I rubbed my forehead. Fucking Heroes. They were always a thorn in my side. "That…wasn't my best moment."

Electra gave a slight laugh. "Yeah, tell me about it. So…"

I patted the pile of straw. "Man, what I wouldn't give for a two-way cell phone connection right about now."

She laughed again but looked relieved all the same. Good, she got my message about where I'd stashed the mirror.

"I got caught talking to your kuudere."

I blinked. "What even is a—you know what? No. I don't want to know." I shook my head.

"Yeah, I figured you'd hear about it from her soon enough." She smirked.

This time it was my turn to breathe a sigh of relief. So, she'd gotten Rel the other mirror. That meant, if everything was still going to plan, she'd contact me the moment it was ready for us to spring our trap.

But she'd already delivered the weapons. It wasn't like I had a big stockpile of scrap metal for another batch after the first, and I'd dismissed most of my sea demons before I went hunting for the killer hummingbirds.

What was she waiting for?

I glanced back to my own status screen. With a quick press of a button, I could find out. Hell, with Electra here, I could probably bust us out on our own.

"How's your hair?" I glanced back over at the Hero. "Looks pretty messy after they got to you."

Electra blinked, then she snorted. If I remembered correctly, that was the same coded phrase she and Wonder Man had used to talk about her charge levels after I'd trapped them both in the trick fortress. She'd let my bots catch her when she still had half a tank and made me believe otherwise.

That was back when I thought she was just another fashion-obsessed, corporate sponsorship-chasing Hero.

"Yeah, they didn't *touch* this 'do." She grinned. She tossed her head, and I saw the barest spark jump from one point to the other. "I…can't say the same for the rest of me…ugh." She rubbed her arms again. "My bruises are gonna have bruises after this."

"Rather." I looked back at my status. "Hey, come look at this."

She glanced over, and I willed myself to share my screen with her. She read the new entries before grinning. "Noice!"

I sighed again. "Is it though?"

She looked at me again. "The heck do you mean?"

I looked between Demon's Sight and Demons Light, holding back a groan at the truly awful pun. "I'm just thinking about what we're going to need…to get out of this mess." My demons were relatively cheap to summon, but they were expensive to maintain. Blue was the most expensive, but even two foundry imps and the five jellyfish demons I'd had took up pretty much all of my mana regen.

I still wasn't back at full, even now. The band at my wrist cut my recovery rate down to almost zero. The upkeep passive would potentially change that, making sure I was ready to go when Rel got the last few pieces into place.

But what if she wasn't putting those pieces into place? What if all of those pieces were exactly where she wanted them?

"C'mon, you can't really be thinking that…"

I looked over at Electra, drumming my fingers on my thigh. "Trust is a two-way street," I said. And really, that's what I'd be saying if I took the Demon's Sight perk, that I didn't trust Rel to do her job, and I needed to double-check all of her work.

Never mind that, outside of this situation, the reduced upkeep would just be infinitely better. I had so many ideas for demons, for what I could use to streamline production, to handle complex tasks like call centers, to build up an industrial base necessary to create the world I'd promised to show one girl.

The one girl I was supposed to be trusting right now.

I…

Electra smacked me upside the back of the head, and I flinched. "What the fuck was that?" I glared at her.

Electra just rolled her eyes. "I know what it looks like when you get all up in your own head." She crossed her arms. "Like, uh, I don't get the why of…uh…" She glanced around the room, trying desperately for a word that wouldn't blow our whole little ruse open.

"Yes," I said. "That."

"Yeah! That!" She grinned. "But anyway, if you're gonna go, might as well go all the way, right?" She rubbed the back of her head. "It's usually how it works out the best for you, isn't it?"

I blinked. "Is it?"

"Well, yeah?" Electra shrugged. "When was the last time you backed down for anything? You know, other than when we blew up your robots in your face and forced you to run away and all of that."

This time, I chuckled. "I guess I do have trouble letting go." I turned back to my screen. "And you're right. I should know what my choices are and stand by them." I selected Demons Light with a mental flex, watching as the skill was added to my character sheet in its new, updated form.

Immediately I felt my mana start to tick up again, and I let out a sigh of relief. I'd been running on as little as I could manage, just to keep all the demons I needed active. It meant that my summon skill had grown quickly, even though the rest had stagnated.

I quickly distributed the rest of my stat points into mana and regeneration.

Status   Unspent Status Points: 0

Physical   Strength: 2

                     Endurance: 3

                     Agility: 5

                     Dexterity: 4

Ethereal   Charm: 3

                     Faith: 1

                     Attunement: 11

                     Soul: 12

"Wow, Empress, your build sucks."

I jerked away from Electra, unsharing her. "That's none of your god-damn business."

She laughed, holding up her hands. "Just saying."

"Just saying, she says." I rolled my eyes. "Shove off."

We were both silent for a moment. Then Electra spoke again. "So, what next?"

I hummed, glancing towards the pile of straw where I'd hidden the mirror. My hand sought its leather pouch unerringly. I pulled the enchanted piece of glass out, looking into its silent depths. Right now, it only showed my reflection.

Nothing more.

"Now," I said. "I guess we wait and see what the people above have in store for us."

"Hurry up and wait, huh?" Electra leaned back, pillowing her head on her shoulder. "Sounds familiar."

"Indeed."

Nothing left to do but wait.

CHAPTER 32

Set 'Em Up

You know." I kicked my heels idly against Electra's sides. "I always wished I could speak Spanish."

Beneath me, hands clasped around my thighs, Electra huffed, though not from my weight, of course. "Spanish?"

"My family's from Central America." I shifted again, flexing my core as my hands did their dastardly work. "But my mom wouldn't teach me any, wanted me to grow up speaking English. Mainly because of my complete imbecile of a father, but still."

"You'd think you coulda learned it on your own."

I pouted, pressing forward slightly. "I suck at languages. Of course, I picked up a bit but—" My shiv screeched against the stone, and I slipped.

Electra swore, taking half a step forward as I threatened to tumble off her shoulders. "God—hecking—darnit, Empress!"

I placed a hand against the wall, pushing myself upright. "Sorry." Looking closer, I could see the brick in the corner had a nice long scratch going across the middle of it. Right through something that looked *very much* like the runes Maarin had shown me.

I scraped at it for a bit more before the shape fizzled, glowing briefly once, then sputtering out. I grinned. "Got it."

"Jeez, Louise." Electra shifted, half kneeling and half shrugging me off of her back. I slipped nimbly back to the ground, and if anyone said otherwise, they were a lying liar who lied.

Completely unrelated, Electra caught my wrist before I could face-plant into a wall. "That did it?" she asked.

"Should have." I took my arm back, brushing off my undersuit. Today, with Electra's help, we'd done a complete canvassing of the cell. That one enchantment in the corner was the only thing we could find; luckily, we'd spotted it before the light vanished completely, and the moon had given me enough to work by for chipping it off.

We could speak freely.

Electra tilted her head and looked at me. "You know, I never really thought about you as Latina."

I paused, blinking once, then again. I sighed. "And we were doing so well too."

"What?"

I shook my head. "Don't worry about it." It was just one more thing I'd blackmail her with later. "For now, do you think you can short out our handcuffs?"

She squinted at me for a moment longer before shrugging. "I don't know." She rolled her wrist, the silver shackle glinting in the light. "You saw when they put it on you, right?"

I grinned with the promise of savage vengeance. "They knocked me out."

And I would remember that.

Electra shifted. "Uh, Em', you're kinda freaking me out here."

I smoothed my features into something more socially acceptable. "I have no idea what you're talking about."

She groaned. "And you say, 'normal you' and 'super evil happy fun time you' are the same person?"

"They are."

Electra rolled her eyes. "'They,' sure." I smiled beatifically up at her. "Anyway, a wizard did something weird with it, and then it kinda melded together seamlessly." She ran her finger around the edge of the shackle, tracing its smooth surface. "I'm not sure what you want me to do here."

I hummed. "How good are you at inducing magnetic fields?"

She blinked, instantly catching onto my plan. "You think I can shatter it?"

"Silver *is* highly conductive, isn't it?" I smirked. "And last I checked, you weren't constrained to actual circuits or anything, just...run a current parallel to the band." I twirled my finger in the air. "Make two magnetic fields that shear at each other at great enough intensity, and *pop*." Oh, sure, I was simplifying a bit, but I'd also seen Electra fry C'thulu when she had enough charge, and she'd been going hard with the generator the last couple of days.

Usually, when you wanted the impossible, it was best to leave the fine details up to the Hero's imagination.

She frowned at the silver band on her wrist, sparking slightly as she fed electricity through it, arcs jumping from the metal to her skin and back again. I knew it wouldn't reduce her charge; she wasn't quite a perpetual motion *engine*, but she had nearly perfect charge retention as long as it arced back to her.

I wasn't kidding when I called her a human-shaped superconductor, and at room temperature no less!

"Maybe," she said quietly. The moonlight cut a sharp line across her features. "But it's metal, if it buckles and warps..."

I hummed. "What's a little blood between friends."

She chuckled. "Be the first time we're shedding blood *for* each other."

"Not true." When Electra glanced over at me, I smiled. "There was that time at the beach. I never did thank you for it, huh?"

She blinked, looking at me for a moment before running a hand through her hair. "Yeah, I guess we did stick it out then." She nodded sharply. "So, when do you want to stage our prison break?"

I sighed, sitting down on the floor. "Not yet."

She cocked an eyebrow, sliding to the ground across from me. "What are we waiting for, then?" She made a show of looking around. "Not like we're gonna get a much better chance."

"If they're expecting something, they'd be expecting it tonight." Idly, I reached out and pulled the pouch containing the hand mirror into my lap. It must have been nearing midnight now, the moon rising ever higher until only a silver sliver spilled through our window. "And we're not the only pieces on the board."

She bit her lip, looking at the dark mirror in my hands.

"When did she say she was going to call?"

I smiled. Still, despite the late hour, my heart was at ease. "We barely got to this part when we spoke about it. I thought we'd have more time to set up something, but if Rel needs more time, she'll have it." I leaned back against the cold stone wall. "I'm not going to spoil my own scheme this time."

Electra snorted. "Been there a bit too often, Em'?"

I flicked her ear. "Don't call me that."

Electra pouted at me, rubbing her ear. "You didn't seem to mind last time."

"Yes, well, last time your head was between my legs." I gave her a cheery smile. "I tend to be more forgiving in circumstances like that."

She sputtered for a second. "Like I would ever go down—!"

Beyond the walls of the cell, the bells in the center of the city chimed once, a long, mournful note. Midnight. The mirror shivered once in my hand, and we both paused.

"Via." A picture slowly formed in its depths. "Lady Via!"

I felt a smile steal unbidden across my face. "Relia."

She sketched a brief bow, head bobbing in the mirror frame. "Lady Via." Her eyes glanced towards the edges of the frame. "Are you alone?"

"Well, they managed to catch Electra and throw her in with me." I waved a hand. "I assume you had something to do with that?"

Rel looked down sheepishly. "I was hoping she'd get away."

Electra snorted. "No, she wasn't."

Rel's head snapped up, and it was funny to see her glare towards the top of the mirror, like she was peering out of it upside down. "Well, maybe if you were a bit *quicker* on the uptake."

"Now, now." I tapped the mirror once. "Play nice, both of you. Besides, it wasn't all bad." I smirked at my erstwhile nemesis. "Electra was just talking about how she'd never—"

"Habah-ba-ba-ba!" Electra leaned forward, arms waving. "That was—that's not important."

Rel frowned again. "What's not important?"

"I'll tell you when you're older." I smiled, leaning back so that Electra was no longer in view. "So, are we ready?"

Rel crossed her arms, but I simply waited.

I'd been waiting all day, after all.

After a moment, she sighed. "Dee and Dum have rounded up every-one. We even managed to use some of the street rats and these mirrors to get more information. She gave a sharp nod. "That's why I couldn't reach out to you earlier, Lady Via. There is a reason the Adventurer's Guild moved against us so quickly. I thought it was because I baited them by promising you had this other project, but that was only part of it."

I raised an eyebrow. "Go on."

She took a slow breath. "They're not the only group of armed thugs in Silverwall," she said. "There's the Guard, of course, but they're better armed and better centralized. Beyond the Guild's reach."

I nodded. "So, who were they after, to need so many...practice weapons from me?"

"The other guilds in the city have leg breakers of their own, espe-cially the Enchanter's Guild. The Adventurer's Guild plans to change that."

I blinked before a wide smile broke out across my face. "When?"

Rel paused, looking off to the side. "Well..."

"Rel, tell me when."

"Tomorrow."

I laughed. I couldn't help it.

"Lady...Via?"

When I came back to myself a moment later, even Rel was looking at me oddly. Electra had gone so far as to scoot back across the cell.

"Don't mind me." I wiped the tears from the corners of my eyes. "That's perfect. Oh, it couldn't be any better if I planned it myself." I looked back to the mirror. "You know where they're going to go?"

Rel let out a breath before a smile started growing on her face. "Yes, Lady Via. We do. They plan to start with the Enchanter's Guild, as they have the most support."

At that, my own answering smile grew even more savage. "And they want your support?"

"They do."

"Perfect. And the other groups? I don't imagine they're going to wait around."

Rel nodded. "From what we have managed to overhear, there will be several other groups going out at once, to hit the smaller guilds."

I nodded. "And our friend, Arlo?" It had been a while since I'd heard from the leader of the Tarnished, the other big gang in the docks.

At that, Rel glanced away. "He…does not want the Guild taking control of the outer city any more than we do, but…he also won't move unless it's worth his while."

I drummed my fingers against the floor, another giggle escaping me as the piece fell into place. "And if we do?"

"Then he can attack many of the smaller groups. But Lady Via, even between the both of us, we don't have enough people. I have heard that—"

"They'll be keeping a few parties back at the Guild in reserve?" At Rel's surprised look, I added. "It's what I would do."

To my side, Electra grinned. "Heh, bet they won't be expecting a prison break."

Rel caught on quickly, eyes glinting. "What should I offer Arlo?"

"Oh, him?" I waved a hand, as the last bits clicked home. "Anything. In fact, he can have it all."

Both women blinked, looking at me in surprise.

"Lady Via?"

"Don't worry about it, Rel. You've set everything up so perfectly, it's like I was there myself." I smiled. "I knew I was right to put my trust in you."

Rel jolted, a flush of red working its way up her neck. "M-my lady!"

"Now," I said. "Get everyone ready. We'll strike as one, the moment they think victory is in hand."

Rel nodded. "They'll begin their attack on the Enchanter's Guild two bells before noon. If we begin then—"

"No, no." I shook my head. Once again, both Rel and Electra looked towards me. "There's no reason to step in and help the enchanters of all people. In fact…" I smiled. "Isn't it just the *perfect* chance to kill two birds with but a single stone?"

CHAPTER 33

Knock 'Em Down

Of course, things would never be so easy.

"Good morning, my little jailbirds."

Electra and I shared a glance as a woman's voice echoed down the stairs to the dungeon. Delia strutted down the stairs into the prison, a sharp little smile curling at the corner of her mouth. Behind her, four other Guildies followed.

I pushed myself to my feet, making a show of brushing off my bodysuit. "To what do we owe the pleasure?" The two of us were still mostly clean, despite two days in a cell. Thank god for super materials.

"Oh, nothing much." The woman smiled at me, tossing her dark red hair over her shoulder. She looked elaborately coiffed—and also more than a little annoyed that we didn't look like filthy peasants, but that was very much a *her* problem.

"It's just that today is an important day, is all."

Electra and I shared another glance. Today was the day the Guild made their power grab for the rest of Silverwall. Of course, neither of us was supposed to *know* that.

Here's hoping that Electra had a better poker face than I suspected.

I scoffed. "I'm sure."

Delia laughed. "Boys, go ahead and grab them."

Electra lowered her stance. "And where the heck do you think you're taking us?"

"Nowhere in particular." Delia examined her nails as the four bully boys entered the cell. "You don't have to play nice; I certainly don't mind if you're a little roughed up before the festivities."

Electra let out a short growl, but then I stepped forward, holding out a hand and smiling winsomely up at the first Adventurer. "Festivities? For me?" I placed a hand on the startled man's chest. "By all means, lead the way."

Delia let out another laugh as I let the two men escort me out of the cell as if I were a princess instead of a pauper. "Oh, Via." She reached out, patting my cheek as one would a pet. "In another life, I'm sure we could have been friends."

"I've never been a fan of the whole servant angle, myself." I smiled back, tilting my head into her palm, even as Electra grumbled but walked out behind me. I knew she wanted to bust out, but it wasn't time yet. Delia was too on her guard. We needed to convince her that she held all the cards first. "But I suppose I wouldn't mind a few nights of working under you."

Delia's smile grew. "And, maybe in another life, I would have taken you up on that, my dear." She patted me again before turning. "But today, we have other plans."

"Really?" I allowed myself to be escorted up the stairs, folding my hands behind my back. "You always struck me as the 'lord over your defeated enemies' type."

My fingers formed into a hand sign. *Information.*

Behind me, Electra huffed. By now, I'm sure she wasn't even surprised that I knew Aegis code. This little batch of sign language, I didn't even have to hack into their servers for. Nope! It came with the employee handbook, actually.

Now, the reason they never got around to changing it after I started building giant robots to take over the city, well…

That was a story for a different time.

"You know me so well." Delia led us through the empty Guild hall above. Electra said it had been bustling when they carted her in, but now it was silent as a grave. "In this case, though, I tend to find that the suggestion of necrophilia rather kills the mood."

I quirked my lips as we were escorted to another small group of adventures by the entrance. "So, it's the gallows then."

"Correct in one!" Delia cast a smile over her shoulder. "Now if only you could have been so prescient beforehand."

I allowed myself a frown. Bitch, I predicted literally this entire string of events. "I'll take another shot in the dark then. You're not supposed to be doing this."

She affected a look of surprise, holding a hand over her mouth. "And whatever gives you that idea?"

"The empty Guild, plus all of your little boy toy Adventurers?" I waved a hand. They still hadn't chained me up. Why would they, with all of my skills locked away? "We're not even the main event, today, are we?" I sniffed. "What a waste. My execution deserves higher billing."

She chuckled. "Egotistical to the last."

"Takes one to know one."

Delia frowned, jerking her head. I ducked mine as the man on my right cuffed my ear. "Watch your tongue."

I smiled. "Truth hurts, huh?" I made a zipping motion before she could decide to hit me herself this time. "Don't worry, I promise to keep it a secret if you will."

She stared at me for a moment more before huffing and turning away. "If you *must* know, the Guild's head wanted to barter you away to the Watch. Outworlders go for a pretty penny in this day and age. But so do their heads." She shrugged. "So, I may have arranged to stay at the Guild today, despite the momentous occasion and, well, if something were to make a big fuss with a public execution…"

"Two birds with one stone?" I made the sign for *wait* next to my thigh. In public would be better, especially if she wanted a show. "So, you're using us as a distraction for something else."

Her eyes narrowed at me, and I snorted. "C'mon, Delia, *darling*." I made a circular motion with my hand. "If you had the pull to send off the entire Guild, you wouldn't need permission to get me hanged in the first place."

She tilted her head at me. "You know, I think you're the first person I've ever met to use the right word."

I smiled. "Been to a lot of hangings?"

"Oh, undoubtedly." With a snap of her fingers, the doors to the Guild were thrown open and our party started out. "They're one of my favorite things."

"Anything to keep the unwashed masses in their place, hmm?"

"You know," Delia said, "I'm beginning to find less enjoyment with your cheek."

"Well, look at the bright side." I shrugged. "A raven will have pecked it out by this time tomorrow."

"Ah yes, that's a much nicer mental image."

"God, Em'." I heard Electra huff behind me. "Are you always so chatty with the people planning to kill you?"

I glanced over my shoulder, meeting her eyes. One of the guards was kind enough to steer me the right way as we turned onto the main thoroughfare. "Well, forcing these fine young men to drag me through the streets sounds like a pain." I rolled a shoulder. "And like hell on my delicate constitution."

A flash of understanding crossed her face, but she continued to slouch. "Don't think I'm as big on the whole 'die with dignity' angle."

Translation: she wasn't going to get *herself* hanged just because I had a flair for the dramatic.

I, of course, just smiled wider. "Don't worry, Ella, it'll all be over soon."

In the distance, a bell began to toll the hour. That would be the start of the raids, and the start of my plan as well.

The mirror, I'd been forced to leave in the cell. I'd even made sure to step on it, part of the reason I was being so theatrical. So, I had no way to contact my people. Luckily, Electra and I had already been planning to bust out on our own.

Things would just have to be a little bit more…ad hoc.

There were already gallows set up by the time we made it to one of the main squares of the city, with more than a few people already milling around.

Bread and circuses.

I made no motion to struggle as the other Adventurers pushed us up onto the stage, fastening a rough noose around my neck.

"Got a plan to get us out of this one?" Electra hissed.

I could sense her faith in our new partnership was already being tested, but I'd made my career as a Supervillain off of one thing and one thing only.

I walked through fire.

Instead of saying anything, I smiled at her. Delia was giving some kind of speech or something. The usual drivel, you know, 'dearly beloved, we are gathered here today.' Oh wait, that was the other kind of tragedy. Right, this was more of a 'these *vile* criminals' kind of speech.

I tilted my head back, letting the words wash over me along with the growing murmurs of the crowd.

It really was a beautiful day. If I tilted my head towards the Merchant's Quarter, I could even see a wisp of smoke rising up from what I assumed was the Enchanter's Guild in the distance, not that anyone was paying any attention.

Maybe Delia had more than air between her ears after all.

"Hey, Empress. I'm getting kind of worried here."

"Don't be." I took a deep breath, feeling something akin to pride growing in my chest. On a nearby rooftop, I saw a flash of blue fur, and that pride morphed into savage glee. "Among villains, it's considered a mark of status to merit a public execution. A nod to the fact that unless they have your body, they could never prove you died."

Electra huffed. "Pretty sure that's not what's happening here, Em'."

"Don't take this from me."

"You'd think you'd be more worried about the people trying to take your *life*," she said.

I hummed. "Yeah, you probably would, wouldn't you?"

There was one guard left on the platform; the rest had ringed the gallows to hold back the crowd. Delia was winding down, and then there was one more man as well.

To pull the lever, presumably.

I probably should be worried about him. It would be a shame to die because I'd waited just a bit too long.

"And now…!" Delia said, raising her hand.

"For my next trick!" My voice rang through the air, and I felt the pressure of a thousand gazes snap to me. I smiled.

This was what I lived for.

"I make my beautiful assistant…*disappear*!"

I slashed my hand through the air.

Blue slashed his maw through the last guard's throat.

The man fell gurgling to the wooden planks, even as Blue's tail knocked lever man from the platform. Blue roared, teeth flashing. The guards on the ground below scrambled back. A cry of *"Demon!"* rose from the crowd.

Chaos erupted.

More than one of the Guildies on the ground were taken off their feet in the surge of people suddenly trying to get away.

I grinned at Delia's face. Her expression went from shock to blistering rage in less than a second. From Blue's back, General Tock, my every loyal spider bot, leapt through the air above our heads.

Then Delia's spear hit the gallows lever, and we dropped like a pair of rocks.

CHAPTER 34

Endgame

For a moment, the noose snapped taut around my neck.

My eyes bulged, arms spasming. I thought I was about to hear the sickening *snap* of my own spine, and then darkness.

I'd always been afraid, you know, of the dark.

The last strand of rope snapped instead. I dropped to the ground, collapsing in a heap as my hands scrambled frantically at the noose. My fingers pulled, and the rope gave. I heaved in a breath of air, chucking the rope away.

"Jesus Christ!"

I glanced up at the words. Electra had likewise yanked off the noose. General Tock had cut clean through her rope on the first go. "Did you think you could cut it a little closer, Empress?"

I rubbed my neck. "I think I did, actually."

I pushed myself to my feet as Electra snorted. "Great. Perfect. Grade-A showmanship."

I held out the arm with the mana inhibitor on it. "Showwomanship."

She rolled her eyes, shattering the shackles with a controlled burst of electricity. The metal gave a whine as it crumpled open, and I felt my skills return. "So, please tell me that you have a plan." She popped her own shackles a moment later.

"Of course I have a plan." I looked around. The two of us were isolated beneath the scaffolding of the gallows. Around us, I could see the crowd almost frothing as people stampeded from the square. Blue was still causing chaos above.

"First," I said. There was a thump as Delia dropped through the floor of the gallows. "…We deal with that."

"You are *totally* pulling that out of your a—out of your butt."

"You can swear, Electra." I buffed my nails as Delia glared at the both of us. "The big bad PR team can't hurt you here."

Electra squawked. "That was one time!"

"How fitting." Delia twirled her spear. "You were a thorn in my side until the very end."

"Oh, honey." I sighed. "You don't seem to know who's driving this thing."

Delia growled and lunged. I waved my hand. My mana pool drained to half, pulling dozens of demons into existence. The redheaded Adventurer slid to a stop right before a hobblefiend eviscerated her.

"You—!"

"What, you thought this old thing would slow me down?" I tapped the twisted remains of the inhibitor cuff, and it fell to the ground. "Oops!"

At my side, Electra grinned. "Not so much fun now that the shoe's on the other foot, huh?"

Delia ground her teeth, settling into a defensive stance. "It will take more than some second-rate skills to beat me."

"Why do they always say that?" I shook my head. With an effort of will, half of my little army of demons spilled up through the gallows. They'd handle the rest of the Guildies in the square, and cause…a little bit of chaos before they were killed.

Like all good employers of questionable ethics, I didn't need to pay my new demons if they died before they'd fulfilled *their* contractual obligations.

"You'll regret taking me lightly."

I snapped my fingers. "No, *that's* what they always say, isn't it?"

"Well." Electra shrugged. "People don't really have genre awareness in this kind of setting, you kn—"

She snapped backwards just in time to avoid Delia's spear.

I threw out a Demon-itize. The inky-black bolt raced through the air, only for Delia to bat it contemptuously aside just like she had at the warehouse. "Didn't I already tell you?" She yanked her spear from the wood of the scaffolding, cutting a demon in half with a negligent flick. "It will take more than some second-rate skills to beat me."

I frowned. "Fucking power creep."

<Warrior lvl 11/Mage Hunter lvl 5>

I was hoping I'd be able to catch her by surprise the second time.

"Still, it's not even a rare class." I clicked my tongue. "No wonder you were so jealous."

The woman flourished her spear. "Come a little closer, darling, and I'll show you exactly how I feel about you."

"You guys really were destined to come to blows, huh." We both stopped, turning towards Electra. The blonde nodded sagely. "The main cast can't support more than one *ara* type."

"Electra?" I said.

"Yeah?"

"Shut the fuck up."

Then Delia skewered the closest demon, and the fight was back on.

I ducked back away from a sweep. For now, I just had to let my mana pool keep refilling. I'd grind her down through sheer attrition.

"Buzzer Bolt!" I felt my hair stand on end as Electra's spell raced through the air.

Delia met it head-on, cutting through the lightning with her spear. I grimaced as she danced through my horde of hobblefiends, leaving only fading corpses in her wake.

I continued backstepping, and she pursued. Her face was calm, almost placid, but the spear was anything but.

"Kia!" She spun, unleashing a blast of air from her weapon, blowing my diminished horde backwards. I hissed when I saw another blast of magical electricity veer into the scaffolds. The Buzzer Bolt blew off a piece of wood, and I grabbed it, throwing it up in front of me just in time to block a thrust from Delia's spear. The wood stung my fingers from the force.

She yanked her weapon back. "Pierce!"

I threw the two-by-four at her face.

The woman ducked, spear flashing up. Its blade glowed red, and the skill cut through the wooden beam like butter. With a huff, I dumped

the rest of my mana into another round of demons. Somehow, I found
my way to Electra's side in the press.

"Any ideas?" Electra scowled. "She keeps blocking my spells."

"What about your real lightning?" I asked.

"Think it'll work?" She cast an eye at me. "Her gear's gotta have
some other enchantments on it."

Left unsaid was that they might block her electricity just as well as
her magic.

"We are quickly running out of alternatives." The dissolving corpse
of a hobblefiend slid to a stop at my feet.

"Right." Electra shook out her hands, hair sparking blue. "Least
she's swinging around that big metal spear."

"Yes," I said as Delia cut through the last of my demons for a second time, "because this would be so much more difficult if she were
unarmed."

I guess quality had a quantity all of its own. Haha.

I let out a low breath. All I had left was Blue. Well, along with Mr.
Burns and Coaline, all much too far away to be any sort of help.

"Is that all you've got?" Delia flicked her hair out of her face. Despite
her bravado, I could see the beads of sweat on the woman's brow. If I
had the mana for another round of demons, we might have worn her
down after all.

But only Heroes worried about could-have-beens.

"You got us." I raised my hands, shifting on my feet. "We are in awe
of your superior ability, please, do whatever you—"

I fell to the side as Delia lunged through the space I'd just been. My
hand snapped down onto the haft of her spear.

She raised an eyebrow, and then kicked me so hard I saw stars.

I hit the far side of the scaffolding with a crack that I felt more than
heard. It drove the air from my lungs, snapping my head back. My
vision went white.

Then there was a flash, the crack of thunder, the burnt smell of
ozone.

I slumped to my hands and knees, trying desperately not to throw
up my own esophagus. By the time I managed to stagger back to my
feet, the scent of burnt flesh was already filling the air.

On the far side of our little cage match, Delia was face down on the cobblestone. Wisps of gray-black smoke rose up from her unmoving corpse.

Runes on her armor sparked one last time. They shattered, protection spent, far short of what she'd needed in the end.

Electra stood next to the body, the tips of her hair still arcing with leftover charge. It occurred to me then, as I saw the tips of her usual updo dip slightly with perspiration, that we'd been in this world for quite a long time.

I took in the pallid expression on my partner's face.

Time made monsters of us all.

I took a raspy breath, forcing myself to my feet. "Good shot."

Electra gave a sharp shrug. "Not like I could miss."

I clenched my fists, fingers still trembling. I could feel the bruise starting to form on my back.

Just another day in the life of the most attractive and successful Supervillain in the continental United States.

I pulled Delia's spear from unresisting fingers, then I checked for a pulse. Nothing. "She's dead."

Electra huffed, looking away. "I didn't know how much current to use."

I nodded. "You did what you had to do." Then I took the spear and chopped Delia's head clean from her corpse.

"Empress!"

I tossed the weapon down at my feet. "A bit late for that, don't you think?" I turned towards the gap in the top of the gallows. "Just because she's dead doesn't mean she'll stay that way. Who knows what kind of resurrection magic this world might have?"

Elektra bit her lip. "Wouldn't that…"

I shook my head. "I don't leave daggers pointed at my back."

She let out a long, slow breath. "Yeah."

"Come on." I clapped her on the shoulder. "Next time, I'll take care of it." Electra grimaced but nodded sharply.

"You were never the type to make someone else do your dirty work."

I gave a small smile. "You know me so well." I jerked my head upwards. "Now let's go. We're not done yet."

She drew in a deep breath. It was hardly her first brush with death, even if it might have been her first time dealing with it, but Electra was made of tougher stuff than your average Hero.

"Need a boost?" she asked.

"*Pendeja*." I rolled my eyes. "You know it."

It was why she'd lasted so long against me.

She formed a step with her hands. I hopped up, bracing my hand against her shoulders. "Was it always like this, for you?" she mumbled into my stomach.

I huffed, grabbing the floor of the gallows. "It's never like anything." I hauled myself up, kicking off her shoulders for that last little boost. Rolling over, I lowered my hand.

Electra looked up at me. "What do you mean?"

"I mean that as a villain, you never have a safety net. You never have a bottom line." I gave a sharp smile. "No two jobs are the same, and at the end of the day, the only person you have to live with is yourself."

She clasped my hand. "Sounds…kinda sad, not gonna lie."

She jumped, I pulled. A few moments later, I got her up onto the platform. I shook my head. "Why do you think I have you and Rel?" She quirked her lip into an almost-smile. Then we both pushed ourselves to our feet and took stock of the damage.

The square was empty of people. I saw the corpses of Delia's little crew, proof that my demons had done their job. Besides that, no casualties. Just like I'd ordered before my little monsters had no doubt run into the guards and died.

I didn't imagine I'd be welcome here in Silverwall for much longer.

A stillness lingered in the air. I could hear people yelling and screaming as the fight between the rest of the guilds continued back and forth across the city. But here, for this little moment, it was calm.

"Busy day," I murmured.

"Here comes the rest of it." Electra pointed. I turned to see Arlo and the Tarnished come around a corner towards the square. My fellow gang leader looked to be in high spirits despite the narrow gash on his temple. I spotted the rest of my boys and girls with his gang as well, looking no worse for the wear.

My eyes sought out Rel unerringly.

She smiled as she met my gaze.

I gave a little wave as the victorious raiders came into the square. Shouts of surprise went up as my gang caught sight of me.

"It's Lady Via!"

"Boss!"

"Empress, it's the Empress!"

I smiled a little wider at that, taking a seat on the edge of the gallows. "What, you didn't think I was gonna let you have all the fun, did you?"

A ragged cheer went up from my equally ragged band. It grew louder as Blue bounded up from the stage behind me, preening pridefully. We'd done it. We defeated the Adventurer's Guild. With their biggest force taken out by Arlo and Rel, and Delia's reserves felled by my hand, the rest of the Guild would be mopped up piecemeal.

Of course, an enterprising villain knew to never rest on her laurels.

Rel split from the crowd, coming forward to clasp my hand for a brief moment. "Did I do well, Mistress?"

I raised an eyebrow, and the woman blushed. Still, credit where credit was due. "Perfectly."

Rel smiled wider.

The Tarnished, the very same gang that had attacked *me* all those weeks ago, came to a stop a bit farther away. Oh, but how the tables had turned, for us and the city both. We had about even numbers between their gang and my little empire, with blades and grins still dripping crimson from the carnage.

We were all of us, red in tooth and claw.

"Arlo!" I waved cheerfully. "How'd things go on your end?"

The gang leader's salt-and-pepper beard twisted sharply around the answering grin. "Couldn't have planned it better myself. The Guild doesn't have a man left on his feet from here to the high wall."

I grinned back. "Excellent." I paused for a moment. "But, my friend, I couldn't help but notice that your boys are all wearing my colors." Black and gold, obviously. "What happened to that thing you had going, with the...silver rings, was it?"

"Well." His grin turned even sharper. "Only one band of hired thugs was invited to join the Guild. It's just how these things go."

"And the fact that I'll be taking all the blame for this little escapade?" I fluttered my eyelashes at him. "I thought we were friends, Arlo."

Some of his rogues and cutthroats shifted at my words, but Arlo just kept laughing. "Can't handle a little heat, girlie?"

"Oh." I kicked my feet idly in the air. "Don't worry about me."

Because the day had been…*all* according to plan.

All According to Plan

A s you can see, Duchess, this cannot be allowed to stand."

Duchess Ivey of Silverwall looked up, golden eyes blinking listlessly. "I'm sorry, Seneschal." Her gaze slipped back towards the window, silver pale hair glinting in the morning light. "I did not quite follow your report."

"It is of no matter." Seneschal Hawkwright dipped his head slightly. "Simply put, the criminal elements in the outer city have gotten out of hand. By your leave, I'll take a detachment of the guard to remind them of their place."

"Hmm." The duchess raised a hand, fingers scratching at the suture marks in the hollow of her throat with trembling fingers. "Tonight."

Hawkwright gave a cough. "My lady?"

"Tonight would be best." She kept scratching. "Don't, don't, don't you always say that criminals come out at night?"

He sighed. "It would be more dangerous."

Duchess Ivey bobbed her head. "Take another detachment or two." The man turned his eyes heavenward.

"Very well." The duchess nodded again, at his words. "Also, there is the matter of her Highness and—"

"Not this moon."

Her voice turned sharp.

Seneschal Hawkwright paused. "Lady Ivey, you yourself are scarcely recovered from last month. Would it not be better if…"

"Not this moon." Her fingers clenched, knuckles white at the hollow of her throat. "This alone is my decision, is it not, Seneschal?"

"I merely…" the man glanced to the side, "am concerned for your health."

"How *kind* of you."

Indeed, her words were near sharp enough to *cut*.

Hawkwright bowed stiffly. "I shall see to the preparations." The duchess looked away, and the door shut sharply behind him a moment later. She let a minute pass in silence before she rang for her niece.

In a few short minutes, the princess, seventeenth in line to the throne of the Vecorvian Republic, arrived. "Auntie," she said.

Royal blood ran true.

Princess Ishanti Melir was a mirror of her maternal aunt. The woman had yet to reach her twentieth year, but her silver-white hair was long and golden eyes still bright. Duchess Ivey scratched at her throat at the sight of her niece's yet-unblemished skin.

She took Ishanti's hand, squeezing it gently. "Tonight."

The young woman blinked once, trembling slightly. She opened her mouth to speak, but a knock came at the door.

"Duchess." A robed physician came into the room, his assistant pushing a cart behind him. "It is time for your treatment."

Ivey took back her hand. "Go." Ishanti swallowed, looking at her aunt. "Go!"

The princess sketched a brief curtsy and went.

She cast a glance over her shoulder as the assistant pushed the door to her aunt's chamber shut. The last thing she saw was a small glass vessel, its contents pulsating with golden light.

Guard Captain Marie marched through the old docks with a singular purpose.

To the west, the sun had just touched the top of the outer wall. She had already sent out her runners in squads of five to cordon off areas of interest. Tonight would be a night to remember.

She'd finally been given dispensation to clear the slums in force, and Marie intended to make use of it.

Three full detachments of her men marched down the dilapidated streets of the old docks in a silver cordon worthy of their city. Breastplates and burnished helmets gleamed in the fading light. The men and women of the Guard were like a ship parting a sea of detritus. The waves knew better than to get in their way.

"Ey, if it isn't Marie, old girl!"

Of course, there were always breakers.

Guard Captain Marie held back a grimace. "Arlo." She gave the old bartender a curt nod. "Tell your boss that we're coming for his balls."

The man gave a jaunty salute as the cavalcade marched past. Marie resisted the urge to spit at his feet. "I work for meself, ma'am, but I'll pass it along." He winked. Marie ignored him.

"Who's the ass?"

Guard Captain Marie reached back and slammed the Armsman's helmet shut. "Who's the ass, *Captain*?"

Maria's second in command held back a snort. "Arlo of Eastside." Eloncio shrugged. He came from these parts before going straight. "Small-time drug pusher, but he knows to keep his hands to himself."

"He's in with the Tarnished," Marie grumbled.

"You've been saying that for years."

"Captain, the warehouse is just up ahead!"

Marie swallowed her retort. "Fan out, men!" After the riot in the Merchant Quarter, damn Duchess Ivey had finally gotten off her royal ass and ordered a retaliation. It wasn't hard to piece together who was responsible for the madness.

Fortunately, the Adventurer's Guild had already gotten their collective asses handed to them. All that was left was the gang who'd instigated the whole mess in the first place.

Marie looked up at the massive warehouse, a smokestack belching soot into the air. "Not like Silverwall's newest gang even tried to hide…"

Her second grinned. "All the better for us, eh Captain?"

Marie just grunted, running a hand through her short, muddy hair. "Let's just get this over with." At her command, a squad of ten men went up to the door, carrying an enchanted battering ram. The rest of her squads fanned out around the street. "We should be doing this as a raid."

The man shrugged. "Seneschal said the duchess wanted a statement."

"Damn Duchess Ivey." The captain sighed. "Alright, boys, bring down the house!"

The squad at the doors hefted up the battering ram and slammed it against the wooden doors. They splintered on impact, flying into the interior of the building.

Marie's jaw dropped in time.

Inside was not a group of surprised workers or a batch of criminals ready for their desperate last stand. Hells, she would have even taken a hastily abandoned building.

Because the warehouse was abandoned, alright. But not *hastily*.

The back wall had been torn down, and everything within stoked into a raging inferno. This wasn't the work of a few hours. It would have taken a day, or more even, to set it all up. Then, the moment her men had been spotted in Eastside, this Empire had sent word back and struck a match.

As she watched, the remains of the roof caved in, ashy black smoke billowing up into the air.

Eloncio nodded to himself. "Leastwise we know where the smoke's coming from."

She reached over and slammed his visor shut.

I closed the messaging mirror with a satisfied click.

The case itself hadn't been hard to put together with a bit of scrap metal, and it added such a wonderful note of finality to the whole affair.

Electra raised an eyebrow. "Well?" She was leaning against the back of the wagon, her slightly longer hair swaying as we trundled down the road, far away from Silverwall. "How'd it go?"

"Flawlessly," I smirked. "I couldn't have timed it better with the Navy Master Clock."

She snorted. "You'd know, Em'."

"It was one time." I rolled my eyes. "I even gave it back after."

"Broken!"

I waved a hand. "This is this and that was that." I glanced over my shoulder. "Any trouble with the rest of the clasp, Rel?"

Electra huffed.

"Almost…got it!" With a grunt, Rel snapped the last connector into place on my lower back. With a soft hiss, my armor's auto seal activated.

"I can't believe you found this." I stroked the glossy neosteel arm-guard. "Thought I'd have to burn down the whole city to get it back."

"The Enchanter's Guild had it, Mistress." Relia straightened up, brushing off her slacks. "They were trying to unravel the durability enchantments."

"Please." I waved a hand. "As if I needed magic to create this suit."

She smirked. "I'm sure it looked magical to *them*."

I cast another glance over my shoulder. "You've gotten snarky." Rel started to reply, but then I gave her a pat on the cheek. "It looks good on you."

I affected not to notice as the woman sputtered quietly. With a flick of my wrist, I popped my armor's power unit open on my chest. "It's been a minute," I murmured.

I didn't have a new reactor. The one inside General Tock—currently in standby mode in the corner of the wagon—didn't have the output to power my suit without shorting out. I could build a new one, but not until I had the tools to build the tools, you know how the saying goes.

Of course, I always had a Plan B.

"Well." I spread my arms out, turning towards Electra. "Gonna top me off?"

Electra stood. "I'd get fired if Aegis ever caught me doing this."

I grinned. "How excellent. I know an enterprising villain that could use a…partner in crime."

"Thought you'd go for a minion, Em'."

"I already have the perfect minion, Elenore." I chuckled. "But don't tell me you haven't wondered what we could accomplish together… what we *will* accomplish together."

Electra stared at me for a long moment but then sighed. "I guess I already made my choice, huh?"

She reached out, touching the socket in my chest plate. With a sharp crack, she unloaded a massive burst of current into my suit. I sighed as the system whirred to life, feeling whole once more. "It's good to be back."

The wagon trundled to a stop, and Dum stuck his head inside from the driver's seat. "We made it, boss."

"Perfect timing." I snapped the power socket shut, leaving behind only the glossy expanse of armor that configured flawlessly to my form. I threw my new black cloak over my shoulders. "Shall we, ladies?"

Electra shoved her hands into her pockets. "Let's get this over with."

Rel just nodded, sliding into her place at my side.

The three of us stepped out of our cart, Dee and Dum falling in step behind me just like they'd never left.

Around us, nearly a dozen different carts and wagons had rolled to a stop. Rel had purchased them all with the funds from my business, including the last sale to the Adventurer's Guild itself. And in those carts were my people, my advancements, my innovations, and even a small kiln for Coaline and Mr. Burns.

I'd taken my empire with me.

Behind us lay a city that I no longer had any use for. In *front* of us, however, lay a small farming village. It was worn and run-down, with fallow fields and not enough men to deal with the monsters plaguing it from the countryside. Even now, the people of the village eyed us warily, too frightened to step forward.

Luckily, the chief owed Electra a favor.

"So, what are we doing this time, boss?" the electric blonde asked.

"The same thing I do every time, El." I smiled. "Trying to take over the world."

Joseph Marcia is the author of fast-paced, character-driven narratives that stretch the definition of genre. Also known as Argentorum, Marcia cut his teeth in the wild world of online fiction. *Be Thou My Good* is the first book in his Devil's Foundry series, which also includes *Be Thou My Brilliant* and *Be Thou My True*.

Podium

DISCOVER
STORIES UNBOUND

PodiumAudio.com